HAYNER PUB. INTO THE SQUARE

P9-DMX-667

RECEIVED
JAN 31 2017
By_____

No Longer the Property of
Hayner Public Library District

HAYNER PUBLIC LIBRARY DISTRICT
ALTON. ILLINOIS

OVERDUES 10 PER DAY, MAXIMUM FINE
COST OF ITEM
ADDITIONAL $5.00 SERVICE CHARGE
APPLIED TO
LOST OR DAMAGED ITEMS

THE
BREAKOUT

RYAN DAVID JAHN

THE
BREAKOUT

THOMAS DUNNE BOOKS / ST. MARTIN'S PRESS ≈ NEW YORK

This is a work of fiction. All of the characters, organizations, and events portrayed in this novel are either products of the author's imagination or are used fictitiously.

THOMAS DUNNE BOOKS.
An imprint of St. Martin's Press.

THE BREAKOUT. Copyright © 2017 by St. Martin's Press, LLC. All rights reserved. Printed in the United States of America. For information, address St. Martin's Press, 175 Fifth Avenue, New York, N.Y. 10010.

www.thomasdunnebooks.com
www.stmartins.com

Designed by Jonathan Bennett

The Library of Congress Cataloging-in-Publication Data is available upon request.

ISBN 978-1-250-07450-8 (hardcover)
ISBN 978-1-4668-8620-9 (e-book)

Our books may be purchased in bulk for promotional, educational, or business use. Please contact your local bookseller or the Macmillan Corporate and Premium Sales Department at 1-800-221-7945, extension 5442, or by e-mail at MacmillanSpecialMarkets@macmillan.com.

First Edition: January 2017

10 9 8 7 6 5 4 3 2 1

3486242

F
JAH

For my daughters,
Francine
&
Matilda

ACKNOWLEDGMENTS

Brenden Deneen and Nicole Sohl guided this book through publication. Thank you.

I'd also like to thank all the men and women in the armed forces, including my brother Nick, who took shrapnel from an IED while stationed in Afghanistan.

You risk your lives and spend months or years away from your families in order to keep your country safe, and while I don't always agree with the decisions that put you in harm's way, your sacrifice is appreciated.

It is impossible to suffer without making someone pay for it;
every complaint already contains revenge.

—FRIEDRICH NIETZSCHE

If an injury has to be done to a man
it should be so severe that his vengeance need not be feared.

—NICCOLO MACHIAVELLI

THE
BREAKOUT

AUTHOR'S NOTE

There are several cities, towns, and suburbs called La Paz, including five in Argentina, two in Mexico, and three in the United States. The town in this novel, however, is based on none of them.

1

Layla Murphy was sitting at a small table in El Niño's Pizza, a dingy joint in La Paz, Mexico, thirty minutes west of Juarez by car. Paintings of sugar skulls and men in sombreros hung crooked on the yellow plaster walls. Layla had her hands clasped in her lap, head tilted down, unwashed ropes of hair hanging in her face. She looked at a hangnail on her right thumb. Nibbled at it, spat it to the floor, and laced her fingers together once more. A slice of pizza sat untouched on a chipped white plate in front of her, oil pooled in the concaved bowls of the pepperoni rounds punctuating its surface. Layla Murphy had ten minutes left to live.

She had blond hair and green eyes. She stood five foot five and weighed just under a hundred pounds, but a year earlier, before she'd gotten hooked on heroin, she'd weighed one hundred and thirty. Her hip bones hadn't jutted. Her cheeks hadn't been hollow. Her joints hadn't looked like large knots on thin branches.

But a lot could change in a year.

She was twenty-four, and had she known she was about to die, it might have crossed her mind she was too young to face such a fate.

She hadn't had a chance to live life yet; she'd never even been in love. But she didn't know death was coming for her so soon; people rarely do.

"I've seen you struggling with your problem."

She looked up at the sound of the voice. The face across from her was pale and handsome and clean shaven except for a small patch of stubble on the outside curve of the chin missed during the last shave. The wavy hair was brown, except at the temples, where age had dusted it gray. The eyes were large and brown and glistening with sympathy.

The man's name was Francis Waters and he was a special agent for the Drug Enforcement Administration. He wore a navy two-button suit, probably off-the-rack Armani, a French-blue shirt, and a red-and-brown diagonally striped tie. The brown in the tie matched both his shoes and the leather band on his Burberry watch. It didn't occur to her that a man working for the DEA was unlikely to be wearing a two-thousand-dollar suit and a fifteen-hundred-dollar watch. Nor did it occur to her that he might be getting additional income from somewhere else, from some*one* else, maybe someone dangerous.

If it had, she might've been more cautious.

"I think this might be a way for you to escape your current situation," Waters said, "a way to get your life back. I know you want that. I can see it in your eyes."

She nodded. More than anything she wanted her life back. She wanted herself back. She missed the person she used to be. All she felt anymore was either lost in the nothingness of the heroin sky or a heavy need to be lost again, to drift away from this world like the balloon she became when she shot up, no longer weighed down by the emotions that normally pressed themselves upon her, her head drifting off while her body sagged limp. At some point she'd become a person she didn't like, a person she hated, and she didn't want to hate herself anymore.

She wanted to be the person she used to be.

"I do," she said.

"I know. Like I said, I can see it in your eyes. They're desperate. You want to know the truth, it's why I chose you to contact. I saw you in the park across from Rocha's estate and I knew. But to get that life back you're gonna have to testify against him. You agree to that, we can keep you safe and get you treatment. Get you straightened out." He paused for a moment, folded his slice of pepperoni in half, and shoved it into his mouth. While chewing he said, "Is that something you're willing to do?"

This question she'd been asking herself for three days now, since the morning Francis Waters sat next to her on that swing in the park and introduced himself. She'd been around Alejandro Rocha and his organization long enough to know if she agreed to testify she might be killed. But death would be better than the life she'd been living. If she could escape herself, find the person she used to be, it might be worth living again; and if she died trying to do that, at least she wouldn't feel the things she felt now, when she felt anything at all.

"It is," she said. "I'll do it."

"That's good. That's very good."

Waters wiped orange grease from the corners of his mouth with a small napkin, balled it up, tossed it on the table. He looked toward the large window facing the parking lot and raised his hand, holding up two fingers, gesturing to someone unseen. The restaurant was lit up while outside it was night, so all she could see in the glass was a dim version of the room reflected back at her, ghosts of herself and the man she was sitting across from, ghosts of the tables and chairs, but the gesture made her nervous. Francis Waters was communicating with someone outside and she was afraid to find out who.

Diego Blanco pushed through the front door, which knocked against a bell, and it clinked a sour note. He stepped inside and stood a moment on the vinyl floor, door swinging closed behind him. His head turned toward the table where she was sitting and his eyes locked on hers. They held no emotion, no clue as to what he might be thinking. Looked as empty and dark as the mouths of caves.

He was a stocky Mexican man about five six with a square head and close-cropped black hair salted with white. His eyes were always bloodshot. He was missing the upper portion of his right ear. A toothpick poked from the left corner of his mouth. He wore black slacks and a white button-down shirt with short sleeves. If it weren't for the green prison tattoos that covered his arms to the wrists, and the knuckle tattoos on his left hand, EWMN, one letter for each finger, he might have looked like a server at a mid-range restaurant.

"Sorry, honey," said Francis Waters. "Money talks and Alejandro Rocha's got plenty."

He shrugged, showed his teeth, a so-sue-me grin that lit up his eyes for a moment, and took another bite of pizza. His nonchalance disturbed her more than what was about to happen. She couldn't understand playing with another person's life so carelessly. She'd played with her own life carelessly, but it was hers to play with.

Diego walked to the table and held out his right hand. She looked at it as if it were an alien thing: the dirty crescents under his fingernails, the blood blister on the side of the middle finger, the three dots tattooed on the webbing between index finger and thumb.

"Let's go, Layla."

She put her hand in his—it was like clamping a small bird in a vise—and he pulled her to her feet. His fat hand was rough and callused. He dragged her forward and together, hand in hand, they walked toward the fingerprinted glass door that would take them outside.

■ Diego walked her through the dark night to the far side of the parking lot where a beat-up Ford pickup truck sat waiting. The local billiards joint was just across the street. Several men and women stood outside, smoking cigarettes and laughing with bottles of sweaty beer gripped in their fists, but they wouldn't help her. No matter what happened they'd pretend not to see. If she called out to them across the street, they'd just look the other way. If things turned violent they'd head back inside, chalk their cues, and rack some balls. But they wouldn't help. They wouldn't even discuss what happened amongst themselves. Alejandro Rocha owned this town. Nobody interfered with his business, or even discussed it, and everybody knew that she was his business.

When they reached the truck he pushed her forward and told her to get in. She pulled open the passenger door and stepped up and inside. The air was thick with the smell of Diego's deodorant and aftershave.

He got in behind the wheel, looked at her with bloodshot eyes, tongued his toothpick from one corner of his mouth to the other, and said, "You're shaking. Let's get you a dose of medicine to calm your nerves."

She nodded despite the fact she knew what was coming. She could fight—push him away, climb out of the truck, and run into the night—but it would only delay the inevitable. She had nowhere to go. La Paz was surrounded on all sides by desert. For miles in every direction one would find only sand and low hills, desert grass, shrubs, and stones.

Francis Waters had been her last hope and he'd betrayed her. It wasn't even a surprise. But she had no more fight left in her. So she sat there while Diego cooked her shot, while he drew the liquid into a syringe, while he unstrapped his belt and wrapped it around her arm. She sat there while he stuck the needle into her, while he drew back the plunger, pulling blood into the syringe to ensure he'd struck a vein, while he thumbed down on the plunger and injected her.

A feeling of warmth washed over her, as if she were suddenly submerged in bathwater, and she sank into it deep. Her vision faded from the periphery toward the center, darkness creeping in from the edges until she could see nothing at all. The warmth overwhelmed her, surrounded her, and then suddenly stopped.

She felt nothing at all.

■ Diego tongue-shifted his toothpick and pushed out of the truck. The warm night air enveloped him. He walked around to the passenger side, looked at Layla's face pressed against the smudged glass, the eyes blank despite the tears still standing in them, the mouth hinged open but incapable of speech, the oily hair hanging down into a face blanched and beaded with sweat.

She'd been beautiful once. Now she was garbage, the only part of her that remained a shucked husk.

Diego pulled open the door. Layla's body fell out of the truck and into his arms. He dragged it around to the back of the truck and heaved it onto the open tailgate. Walked back to the side of the truck and picked up a shoe that had fallen off her left foot. With the shoe in hand he climbed up after the body and dragged it into place, putting it on top of a tarp spread across the bed of the truck. He replaced the shoe and folded the tarp around the body. While he did this he thought of a butcher wrapping a cut of meat. He tied the tarp into place with twine, jumped from the tailgate, truck springs creaking, and walked around to the cab. Got in behind the wheel. His right hand turned the key in the ignition while his left foot pressed down on the clutch. The engine sputtered, backfired, and roared to life.

He jammed the transmission into reverse and released some of the pressure on the clutch while simultaneously gassing the engine. The truck jerked backward out of its unmarked parking spot. His hand shoved the transmission into first and the truck jerked forward. He turned the wheel left while the truck rolled off the curb and onto a narrow, cracked street.

He reached out and twisted a knob. The headlights splashed angles of light onto the street and the truck chased down the darkness in front of the beams. He headed northwest until he hit Avenida Hidalgo, then made a soft right without bothering to stop at the graffiti-besmirched ALTO sign. He continued north on Hidalgo, passing several businesses along the way.

Finally he reached the northernmost point of the city, a large white church with a forty-foot spire. A crucified Jesus hung on a large wooden cross at the top. The street led directly into the driveway, faded asphalt giving way to gravel, which ground like teeth and popped from the pressure as the truck rolled across it. He parked in front of the church's concrete steps, pushed open the driver's-side door with a creak of hinges, and stepped out onto the gravel. Walked through the warm night air to the back of the truck and pulled the wrapped body out. Saddled it over his shoulder with a grunt. Headed up the steps to the church's double doors, grabbed one of the door handles, thumbed the paddle, and pulled.

The door swung open, revealing the dim interior of a large, empty church. It smelled of aging wood, old bibles, and the smoke of candles that had guttered out.

He carried the body down the center aisle, past several rows of empty pews.

The only illumination in the room was what splashed in through the stained-glass windows, both from the moon and sodium-vapor streetlamps, multicolored angles of light slanting against time-yellowed plaster walls and mahogany wainscoting.

He carried the body to the raised platform from which the people of La Paz received their sermons every Sunday and Thursday. Bent at the knees and set it down gently.

He walked back out to his truck, grabbed a length of rope, and returned. Tied the rope around the corpse's ankles, and with that done, walked to a hand-carved Jesus at the back of the stage. Stained oak with fine chisel marks, the face a permanent mask of pain. He reached around behind it and yanked up on a metal lever. Pulled at the plinth on which Jesus stood with spiked feet. Jesus pivoted clockwise while hinging around a metal pin in the front left corner of the plinth, the open palms and pained eyes turning to face the left wall. As Jesus turned, as the plinth hinged out of place, a concrete tunnel leading straight down into darkness was revealed.

Diego dragged the body to the tunnel, and using the rope, lowered it into the darkness below. When El Paso police found the body it needed to look like a simple overdose, nothing more, which meant it couldn't have broken bones or an excess of posthumous damage. He'd been down that road before and it always led to serious investigations, and investigations led to questions that needed answers, and answers led to him.

No fucking thank you.

Once he felt the body settle on the floor below he let go of the rope. It coiled into the darkness. He followed it, climbing down a wooden ladder until he reached bottom. He rolled the body onto a flatbed cart usually reserved for cocaine, grabbed the rope and coiled it on top of the corpse, and began pushing it through a tunnel lit only by periodic forty-watt bulbs, thin metal chains hanging down from them. The tunnel extended for over a thousand yards, something more than half a mile. The front left wheel squeaked and rattled while he pushed. He had to fight to keep the cart from swerving into the tunnel wall, and he made a mental note to bring WD-40 next time he planned to be here.

By the time he reached the other end of the tunnel he was covered in a layer of sweat, his own stink hanging thick around him. He'd have to take a second shower when he got home. But his part was almost finished, which was a relief. He didn't mind killing, so long as it was someone he had no feelings for, but he disliked dealing with dead bodies, one to two hundred pounds of incriminating evidence. Even in La Paz it made him nervous.

While walking underground he'd crossed the border between Mexico and the United States. Alejandro Rocha didn't want the corpses of Americans found in Mexico. It caused all sorts of trouble, and though La Paz police were paid well, there was only so much trouble could fall on a person before that person broke under the weight. Best for everybody if La Paz seemed a quiet desert town and nothing more. Best for everybody if dead Americans were found in America. Especially pretty white girls.

He buried bodies when he had to, but when you buried a body you ended up waiting for discovery, and unintentional discovery was a nightmare. Best to determine when and how a body was found, to control the circumstances before it happened.

He picked up the end of the rope tied around the corpse, and holding onto it, climbed up a wooden ladder, emerging from the floor of a feed shed on an ostrich farm just north of an unnamed county road in New Mexico. He pinned the rope under a brick and pushed out through the feed shed doors. Looked left and saw a dirt driveway leading south to the road, a two-lane stretch of blacktop surrounded by sand, stones, desert shrubbery, and not much else. Farther to the south, two border fences had been erected, chain link lined with tattered tar paper, and in the hundred-foot gap between these fences stood glowing sodium-vapor lamps meant to illuminate any border jumpers, but he'd bypassed all of that.

A dusty gray Nissan Sentra sat parked in the driveway, a man leaning against the front right fender smoking a cigarette. The ember glowed bright orange as he took a drag. He exhaled through his nostrils, the smoke drifting on the still night air.

"Help me pull her up."

The man pushed off the car, flicked his cigarette away, and walked over. The two of them hauled the corpse up out of the tunnel and put it into the trunk of the Nissan. The man slammed down the lid.

"Guess we're done here," Diego said.

The man nodded, lit another cigarette, held out his open pack.

Diego tongued his toothpick and said, "Quit last month." He turned around, walked back to the feed shed, and glanced left at the ostriches sleeping behind a tall cedar fence. A breeze blew into his face, and their stink came with it. He stepped inside, made his way to the tunnel, and climbed down into darkness.

He trudged back toward Mexico, pushing the cart in front of him, that squeaky wheel whining at him the entire fucking time.

The man with the Nissan would drive the corpse into El Paso. He'd find a building where drug users were known to squat, or an alley where junkies were sometimes arrested, and dump the body there, making it look as though that was where Layla had overdosed.

The dead body might lie there for two or three days before the smell got bad enough for someone to realize something was wrong. Junkies weren't the most observant of people, and regular folk tended to avoid places where junkies hung out. Once the corpse was found, police would arrive, see she'd given herself a shot of bad medicine, and the case would be closed before it was opened. Accidental death due to overdose. End of story.

Diego climbed out of the tunnel Mexico-side and pushed Jesus back into place. Walked out of the church, down the steps, and across the gravel driveway to his truck. Slid in behind the wheel, started the engine, and shoved the transmission into gear.

He drove away from there and almost immediately forgot about Layla.

But he'd soon get a hard reminder.

2

James Murphy was arrested on a Wednesday.

He was sitting behind the wheel of a rented Ford Taurus, key in the ignition and engine running, but only so he could keep the air conditioner on. The car faced south, sun shining in through the passenger window as midday gave way to evening. A park lay to his right, a well-kept hundred acres of grass, playground equipment, walking paths, and benches shaded by the dense leaves of summer trees. But none of that was of interest to him. Nor were the shadows stretching long in his direction and growing longer as the sun made its descent.

He was watching an estate several hundred yards to the south, watching cars enter and leave. He'd crossed the border into Juarez around nine o'clock Monday night, but spent no time there. Instead, he drove straight through, heading west to La Paz, the place his sister had been living before her dead body turned up in El Paso.

It was a thirty-minute drive from Juarez.

You passed through empty desert along a two-lane strip of faded asphalt. Wild shrubs and cacti dotted the landscape on either side of you. Headlight beams splashed across roadkill, guts spilled out like tangled rope. Aside from the road you were traveling on, you saw no signs of human life. Almost half an hour passed before La Paz came into view in the distance, flickering dim in the night. Five minutes after that you turned right onto Avenida Hidalgo, and as soon as you did, you were in La Paz, a nondescript Mexican town of interest only because it was home to the man you blamed for your sister's death.

He'd checked into Hotel Amigo, where he was now staying, and after taking a shower and changing clothes, walked across the street to Los Parados, a local dive bar he'd seen while parking. It was dark inside, only neon beer signs and a lamp above the scuffed pool table illuminating the place. About two dozen people inside, either sitting at small round tables or the bar; a couple drunk men throwing darts against the far wall. He sat on a duct-taped stool at the counter and poured a few beers down his throat, staring at nothing and thinking about his sister. He wondered if she'd ever come in here, wondered if she ever sat where he was sitting.

A prostitute, perhaps forty, approached him. She said he was handsome and asked if he had a room across the street. He told he wasn't interested. She pretended to be offended, hoping he'd buy her an apology drink, but when he didn't, she moved on to the next guy. After an hour he went back to his room and lay down, hoping to get some sleep, but ended up staring at the ceiling, listening to Mexican television until sunlight broke through the window.

Since then, he'd spent at least twenty cumulative hours parked here, watching, but hadn't seen Alejandro Rocha. Others had come and gone, but Rocha remained unseen, hidden behind the walls of a house larger than the apartment complex James had lived in before joining the Marines, all twenty-five units, the house itself hidden behind a sturdy stucco wall and wrought-iron gate, set at the back of a long cobblestone drive bifurcated by a fountain, a small nude boy pissing into a cast stone bowl.

He looked through his dirty, wiper-streaked windshield, watching as cars and trucks entered or left the estate, looked through binoculars to see the faces of the people in those vehicles, hoping each time the face he saw belonged to the motherfucker he wanted to kill. But each time he saw someone else, someone he didn't recognize. He'd been hoping to find some sort of pattern in Alejandro Rocha's behavior, but he hadn't seen Rocha at all.

He glanced now to his passenger seat and the jug of water sitting there. He picked it up and took a drink. He thought about the M40A3 sniper rifle wrapped in a blanket under his hotel room bed.

Once he knew more about Rocha's behavioral patterns, he'd bring it out, set up a good distance from the man's estate, anywhere from five to eight hundred yards, kill the son of a bitch, and be gone before anyone even knew what had happened. Before the mist of blood hanging in the air had even settled to the ground.

He'd imagined squeezing his trigger dozens of times since he learned of his sister's death, since her body had been discovered next to a dumpster in El Paso by two boys taking a shortcut to school. He imagined the view through his scope, imagined squeezing his trigger and feeling the rifle kick against the crook of his shoulder. The head snapping back. The skull opening, exploding outward, ejecting a messy triangle of brains, blood, and bone shards.

Two blue-and-white police cruisers turned left off the cross street to the south and rolled toward him, their light bars flashing. The lead car rumbled past, swinging left to block him in from behind, while the other car pulled up to his front bumper and stopped only after it made contact with the Ford Taurus.

James keyed off the engine and put his hands on the steering wheel, in plain sight, hoping to keep everything cool.

A uniformed police officer stepped from each vehicle. They wore navy pants and light blue shirts with navy pocket flaps and shoulder straps. Their badges caught the fading sunlight as they walked toward him, right hands resting on their duty weapons. One was tall and thin and clean shaven, the other short and heavyset with facial hair trimmed into a Van Dyke.

"Good afternoon, sir," said Van Dyke in English, squinting down at him.

"Something the matter?"

"There any reason you've been parked here for the last several hours?"

"It *is* a park."

"It's suspicious is what it is."

"In what way?"

"Why are you parked here, sir?"

"No good reason."

"You were parked here yesterday as well."

"Did someone complain?"

"This is a good neighborhood, the wealthiest citizens of La Paz live near here, and strange cars make them nervous. We've received several phone calls."

"I haven't done anything illegal."

"Nobody accused you of illegal activity, sir. Why would you mention it?"

"You're the police."

"We'll need to see your driver's license."

James unfolded his leather wallet, slipped his license from its sleeve, and held it out pinched between his index and middle fingers. Van Dyke yanked it away, held it about a foot in front of his face, and squinted at it.

"Austin, Texas."

"Yes, sir." He'd been living in El Paso for the last month, since he'd returned from Afghanistan, but his license still listed the address at which he'd lived before joining the Marines six years earlier.

"What brings you to Mexico?"

"Had a little time off from work, thought I'd check it out."

"What sort of work do you do?"

"Marine Corps sergeant."

"Stationed at Fort Bliss?"

"For the time being. Got back from Afghanistan last month."

"Fort Bliss is an Army base."

"Marine Corps detachment."

Van Dyke handed James back his license. "Step out of your vehicle, sir."

"I'm not sure that's necessary."

"We're gonna search your car."

"No, you're not."

Van Dyke thumbed the strap off his holster. "I wasn't asking permission, Mr. Murphy. Step out of your vehicle."

"No. Last time I checked it wasn't illegal to sit in a parked car. You've got no probable cause to search my vehicle."

Van Dyke drew his duty weapon, aimed it at James. "Step out of the vehicle now, and keep your hands visible. My reason for searching your car is that I choose to. You're not in the United States and you'd be smart to remember that."

James hesitated a moment before he pushed open the door and stepped out onto the street, hands raised to his shoulders. Van Dyke turned him around, kicked his feet apart, and frisked him, finding nothing.

"Stay here," he said to James. To the other cop he said, *"Buscar el coche."*

James sat on the hood of the car and waited for the harassment to be finished.

The thin cop searched the interior, coming up eventually with several computer printouts of articles about Alejandro Rocha, but nothing more. He pulled the key from the ignition, walked around to the trunk, opened it, and searched inside.

"Qué chingados," he said, holding up two bricks of what looked like cocaine.

James stood up and said, "Now, wait a minute. Those aren't mine." But even before the words left his mouth, he knew there was no point in speaking them. The cocaine had been planted and the only people who might've done it were the cops about to arrest him.

"We're taking you in," Van Dyke said, his duty weapon raised. "Turn around and put your hands on the hood of the car."

"I'm not sure I'm gonna do that," James said.

"You will unless you want to get shot. Turn around."

"We all know those drugs were planted."

Van Dyke swung his weapon toward James's left temple.

James reached up and grabbed the wrist, pulled the gun out of Van Dyke's hand, and turned it around on him. He did this on instinct, without thinking of the consequences, and as soon as it was done he regretted it. It put him in a situation even worse than his last one. He was sure his license plate had been punched into the system. If he killed these men, La Paz Police Department would trace the rental car back to Hertz, which would trace it to him, and he'd end up going down for murder instead of drugs. Not exactly an improvement.

Now he needed to figure out how to extract himself from this situation.

"Why don't I just get in my car and drive away?"

The thin cop stepped around the trunk with his own weapon raised. In poor English, he said, "Drop . . . or I . . . shoot you."

"Your hand is shaking," James said. "You'll miss. Why don't *you* drop your weapon and let me leave?"

"No," the thin cop said. "Do as I say . . . or die."

Either James overtook these men, which might lead to one or both of them getting killed, or he let himself be arrested—those were his choices—and though part of him leaned toward overtaking them, consequences be damned, he knew he needed to think about his reason for being in Mexico. He was here for Alejandro Rocha, the man responsible for his sister's death, and he didn't intend to leave until the man had paid for it.

"Okay," he said. He leaned down and set the gun on the asphalt.

As soon as he did, Van Dyke kicked him in the face, bloodying his nose. "That's for pointing my own gun at me, *pendejo*."

James had to resist the urge to fight back, and instead let Van Dyke grab his right wrist, twist his arm behind his back, and slam him down onto the car hood. His cheek lay against the hot metal. Sweat dripped from his nose. Van Dyke slapped a handcuff around his right wrist, pulled his left arm behind his back, and cuffed that one too. He pulled James up, walked him to the police cruiser parked behind the Ford Taurus, yanked open the rear door, and shoved James into the backseat. He slammed the door shut.

◼ Van Dyke drove him to La Paz police station, which was located in an all-purpose municipal building, a sign on the beige-painted stucco façade reading MUNICIPIO DE LA PAZ, and on each glass door a vinyl sign identified the organization behind it, including, on the third door from the left, POLICIA. The building sat at the end of Calle Tortuga on the west end of town, several dust-covered police cars parked along the shoulder of the road leading up to the building. There was an empty space right out front. Van Dyke pulled the cruiser into it. He killed the engine, pushed out into the bright, hot day, stood a moment under a Mexican sun that had melted a hole in the blue firmament, and pulled open the back door. He grabbed James by the shirt collar and yanked him from the cruiser. Pushed him toward the police station, up the steps, and through the glass door. The door sighed shut behind them.

Tepid air blew from several vents, making the station almost comfortable.

The desk sergeant glanced up at them with low-lidded eyes, stared a moment, and looked back down to the manual typewriter in front of him, tapping out his words slowly and with great force to ensure each whack marked all three carbon copies. Yellow, pink, blue.

Van Dyke led him past the desk sergeant and a squad room littered with cheap fiberboard desks—and a few disheveled cops—to a room containing only a metal table and two foldout chairs. He shoved James into the room and yanked the door shut.

A moment later it locked with the solid metal clack of a dead bolt.

◼ Almost an hour later, a man of about fifty, with a thick comb of a mustache that covered his upper lip and deep crow's feet around the eyes, walked into the room. He wore a brown suit. His black hair was greased back except for a strand that hung loose over his right eyebrow, curling back up on itself like a fishhook. He nodded at James and without a word unhooked the cuff from his left wrist. He sat him down in one of the foldout chairs and clasped the loose cuff around a thick steel staple welded to the edge of the table. Sat down across from James, pulled out a pack of cigarettes, and stuck one between his lips. Lit it with a scratched Zippo, took a deep drag, exhaled through his nostrils. He held the cigarette pinched between index finger and thumb. Used his teeth to peel a flake of dry skin from his bottom lip and spat it to the floor.

"I'm Detective Ernesto Huerta and I have many questions for you, James Murphy."

"I don't have any answers. The cops planted that cocaine in my trunk."

Detective Huerta waved away the statement with a lazy sweep of his left hand, as if shooing away a fly. "My questions don't concern the cocaine in your trunk."

"What *do* they concern?"

"Your interest in Alejandro Rocha—and the rifle my men found in room two thirteen."

"You searched my hotel room?"

"We've been aware of you since your arrival, Mr. Murphy. La Paz isn't a town people regularly visit. What's your interest in Rocha?"

"Who?"

"Don't pretend you know not whom I speak of."

"I'm not pretending."

"You had twenty-seven news articles about him in your car."

"I might have heard of him."

"So what's your interest?"

"I don't see how that's any business of yours."

"It is if it's related to the rifle."

"I'm licensed to carry that gun."

"Not in Mexico. Drug and weapons charges are very serious business. Especially with the amount of cocaine found in your trunk."

"I told you already, those drugs were planted."

"That argument will not go very far with a judge."

"How's it going with you?"

"What's your interest in Alejandro Rocha?"

James only stared. Said nothing.

"This will go better if you cooperate."

"I'm not interested in cooperation. Not with the bought-and-paid-for cops of La Paz Police Department."

"Trust me, Mr. Murphy, you *do* want to cooperate. You want to do this the easy way."

"You don't have a clue what I want," James said. "If cooperating with you is the easy way, I'll go the hard way."

Detective Huerta shrugged. "So be it. I'll take you to La Paz City Jail where you'll be held until your trial's finished, at which point you'll either be moved to one of the long-term blocks at the jail or transferred to Cereso state prison in Juarez. Your conviction, however, is not in question."

"When can I expect the arraignment?"

"It could be ninety days; it could be six months. There's no hurry to get this done. But it doesn't matter. As soon as you're there, prison will be your home until you die. You fucked with the wrong individual."

"I didn't fuck with anybody." But James now regretted allowing himself to be arrested. Rocha must have seen James—or been told about him—and sent the police out to bring him in. A man watching his estate was a man worth taking an interest in, and cops were good at getting information out of people. They'd already learned more than he wanted them to know, and they'd surely pass along what they'd learned to Rocha.

"You said you wanted the hard way," Detective Huerta said. "You'll get it."

◼ Detective Ernesto Huerta shoved James into the back of a black sedan, slammed shut the door, and got into the driver's seat. Started the car and slid it into gear. The fan belt squealed. He looked in the rearview mirror at James and James looked back. Detective

Huerta slipped a cigarette between his lips and set the end on fire. Cracked his dust-covered window and blew smoke out the side of his mouth.

"You still have a chance to talk."

James continued to stare into Detective Huerta's eyes in the rear-view mirror. His lips remained sealed. He blinked.

"Okay," Detective Huerta said.

He pulled his foot off the brake and moved it to the gas. The car eased forward. He drove them south along Tortuga until they hit Calle El Tule, where he made a right. They headed west through the desert toward a crescent of large brown hills and continued on for another ten miles before driving into the desert valley at the base of those hills.

The jail came into view in the distance, wavering unsteadily behind heat vapors. Several low cinder block buildings surrounded by guard towers. Three rows of chain-link fence topped with razor wire. If you made it over the first fence you'd still have two more to get past, a gap between each of them. No chance of doing that before one of the towered guards saw you and put a .308 Winchester into your back.

James felt his stomach go sour.

■ Detective Huerta pulled the car up to a cinder block building with TRATAMIENTO hand-stenciled above the rusting metal door. He stepped outside, walked to the car's back door, swung it open. Pulled James out, took him into the building, and handed him over to two guards.

"You'll regret not talking," Detective Huerta said. Then he was gone and the rusting metal door latched behind him, the light from outside cut off.

The two guards took his personal property, including his watch, his wallet, his cell phone, and his clothes (except his Puma sneakers). They took him to a shower and handed him a hotel-sized bar of soap. He stood under the cold spray and washed for five minutes before one of the guards shut off the water, soap still in his hair and under his arms. One of them tossed a scoop of delousing powder onto his head and another onto his groin. It stung his eyes. He wiped the powder away with a threadbare towel. The second guard yanked the towel away and handed him a gray jumpsuit. He put on the jumpsuit and his shoes. They walked him out of processing and handed him over to another guard and, in Spanish, told the guard to take him to Block A, cell 16. The guard shoved him forward and marched him down various corridors. A few inmates shouted at him:

"*¡Yo cago en la leche de tu puta madre!*"

"*¡Cagaste y saltaste en la caca!*"

"*¡La concha de tu madre!*"

But mostly they just looked out through their bars in silence.

Finally they reached his cell. The guard shoved James inside and swung shut the barred door. It hit with a loud but hollow clank and latched.

In English the guard said, "You should be careful in here, *bolillo*. People die."

He pivoted and walked away. The echoes of his footfalls, loud at first, faded to nothing.

James turned in a slow circle, looking at his cell, taking in his new surroundings. The cell was about eight feet deep and six feet wide. He could stretch out his arms and touch each wall with his fingertips. The walls were cinder block. Several of the previous inmates had carved their names or initials into them. Others had carved or written crude phrases: ME CAGO EN LA LECHE, TENGO GANAS, and VETE A LA VERGA CULERO. Against the back wall was a steel toilet and a basin. A barred window above the toilet looked out on a lamp-lit yard. A cot against the left wall held a folded white sheet, a thin blanket, and an uncased pillow. The pillow was ringed with yellow sweat stains. A metal desk sat against the right wall, bolted to the floor, a chair pushed up to it. He walked to the desk, shoved the chair aside, and pulled open the single drawer. Inside he found a pad of paper, a rubber band, and a metal pen casing from which someone had removed the ink tube, and a small spring.

He pushed the drawer shut and walked to the cot. He unfolded the sheet, threw it over the cot's thin mattress, and tucked it in. Draped the blanket over the sheet and put the pillow at the head of the bed. Lay down and looked up at the concrete ceiling. Thought of his time in boot camp, sleeping on the cots in the barracks there. This was very similar—and totally different.

People die. That was what the guard had said, and he knew it was true. Everyone born would one day die. Like his sister had died.

He thought about his history with her.

He was four years old on the day she screamed into the world. He remembered being in the delivery room—his parents had wanted him to understand what was happening—and believed now her birth was his earliest memory. It wasn't clear in his mind. Rather than being a mental movie, the memory was a series of out-of-focus still photographs. Yet he remembered.

There he was, four years old, standing at the foot of his mother's birthing bed. There was his mother with her legs spread, knees bent. A thatch of wet blond hair sticking out between his mother's legs: just that disembodied blond hair tinted pink with amniotic fluids. Layla's purple face pushed out from between their mother's legs, eyes and lips shut tight, face like a prune. A doctor holding her, so tiny. His father with a large pair of scissors cutting the umbilical cord, a shocked expression on his face, as if he'd just witnessed something he was not prepared for.

James loved her from the beginning. He gave her bottles, played with her on the carpeted floor, napped with her in the crib even though he was a big boy and slept in a bed.

He was also protective of her. He was going into fourth grade as she was entering kindergarten, and on the first day he insisted on walking her to class, and she hugged him tight and cried, and he told her it would be fun. At the end of the day she said he was right. The first day of school *had* been fun. They'd sung the alphabet song and played kazoos and she'd made new friends, Brynlee and Caydence, and they'd get to see each other tomorrow. He walked her home, holding her hand the whole time. He was only nine, but her hand felt small in his.

They talked about everything. Siblings who were close could discuss matters with one another they'd never bring up to their parents or their friends from school. He had a bond with his baby sister that combined familial love with absolute trust, and because he was four years older, she often talked to him about her troubles and asked him for advice.

He did the best he could for her. He helped her with schoolwork he'd already had to do. He took her to the park and pushed her on swings. Later, when she had boyfriends who treated her poorly, he bloodied their noses and bruised their ribs.

Yes, he'd been protective, but he hadn't saved her.

If he hadn't been in Afghanistan, she might have come to him for help, and he might have been able to protect her from the people who'd dragged her to her death. But he'd been gone when she needed him most.

So he knew full well the guard's words were true. People die.

But he knew something else as well, something the guard hadn't said, which was that sometimes those deaths must be paid for. Everybody died but not every death was equal. Some lives were stolen, as his sister's life had been stolen, and even though a stolen life couldn't be recovered, you could make someone pay for it.

He had every intention of making the man who took his sister's life pay in full.

It didn't matter that he was in jail. He would find a way.

He had to.

■ James woke up to the sound of his cell door swinging open. Two man-shaped shadows entered the room. Dark silhouettes, bulky. They grabbed him and pulled him from his cot. They threw him down. He whacked the side of his head against concrete, then looked up at the silhouettes. His left arm was asleep. His fingers tingled and ached as blood returned to them. He asked what the hell was going on.

"You have a visitor," one of the men said in Spanish.

Footsteps echoed in the corridor outside his cell. A man appeared in the unbarred doorway. He was backlit by dim yellow bulbs in the hall. He said in Spanish that he wanted the light on in this cell. One of the guards told him all the lights were connected to the same circuit, that the only way to turn on this light was to turn them all on.

"Then turn them all on."

"Yes, sir."

One of the guards left, his footsteps, loud at first, fading as he walked to the end of the corridor. The naked yellow bulb in the ceiling flashed to life, as did the bulbs in every other cell in this block, humming with electricity. Other inmates cursed and shouted. The guard standing over James yelled for them to shut their *bocas malditos*.

James looked from the guard to the man standing in the doorway. He recognized him immediately. He'd seen his picture illustrating dozens of news articles. Alejandro Rocha. He was handsome, about forty years old, and stood five ten. He had prominent cheekbones and a widow's peak. His brown eyes were almond shaped. He wore a tailored seersucker suit, white, a white cotton shirt, a baby blue tie, baby blue pocket square, and baby blue socks. His hands were clasped behind his back. A smirk touched his lips.

"Mr. James Murphy," Rocha said in unaccented English. "I have a few things I'd like to discuss with you. May I enter?"

James sat up, nodded.

Rocha entered the cell, glanced at the guard, told him in Spanish to get out and shut the door. The guard did as he was told. Alejandro Rocha's organization wasn't as large as the Juarez cartel, but it brought in millions of dollars a year, and a percentage of his income could easily buy a town the size of La Paz—law enforcement officials, politicians, and anybody else who might need to hear a monetary argument to see things his way—and he'd used his money to do just that. It was the only way for an illegal operation of that size to function.

James knew this, but watching a prison guard take orders from a man who deserved to be behind bars put a coil of rage in his belly, and as he watched Rocha sit casually on the edge of the cot and cross his legs, that coil tightened, the pressure increasing.

"I understand you've done some research on me, Mr. Murphy, but did you know that I'm an educated man?" He looked at James, waited for a response.

Through clenched teeth: "No."

"Business degree from Harvard. I've done so well in business, in fact, that I finished paying off my student loans years ago." He smiled. "My education paid for itself. The American dream realized in Mexico."

It was the smile that did it. How smug it looked plastered on the tan face.

The coiled pressure couldn't be contained.

James dove for him, shoulder slamming into Alejandro Rocha's stomach. The air escaped Rocha's lungs and he doubled over while the momentum of the blow slammed him back against the wall. He whacked his head on a cinder block. James got to his feet and swung, punching the son of a bitch in the nose. Blood poured from his nostrils, ran over his mouth, dripped onto the white shirt. James swung again.

The cell door opened. Both guards rushed in. They grabbed James by the arms and flung him away. He whacked his head on the steel toilet and dropped to the floor. The guards moved in on him, drawing their saps.

"Stop," Rocha said in Spanish. "We're fine. Leave us to our conversation."

He pulled the blue pocket square from his coat, snapped it open, and wiped at his bloodied face.

The guards left the cell again, shut the door.

James pushed off the floor and sat down on the edge of the toilet. He looked across the small cell to Alejandro Rocha. The man blew his bleeding nose into the pocket square, folded it, and slipped it away.

"I admire a man who's in touch with his emotions. So many men are closed off, but I'm going to have to ask you to refrain from violence for the time being. What's your interest in me, Mr. Murphy?"

"There's nothing interesting about you."

"You did a lot of reading up for a man with no interest in who or what I am."

"I'll read a bottle of toilet cleaner if I'm taking a shit and there's nothing else handy."

"You may choose to deflect, Mr. Murphy, but eventually I'll get to the bottom of this matter."

James thought: *You'll get to the bottom of a hole in the ground, and I'll cover you in dirt, you motherfucker.*

He said: "Why did you have me locked up?"

"I like to know where a man is when I have questions for him. Did you intend to use the weapon the police found in your hotel room on me?"

"It was for protection."

"A sniper rifle for protection?"

"I like to keep danger at a distance."

"Who are you working for?"

"Amway. I was hoping you'd want to host a party. I think your estate would really impress people. I'm not saying we should lie, but maybe imply that Amway got you the place."

Rocha smiled without humor. "I see. So this conversation is going nowhere."

"You'll get where you're going faster by running on a treadmill."

Rocha got to his feet. "Very well. But you need to understand something. I can make the charges against you disappear. It's nothing to me. I mutter a few sentences and you're free. I'm also more than willing to buy my way out of trouble. I assume you have access to the people who hired you. I believe turnabout is fair play. But so long as I have questions about your intentions, so long as I don't feel safe with you walking the streets, you'll remain behind bars."

"Or you'll have me killed."

"Don't be foolish. I know better than to burn a book before I've

26

read it. Of course, if a book is very tightly bound, sometimes you *do* need to break the spine to get at the information you want. I suspect we'll be talking again soon."

Alejandro walked to the cell door and told the guards to let him out, which they did. The door swung shut again with a metal clack. Rocha looked at him through the bars. "Try to stay safe, Mr. Murphy. Many terrible things can happen in jail."

He turned and walked away, his footsteps echoing loud in the otherwise quiet corridor. The guards followed behind him. James stood at the cell door and listened until he heard only silence. He walked back to his cot, lay down, stared at the ceiling.

He wondered how long it would be before Rocha grew impatient and decided to kill him. He wondered what he'd do about it, what he'd be *able* to do about it.

3

Alejandro Rocha pulled a fold of cash from his pocket and slipped it from its platinum money clip. He peeled five hundred dollars off the outside of the fold and handed the cash to the guard on the left, whom he trusted more than the other, before sliding the clip over what cash remained, somewhere in the neighborhood of three thousand dollars, and putting it back into his inside coat pocket.

"That man needs to be hurt," he said in Spanish. "He shouldn't be killed. Not yet. He has information I intend to obtain. I merely want him to understand that killing him would be a trivial matter—and that he *will* be killed if he continues to refuse to talk."

The guard slid the cash into his pocket and nodded. "It will be taken care of."

"What did I say?"

"You said he's to be hurt."

"But."

A pause as the guard thought about what was expected of him. "But not killed."

"That last part is important. Do you understand?"

"Yes, sir."

"Make sure the man you hire understands as well."

"Yes, sir."

"Have it done tomorrow. On the yard."

"Yes, sir."

"Okay." Alejandro stepped outside. He pulled out the pocket square and wiped at his seeping nose. He snorted and spat a wad of blood into the dirt. It formed a bead as the dry sand absorbed the moisture. He squinted at the eastern horizon and saw the sun's nimbus arcing over the edge of the world, though the sun itself was still hidden. The low sky was heather gray, but higher up the air turned dark purple. Stars were visible in what remained of the plum night, dotting it like backlit pinpricks in a dark sheet.

He folded the pocket square, shoved it away, and walked toward his car, an ibis-white Audi A7 Prestige with twenty-inch wheels. He unlocked it as he approached, pulled open the door, and slid onto the soft beige leather driving seat. He started the car. The engine purred. He had a Los Dynamite CD in the stereo system, and as soon the car was started, *"No Me Sueltes"* began blasting through the speakers. He turned up the volume, slid the car into gear, and rolled toward the gates.

The guard who controlled them, recognizing the car, had all three rolling open before Alejandro was anywhere near. He drove through, dust drifting into the air behind him, and moved along an unpaved road that was little more than tire grooves in the sand. He made his way around the east side of the jail to the unnamed street that would become Calle El Tule when he reached La Paz. He cracked the window as he drove—he disliked still air—and watched the sunrise in the distance.

He entered the city about fifteen minutes after sliding in behind the wheel of his car. Rolled through the slums, small houses and dilapidatcd apartment buildings packed together tightly. Leaking roofs with tarps thrown over them; laundry drying on lines in grassless yards; cars and pickup trucks sitting on blocks; dogs chained to trees barking furiously at his car as he rolled by.

As he crossed Avenida la Cruz, the city turned middle class. He drove past Parque de los Niños, both the primary and secondary schools, the Slim Office Building, and La Valentina, the best restaurant in town, which he happened to own.

He thought about James Murphy. The man had something against him. His violence had been angry and that meant it was personal. Alejandro intended to find out who, if anyone, was behind him. Men of importance knew how to exploit lesser men for their own ends—he did this himself—and he suspected someone had seen the violence in James Murphy and pointed the man in his direction, as one might aim a gun. He wanted to know who.

When he reached his estate he turned right into the cobblestone driveway. He slid his window down and punched in the key code. The gate opened and he drove through. He glanced at his rearview mirror as the gate swung shut behind him, and then rolled past the fountain that split his driveway, a small quail bathing in it, and parked in a four-car garage to the right of the house, sliding in between a BMW 650i Gran Coupe and a Jaguar F-Type. He stepped out into the quickly brightening morning, walked to the front of the house, past two armed guards in black suits—they stared straight ahead, unmoving—and up a short flight of concrete steps. Pushed open the thick door and stepped into the air-conditioned house.

White Carrara marble lined the foyer. Beyond it lay a recessed living room with Macassar ebony floors, a hand-woven area rug rolled out across the wood, the room furnished with a coffee table and three couches.

Beautiful women lay across the couches, two on each of them, their legs tangled together. They were still awake from last night, not up early, lazily watching the sixty-inch Samsung HDTV mounted on the south wall above the never-used fireplace. The women glanced toward him as he stepped inside, one of them saying, "Welcome home, Alejandro." He nodded his greeting and they turned back to the TV. They didn't even notice the blood on his clothes. Or perhaps they knew better than to ask.

He glanced at the screen, saw they were watching Daniel Craig in *Casino Royale*. He watched for a moment himself before heading to the right, where a spiral staircase would take him to the second floor.

He walked upstairs and made his way down a long door-lined hallway to the master bedroom. As soon as he stepped through the door he began stripping himself of his seersucker suit, dropping clothes to the wood floor. Once he was naked he walked to the bathroom and turned on the cold water in the shower. He stepped under its spray. Washed himself, spat blood into the metal drain, brushed his teeth, shaved with a Panasonic wet-dry electric razor, and stood with his face tilted toward the showerhead, eyes closed, the spray massaging his eyelids and cheeks.

Several minutes passed.

Finally he turned off the shower, pushed through the glass door, stepped onto the thick bathmat, and grabbed an Egyptian cotton towel from the heated rod. He dried himself off and tossed the towel to the floor. He returned to the bedroom, pulled a pair of blue Armani bikini briefs from the top left drawer of his dresser. Stepped into them, slid them up—adjusting himself in the front pocket—and walked to the balcony. Opened the French doors and stepped out into the day, the tile cool beneath his feet. He squinted into the distance. The sun was now hovering above the horizon, the morning shadows stretched out long, pointing in his direction.

Beyond the Olympic-sized swimming pool and the well-kept lawn, beyond the clay tennis court and the cedar-enclosed backyard shower, beyond the koi pond and the guesthouse, beyond the back wall of the estate and the four armed guards posted along it, the desert stretched out for miles, heat vapors already beginning to distort the air with their wavering dance. Mesquite and guayule and ocotillo erupted from the orange sand. Rattlesnakes lay stretched out on boulders. Tarantulas hid in the shade under the shrubs. Lizards scurried.

He looked down at the pool area. Several women in bikinis lay in tanning chairs—some up early, some up late—drinks beside them on small glass-topped tables, lipstick-stained cigarettes angled in ashtrays sending ribbons of smoke into the desert air. Yet another woman was sitting on the pool's verge, her feet in the water kicking lazily, sending ripples out through the otherwise glassy surface.

He stood there for a long time before he turned, walked inside, and grabbed a Glock 22 from his dresser. He walked out of the bedroom and made his way downstairs to the kitchen. Pulled open the stainless steel refrigerator's top drawer, grabbed a Corona, popped the top with a bottle opener screwed into the wall, and headed out to the pool.

He took a drink of his beer, walked to an empty tanning chair, and lay down. He moved his Glock hand to his lap and rested it there. Glanced to his right. A fringe-toed lizard crawled along the concrete, moving toward the back of the property. Alejandro took another sip of beer, aimed, and fired. The gun kicked in his hand. The lizard vanished. One second it was there. The next it was gone. All that remained was a small triangular streak of blood on the concrete, making it look as though a ketchup packet had been stomped.

Several of the girls jumped and screamed.

Alejandro laughed, took another sip of his beer, and lay back again. He closed his eyes and let the heat of the sun warm his face. The insides of his eyelids were red.

■ Diego Blanco and Gael Morales drove through the west side of the city in a white Ford Econoline van. They weaved their way up and down the grid of the slums, looking for a kid named Paco. Skinny little punk about eighteen years old with a pathetic twelve-hair mustache, liked to wear Dodgers baseball caps backward. They'd been cruising the streets for almost an hour but had yet to see him. Diego tongued the toothpick in his mouth and thought about knocking a few heads together, asking questions, but the problem was that word might reach Paco before they did. If that happened, he'd run, and the last thing Diego wanted was to have to track him down in Juarez. He'd be damn near impossible to find, but Alejandro would demand it be done.

He scratched at the scar on the top of his right ear and turned left onto Avenida Violeta. They rolled toward a McDonald's.

"You hungry?" Diego asked in Spanish.

"A little," Gael said. "All I had this morning was a Pop-Tart."

Diego pulled into the McDonald's parking lot, rolled to the back of the six-car drive-thru line, and said: "What do you want?"

"Huevos con jamon."

"We're driving. No fork food."

"Then a McMuffin. What are you getting?"

"McMolletes."

"Coffee?"

"Yeah. You?"

"Orange juice. No. A small Coca-Cola with extra ice."

"For breakfast?"

Gael shrugged. "I like Coca-Cola."

The line moved forward. Diego glanced left to the building and saw Paco sitting at a table in front of the dust-covered picture window, shoving a *cuernito de jamon y queso* into his idiot face. He had on a backward baseball cap and a white jersey. He took a bite, slurped coffee, then—possibly feeling himself being watched—glanced out the window. For a moment he looked out blankly. Finally, their eyes locked, but neither of them moved. Recognition and fear transformed Paco's face. He panicked, got to his feet, and ran, abandoning his breakfast on the Formica table.

"Cabeza de mierda."

Diego slammed the transmission into park, shoved out of the van, leaving the driver's-side door open, and went running around to the front of the stucco building. Paco shoved through the front door just as Diego turned the corner, glanced toward him, and darted in the opposite direction, heading down Calle de Oro. Diego chased after him, staring at the KERSHAW on the back of the kid's jersey. He pulled a pistol from his waistband while he ran.

"Stop or I'll fucking kill you!"

But Paco didn't stop. He pivoted right, down Avenida la Cruz, losing one of his untied Jordans as he turned the corner. The shoe flipped end over end before settling on its side.

Diego kicked the shoe out of his way and continued to chase the little shit, knowing he couldn't shoot but wanting to put an end to this. Kid might have to die, but that was Alejandro's call, not his. He'd been tasked with delivering Paco alive and that was what he'd do.

He stumbled over a second shoe as he ran and almost fell. Kid must have kicked it off after losing the first. They continued south, the distance between them growing. Diego was too old for this, too fucking fat, but if he lost Paco, he'd be in the shit up to his nostrils. So he ignored the stitch in his side and worked up to a full-on sprint.

They ran toward Calle Fidel Avila, Diego slowly gaining on his prey. Kid started across the street but only made it halfway before the Ford Econoline screeched into the intersection from the west and slammed into him.

Paco went sprawling onto the cracked asphalt, head slamming against it even as he slid across the rough surface. Gael Morales shoved out of the driver's-side door, hurried to the kid, and pulled him to his feet by the collar of his jersey.

Diego caught up with them, out of breath, glad it was over.

"That's one way to do it."

"I know you hate to run."

Diego took over. Bashed Paco in the head with his pistol, grabbed a fistful of hair, and dragged him to the van. Kid's left arm and cheek were covered in road rash, blood beginning to seep from the shallow wounds. A patch of hair had been road-shaved from his head. Pieces of gravel were embedded in his flesh. But Diego was hardly inclined to feel sympathy. Little *hijo de perra* had made him run, and as Gael had mentioned, he fucking *hated* to run. He slid open the back door and shoved Paco inside. Followed him in, keeping his pistol aimed. Kid sat on the bench seat and Diego sat beside him.

"Please," the kid said.

"Yo cago en la leche de tu puta madre."

Gael leaned in through the sliding door. "You want me to drive, then?"

"If you don't mind."

Gael nodded, slid shut the door, and walked around to the driver's side.

Gael Morales had been on Alejandro's payroll a little more than six months now. He was about thirty years old, thin, maybe five foot eight, handsome, with dark skin and large green eyes—which meant one of his parents was probably white—wore Original Penguin polo shirts and cuffed raw-denim Levi's almost every day, smoked un-filtered Camels, and was always spitting flecks of tobacco from the end of his tongue. Said he smoked unfiltered because other people hated them. Meant nobody tried to bum.

Diego liked the guy. He was up for just about anything, didn't ask too many questions, and didn't cause trouble. Pretty soon, once Alejandro was comfortable with him, he might make real money. Until then, Diego slipped him a little extra on the side, just to make sure he stuck around. Guy like him would be able to make money somewhere and Diego wanted it to be here.

It was hard to find good men.

■ Alejandro's guys dragged Paco into the backyard. He heard them before he saw them, turned his head, and squinted as they hauled the kid through the gate at the side of the house. They dragged Paco toward him, one on each arm, and when they arrived shoved him forward. Kid was crying, tears streaming down his face.

"*Lo siento, lo siento, lo siento.*"

"*Puse mi polla en la boca para que te calles.*" He said it softly, al-most as if he were comforting the kid rather than telling him he'd put his dick in his mouth to shut him up, but that didn't matter. Kid pissed himself, a dark splotch spreading across the front of his jeans, liquid dripping from his pants and pooling around his shoeless feet. Alejandro didn't even want to know how the kid had lost his kicks. It didn't matter. What mattered was this:

"You stole from me, Paco."

35

"I was gonna pay you back. My father needed the money for—"

"Your father's gambling debts are of no concern to me."

"They were gonna kill him."

"So you stole from *me*?"

"I was gonna pay you back."

"What did you think would happen when I found out?"

"I didn't think—"

"You didn't think I *would* find out."

"No, sir."

"Why would you pay me back, then?"

"Because I don't steal."

"But you *did* steal. You walked into my convenience store and you emptied my register."

"It wasn't very much money."

"It isn't about the money, Paco. It's the principle. You could have come to me and asked for work. I might've found something for you. You might've been able to *earn* the money. You know I take care of my city and the people in it."

"I was going—"

"To pay me back. I know. But people can't think that it's okay to steal from me."

"They don't."

"I know they don't. Because when people *do* steal from me, I do to them what I'm about to do to you."

"Please."

"Please what?"

"I'll work it off."

"It's too late for that."

"I'll work *hard*."

"It isn't about the money, Paco. You could have robbed any number of places I don't own, but you robbed one of mine instead."

"I'll do whatever you wish. I'll do anything."

Alejandro cocked an eyebrow. "Anything?"

"Anything at all."

"Good. Then I'm going to request that you die."

He raised the Glock and squeezed the trigger. The sound was loud. The head jerked back. A red dot appeared above the right eyebrow. Blood seeped from the dot, ran down the forehead, rolled across the ridge of the eyebrow, and down the cheek. It dripped onto the white jersey. The kid took two steps back and fell into the swimming pool. Blood spread out from the head, turning the clear water red.

"Damn it," Alejandro said. "Now I won't be able to swim." He slammed the Glock down on the table beside him. "Gael, get this motherfucker out of my swimming pool."

■ While the kid pissed himself and cried, Gael pulled a pack of Camels from the breast pocket of his navy polo shirt, tapped out a cigarette, put it between his lips, and set it on fire. He took a drag from the cigarette and exhaled through his nostrils. He spat a flake of tobacco from the end of his tongue. Thought about what he was doing here.

These people knew him as Gael Morales, but the name on his birth certificate was Gael Castillo Jimenez. He was thirty years old, son of Jorge Castillo Jimenez and Lois Castillo Jimenez, née Gordon. Born in Buena Park, California, 1985. Bachelor's degree in criminology from California State University, Long Beach. Master's from the University of Maryland.

He'd joined the DEA with the ink on his master's still wet, one of a small percentage of recruits who didn't have prior law enforcement experience, and spent eighteen weeks at Quantico receiving firearms training, learning about drug recognition, and going through a defensive tactics regimen, after which he spent another nine weeks undergoing intelligence training. He was assigned to the El Paso field office and had since been involved in dozens of cases, dozens of arrests.

This was his fourth undercover assignment.

But he no longer believed drugs should be illegal, which was the foundation on which the job was built. He saw himself and the DEA as fighting an unwinnable war, a war they didn't even have real incentive to win. Eliminate drugs and the reason for the DEA to exist was eliminated as well. No organization would work effectively toward its own eradication. It would be stupid to do so. But it was a war they probably shouldn't be fighting in the first place. The drugs themselves weren't the real problem, not the biggest problem. It was the violence of the trade that needed to stop, and you didn't have to eliminate drugs to stop it. Drugs couldn't be stopped. Might as well try to stop the tides.

Legalizing them would end the violence. Eliminate the incentive to traffic. Prices would drop dramatically, as the prices for marijuana dropped in states that legalized.

End drug prohibition altogether, legalize everything from cocaine to heroin, create safety guidelines. Have drugs sold in regulated locations, in regulated amounts. Tax them. Use the tax money to build and run rehabilitation centers for those who develop problems. Drug violence drops to almost nothing, both the violence of dealers fighting over territory and the violence of desperate people looking for cash to buy their next overpriced fix. Addicts can seek free treatment, treatment they already paid for by purchasing taxed drugs. No more smuggling. No more drug wars between cartels. No more nonviolent offenders filling the prisons.

No more mothers crying over the bodies of teenage sons shot during drug deals gone wrong or busts turned ugly.

The prohibition on alcohol had been tried, and it had failed for the same reasons the drug prohibition would fail, for the same reasons it had already failed. Prohibition did nothing but create an avoidable criminal class.

But full legalization would never happen.

Too many people needed drug prohibition to continue—politicians, law enforcement agencies, prison systems justifying their bloated budgets—which meant there'd always be violent men running violent cartels, filling a need that would be filled no matter how many beat cops walked the streets, no matter what the punishment for possession or trafficking became.

And those men needed to be stopped.

This he believed, despite no longer believing in prohibition itself. Individual bad men must be brought down. You might not be able to stop drugs, but you could stop the most violent of the men who ran them. So he continued to fight his battles, knowing all the while the war was already lost, but believing that, if individual situations were handled correctly, the violence could be lessened.

He'd gone undercover six months ago, befriended one of Alejandro Rocha's low-level employees, and talked himself onto the payroll. To earn Rocha's trust, he did things he'd never do in real life, violent things that made him part of what he was trying to stop, but he told himself it was for the greater good. He might have to be violent, but his small-scale violence would lead to stopping the large-scale violence, and that made it worth it.

Since going undercover he'd learned a great deal. He could prove very little of it, but he was getting there, getting closer every day.

He knew, for instance, that Alejandro Rocha used underground tunnels to smuggle drugs across the border. He knew that he kept girls hooked on junk so he could manipulate them into doing what he wanted, which might involve smuggling balloons of heroin across the border or whoring themselves out for their next fix.

He knew Rocha was responsible for dozens of murders.

The murders he could prove, but he had no jurisdiction over homicide in Mexico, and those who did had been bought and paid for. Rocha could shoot a man in the face on the steps of La Paz police station and walk away without so much as a stern talking-to.

But Gael thought he might be getting close to something. Yesterday he'd sneaked into Rocha's office and collected phone bills, wire transfer receipts, and a few other pieces of paperwork, and when he next had the opportunity he'd take these things to the dead drop so his stateside handler on this case, George Rankin, could collect them and start checking phone numbers and bank account information.

Every day he was getting closer, but for now he was here, in the middle of it, deeply involved in what he was—

The sound of a gunshot shocked him from his thoughts. He

39

watched Paco's head snap back. Watched blood run down his forehead and face. Watched it drip onto his jersey even as he stumbled backward and fell into the swimming pool. Blood spread in the water.

"Damn it," Rocha said. "Now I won't be able to swim. Gael, get this motherfucker out of my swimming pool."

But for a moment Gael remained frozen in place. He only looked at the kid floating dead in the pool, eyes blank as broken television screens. He'd brought Paco here and now he was dead. It was his fault. He told himself again that he had to take part in these things to earn Rocha's trust, but that didn't make him feel better about it. This kid had robbed a convenience store, but he'd hurt nobody, and now he was dead. Dead because Gael had brought him here when he could have let him escape.

"Gael," Alejandro said.

"What? Sorry."

"*Get* this *motherfucker* out of my *swimming pool*."

Gael nodded and butted out his cigarette in an ashtray. He walked to the edge of the pool, got down on his hands and knees, reached out to grab the kid. Got hold of the left foot and pulled him toward the verge. Yanked him up onto the concrete, wet, blood seeping from the hole in his head. Within the hour Gael would be driving the body into the desert for burial.

Paco's parents would never know what became of him.

Gael got to his feet and headed toward the garage to get a roll of plastic sheeting.

4

Vincent Cooper was sitting at the counter in a dive bar in El Paso, Texas, shoving the last bite of a mustard-smeared Nathan's into his mouth, when this girl walked over and sat on the stool next to him. He figured women only sat next to men in bars if they were interested, so he turned to check her out. She was maybe twenty-two, brunette, and pretty enough that she might have been the fifth most popular girl in high school. She tapped the bar's surface with a blue-polished nail and waited for the guy on the other side to notice her so she could order.

"I'm Coop," he said.

"Good for you." She glanced at him, and, after hesitating, said: "Patricia."

"Can I buy you a drink?"

"If you want to."

"What'll it be?"

"Whiskey and Coke."

"Well whiskey?"

She nodded.

He looked toward the bartender, a skinny guy about forty with tattooed sleeves in a black Bukowski T-shirt with pomaded hair and a bushy beard, streaks of gray on either side of his chin. He caught his eye.

"Another Bud?"

"Please. And a whiskey and Coke for the lady."

Bartender nodded, and less than a minute later, set the drinks down in front of them. Coop paid with a ten spot, got his change, and left a dollar on the counter. He looked toward Patricia, held up his beer, and said, "Cheers."

She raised her own glass, tilted it toward him, and took a drink.

"What do you do, Patricia?"

She hesitated again, looked at him in silence for a long time, and said, "I'm not gonna sleep with you if that's what you're after."

"I didn't realize we'd gotten to the rejection part of the conversation just yet."

"I don't want you to get your hopes up is all."

"Is it because I'm black? Don't date the negroes?"

"That's got nothing to do with it."

"What is it?"

"It's because when you go to work on Monday it'll be at Fort Bliss. I don't date soldiers."

"I'm not a soldier."

"You've got a military haircut. Military posture. You're wearing combat boots with your cargo shorts and you got a pack of Newports in your T-shirt pocket. I've lived in this town my whole life. I know a soldier when I see one, and I don't date soldiers. It's nothing personal."

"Soldiers are Army. I'm a Marine."

"What's the difference?"

"Why don't you ask a doctor what's the difference between him and a paramedic."

"Whatever. I just didn't want you to waste your time hammering at something you couldn't nail down."

"Nice metaphor, but I was only counting on conversation."

"I don't believe you."

"Then I guess we're done here."

"I guess we are."

He picked up her drink, finished it in a single draught, ice clinking, and set the glass back down on the bar. He grabbed his beer and got to his feet. Started to walk away and managed two steps before the girl called him an asshole. He stopped, thought about responding, but decided against it. He wasn't nearly drunk enough to pick a fight with some chick he didn't know. Instead he walked to the jukebox while fishing in his pocket for a few loose bills. He was feeding the first dollar into the machine when someone behind him called his name. He looked over his shoulder to see who it was.

Norman Kassube, short guy with blond hair and blue eyes, was standing with a beer in hand, looking back and forth between the TV above the bar and Coop. He wore cutoff shorts, Emerica skate shoes, and a Slint T-shirt with cutoff sleeves. On his right shin was a tattoo of Johnny Cash. On his left was one of Willie Nelson. He looked upset about something.

"What is it, Normal?" Nobody called Norman by his given name, not even his parents. Coop had asked him once how he'd gotten the nickname but he'd said he didn't know. Couldn't remember a time when he'd been anything but Normal.

"Get over here, man."

Coop walked over and asked the question again.

"On the TV. It's coming up."

Coop looked toward the TV. A few commercials flashed across the screen, and after the last of them flickered away, a blond newscaster with thick makeup in reds and blues appeared on-screen. She wore a low-cut red blouse. She smiled, and through too-white teeth, said:

"Welcome back. Tonight we bring you the story of a local Marine Corps sergeant arrested in La Paz, Mexico, a desert town thirty miles west of Ciudad Juarez. James Ian Murphy, twenty-eight, was born in the small town of Bulls Mouth, Texas, and grew up in Austin. With a football scholarship, he received a bachelor's degree in anthropology at Texas A&M before enlisting in the Marine Corps as a private, despite being eligible to join as a second lieutenant. One month ago he returned home after a year in Afghanistan. He is considered by those who know him to be an all-American hero. But last night it was discovered that he was arrested in Mexico with five kilograms of cocaine in the trunk of his rented car. A later search of his hotel room revealed that he also had illegal arms in his possession. La Paz Police Department intends to indict him on charges of possession with intent to sell, and arms trafficking. According to Mexican law, anyone possessing more than half a gram of cocaine is subject to three to six years in prison, but because of the quantity found in Mr. Murphy's trunk, he could face as many as eighteen years. With the addition of weapons charges, this could add up to more than thirty years in prison.

"The United States Embassy's Consulate Office regularly makes phone calls to police departments throughout Mexico to learn about any U.S. citizens who have faced arrest, and was informed yesterday about the charges filed against Murphy. An arraignment has not yet been scheduled, but we will keep you updated on the progress of the case. The Consulate Office is expected to send a representative to La Paz by next Friday, and we hope to learn more then."

Coop looked at Normal. "What the fuck was he even doing in Mexico?"

"I don't know, man."

"Did you know anything about it?"

"No," Normal said. "I thought he was in Austin for his sister's funeral."

"There's no way he was trafficking drugs."

"I know. He's the most straight-edge dude I know."

"Especially not after what happened with his sister."

"I *know*, man."

"It doesn't make any fucking sense. We have to find out what happened."

"How are we supposed to do that?" Normal said.

"Pilar might know something."

"Wasn't she supposed to go to Austin with him?"

"He didn't go to Austin. Let's go see her."

"It's almost midnight."

"I don't give a fuck what time it is. There's something wrong about this."

Coop set his almost-full beer down on the bar and headed for the door. He pushed out into the warm night air. Normal walked out behind him.

◙ Pilar Gutierrez was rolling around in bed with some guy whose name she'd already forgotten. She'd been drinking at Shamrock's Irish Pub with a girlfriend when this Army captain started buying her vodka tonics. He was nice enough, but she knew she shouldn't be doing this. She and James had broken up the day he left for his sister's funeral, five days ago now, but as mad as she was at the way he'd left it, she knew his sister's death had made him into something he wasn't. He'd apologize when he got back and they'd be a couple again. Which meant their breakup was a technicality at best. But she'd been angry when she invited this guy into their apartment. She'd waited for James in North Carolina while he was overseas, dropped everything to be with him in El Paso, and he'd dumped her after being stateside only a month. But now that she was in bed with this stranger—in *their* bed—all she could think about was how to extricate herself from the situation. She wanted this guy off the bed she shared with James, wanted him off the bed and out of the fucking apartment.

A knock at the door did it, three hard bangs with the side of a fist.

She pulled away, relieved, and said, "I better get that."

She pushed off the bed and got to her feet. The room spun and she held out her arms, waiting for the dizziness to pass, and after a moment the room stopped moving and tilting around her. She made her way out of the bedroom, down the hall, to the front door. Unlocked it, grabbed the doorknob, and pulled.

Coop and Normal stood facing her in the darkness. Normal was scraping at the inside of his right nostril with a thumbnail, but when he realized she'd answered the knock, he pulled his thumb from his nose and wiped it on his cutoff shorts.

"Gross," she said.

"I didn't think you'd answer."

"You knocked."

"Coop knocked."

"Not the point, Normal."

"It was hanging like a Christmas ornament."

"I don't care. You don't knock on someone's door and then pick your nose."

"Coop knocked."

"For God's sake, Normal, that's not the *point*. What do you guys want?"

"What's James doing in Mexico?" Coop said.

"James is in Austin."

"No, he's in Mexico, and he just got arrested."

"What?"

Coop nodded. "I know."

"Arrested for what?"

"Possession with intent to sell and arms trafficking. Cops found five kilograms of cocaine in his trunk."

"No way."

"That's what I said, but apparently it's the facts. Any idea what might've happened?"

Pilar looked over her shoulder toward her bedroom, thought about the man in her bed, the man in *James's* bed. She didn't want Coop or Normal to find out he was back there. They'd tell James, and he had enough to worry about. She'd known it was a mistake as soon as they'd come here, and that knowledge was confirmed now by the guilt she felt.

"Hold on," she said.

She closed the door in their faces and made her way to the bedroom. Looked at the man in her bed. He was sitting up, leaning against the headboard, legs crossed at the ankles. When she stepped into the doorway he turned away from the muted TV he'd been watching, looked her in the eyes.

"Everything all right?"

"You gotta go."

"What's going on?"

She shook her head. "Don't worry about it. I just need you to leave."

The guy nodded. "Okay." He sat on the edge of the bed and slipped his socks and sneakers on.

"Go out the back door."

He got to his feet, ran his fingers through his hair. "You have a boyfriend."

"Kind of."

He nodded. "That answers my question about whether I can call you."

"Sorry."

"It's okay. I'm glad it didn't go further."

"Me too," Pilar said. "You're a nice guy, but—"

"It's fine. I'm used to being the nice guy who doesn't get laid. I'll go home and rub one out. See you around." He walked past her and turned left down the hallway. She watched as he pushed out the back door.

As soon as it latched behind him she felt relief wash over her, but the relief was short-lived. James was stuck in a Mexican jail and she had no idea what had happened to get him there.

She walked back to the front door and pulled it open.

"Come in. Sit down."

Coop and Normal stepped inside and sat on the couch. Pilar took a seat in a chair across from them, looked from one to the other. "Tell me what's going on."

"We don't know any more than what we told you," Coop said. "It was on the news tonight. James was in Mexico and got arrested with cocaine and guns. Normal and I both agree there's no way he was trying to deal coke or sell weapons. We just don't know what the hell he *was* doing or how this might've happened."

"I don't either. Unless it's somehow related to his sister."

Pilar and James had been talking about visiting his family for some time, about James introducing her to his parents, and despite the circumstances she'd assumed she would go to the funeral. She wanted to be there for him. He loved his sister and when he learned of her death, he'd cried. It was the only time she'd ever seen him reveal a vulnerable side. But on Monday, as he was packing his duffel bag and preparing to leave, he told her he was going by himself. They fought about it. She said that if he didn't love her enough to have her there for his sister's funeral, maybe he didn't love her at all—maybe they should break up.

He surprised her by agreeing. "If you're gonna be a bitch about it, then you're right. This isn't about *you*, Pilar. My fucking sister's dead." He snatched his duffel and stormed out the front door, slamming it behind him. She waited for him to call, to apologize, but it never happened. He was just gone.

Now it turned out, if she was interpreting the situation correctly, he'd been shielding her from what he was really up to. He'd missed his sister's funeral to go to Mexico, but his trip *had* to have something to do with her death.

"How could it be related to Layla?"

Coop knew less than she did. James didn't talk about personal matters with friends, didn't even talk much about personal matters with her, only what she could pry from the back of his clamped teeth. He generally kept himself to himself. So she didn't know how much to share, didn't want to betray his trust, but she also believed they might have to do something about James being arrested, which meant Coop and Normal should be given at least some information.

She exhaled, paused a moment in thought, and said, "Layla was living with a drug dealer in Mexico before she died."

"Could James have been working with the drug dealer?"

Pilar threw Normal a look of contempt, and it must have been withering, because he dropped his gaze to his lap. "I didn't think it. I was just asking."

"Layla's drug dealer boyfriend must've had something to do with the cocaine the cops found."

"We should go down there and talk to James," Normal said.

Coop agreed: "I was thinking the same thing."

They decided they'd all had too much to drink to head out right away; they'd get some rest and leave in the morning. Wouldn't be able to accomplish anything tonight anyway.

Coop and Normal left. Pilar watched them step outside, closed the door behind them, and latched the dead bolt. Stumbled back to her bedroom and lay in bed, staring at the ceiling. She asked herself what James had been doing in Mexico, what he'd *really* done to get himself arrested, but couldn't begin to guess.

She rolled onto her side and pulled his pillow close to her. She inhaled its scent and wondered if she'd ever get to hold him again, wondered if there'd always be bars between them. She thought about their last conversation, the angry words between them, and felt a sad regret seep into her heart.

"What the hell kind of trouble did you get yourself into, James?"

■ Bogart Thompson woke up to the sound of the living room TV, its muffled vibrations coming in through his thin bedroom wall, Wile E. Coyote getting his ass handed to him yet again as he chased after the Road Runner. He didn't remember leaving it on, but then he'd been so drunk and high he barely remembered coming home.

He sat up in bed, rubbed his eyes. His head ached and his mouth tasted like he'd licked the bottom of a hamster cage. He looked at the glass bong sitting on his nightstand, picked it up, sniffed the tea-colored water, and cringed. It needed to be changed, but he wasn't going to bother right now. He grabbed an orange prescription pill bottle, pulled out a chunk of sour diesel sativa, something to ease him into the day, broke it up, and loaded the bong. Took a big hit, removing the bowl and thumbing the carb once it was filled with thick smoke. Inhaled deeply. Held it in for as long as he could before sending out a chain of throaty coughs. Once the coughing subsided, he took a second hit, finishing what he'd loaded. Tapped

49

out his leavings in a glass ashtray. Got to his feet and stood a moment looking out the window, thinking nothing at all, the morning sun slanting through the dirty glass.

His lips began to tingle from the sour diesel.

His thoughts, scattered across the messy floor of his mind, put themselves together, allowing him to find focus.

He'd first smoked marijuana while in Afghanistan. Life there was both boring and dangerous, an unsettling combination, and brutal violence could erupt out of nowhere. Pot kept his nerves under control, and when he needed to take action, helped him focus.

Up until a month ago, he and the rest of his scout-sniper platoon had been stationed with the Second Reconnaissance Battalion in Nad Ali, and while much of their job consisted of reconnoitering the landscape to gain intelligence, on eleven occasions he'd been tasked with assassinating specific enemy targets.

Pot also helped him smudge the otherwise crisp memories he had of what he'd seen through his scope, both before and after squeezing his trigger.

After a while he turned, walked to the bathroom, flipped up the seat with his bare foot, and pulled down his waistband. Urine splashed into the bowl, hitting the water with great force. He drained for a long time, feeling like he must've had a gallon of piss in him, but finally sent out the last few splashes with a shiver.

"That your first piss in a week? Sounds like a fire hose in there."

He jumped, splashing the edge of the bowl, then shook off and made his way out to the living room. Coop was sitting on the couch watching cartoons. He sipped coffee from a Dunkin' Donuts cup, popped a hash brown into his mouth.

"I got you coffee but left it in the rental car."

"What are you doing here?"

"You got a little pee-pee on your undies."

Bogart looked down and saw a quarter-sized wet spot on the front of his briefs. "It'll dry. What are you doing here?"

"We're going to Mexico."

"Who are?"

"We are."

"How come?"

"Do you care?"

"Not really. When are we going?"

"Now."

"Be back before Monday?"

"That's the plan."

"Let me get my weed."

"Most people smuggle drugs *out* of Mexico, Bogart."

"I'm not smuggling. It's for personal use."

"All right, get your weed. You might wanna put some pants on too."

"I'll think about it."

■ They were on the road by ten o'clock. Coop sat behind the wheel of the rented Toyota Corolla, feeling jittery, wishing he'd skipped the third cup of coffee. Pilar in the passenger seat to his right. Bogart and Normal in back. Coop had picked up Normal last, and he'd made them stop at a convenience store to grab some sour chews. He and Bogart were fighting over who got to eat the red ones.

"I bought them, motherfucker."

"But I hate the green ones. You like them."

"Not as much as the reds."

Coop turned up the radio, which was playing The Fall's cover of "Mr. Pharmacist," and tried to tune out the braying donkeys in the backseat. He lit a Newport, cracked his window, and eased them onto US-54. While he drove he thought about what they were doing, going to Mexico with no idea what they might find there, but he was pretty damn sure they were rolling into trouble. Whatever James had been doing in La Paz, he'd gotten himself tangled in a mess, and they'd have to climb into it to get him out.

Coop was born in Rochester, New York, to a lawyer father and a schoolteacher mother, and they were both upset when he started talking about joining the Marine Corps. His father told him that black people signed up for military service to get opportunities they wouldn't otherwise have, but since he already *had* those opportunities—good grades from a suburban school (with a weighted GPA of 4.6), a college fund ($62,000), and supportive parents—he didn't need the signing bonus or the GI Bill to continue his education. He tried to explain that he was joining for the experience, joining so that he could see something other than upstate New York before he went on with his life, but his father only told him he should take a sabbatical year and travel Europe if that's what he was after. That wasn't the kind of experience he was looking for, though, so he signed up against his parents' wishes, and saw things he never would have imagined, did things he never would have believed.

He'd learned more about himself in the last eleven years, learned more about what he was capable of, than most people ever did.

For instance, he knew without doubt that he would risk his own life to save the life of a friend. James Murphy was one of his *best* friends, which meant it didn't matter what kind of trouble James had gotten himself into, Coop was going to do what he could to get him out of it, and he wouldn't hesitate in his actions.

He pressed down on the gas pedal and drove on, angling toward Mexico and whatever was waiting for him there.

◼ Pilar looked out the passenger window at the hot blur of the world while Coop slanted the car off US-54, brought it to a stop at an intersection, and turned right onto East Paisano Drive. He turned the car left onto I-110, and they headed south toward Mexico once more, but only drove a few hundred feet before traffic brought them to a crawl, backed up at the border. Pilar looked past Coop to the driver's-side window and the world beyond it. To their left was the El Paso BOTA Port of Entry, twelve lanes of slow-moving traffic merging into four lanes of stopped traffic that snaked south for at least a mile. They'd be in Mexico within ten minutes. Those near the end of the line on the Mexico side wouldn't enter the United States for hours. Coop pulled his foot off the brake and eased the car forward.

They'd soon be entering Mexico, and though it had only been a twenty minute drive, it already felt like they were on a different planet.

For the last several days, James had been no more than forty-five miles away, but what he was involved in had so little to do with normal life that it felt as though he were much farther. Pilar knew that to be true without knowing exactly what he'd been involved in.

She'd felt the same when, as a girl, she visited her uncle Arturo in Mexico City. Two weeks each summer from the time she was seven until she was seventeen. Her parents thought it would keep her connected to her ancestry. Three generations of family lived in Mexico while she and her parents lived in Jacksonville, North Carolina, where she'd met James while he was stationed at Camp Lejeune.

Uncle Arturo managed an armored truck company with six branches in Mexico. He was fat and funny and crude, with a big round face and a goatee that only drew attention to the second chin he tried to hide. She liked him a great deal. She also believed that, every once in a while, he organized the heist of one of his company's trucks. She had no evidence to confirm this, no proof, but every now and then Uncle Arturo had a lot of money on hand without explanation. He'd spend more freely, buy expensive meals, send toys or several hundred dollars in a birthday card whether it was her birthday or not. He was smart enough that he wouldn't spend like that if one of his trucks had been robbed recently. But if you checked the newspapers, something she'd never done, she bet you'd find an article from six or nine months earlier about an ATC truck being robbed somewhere, probably right after a large collection from a bank or department store. Police might believe the way the robbery went down meant they were dealing with professionals who spent weeks planning their heist. But an inside man who knew all the details could get even common hoodlums to do a professional job, and such a man could also get away with paying those hoodlums a very small cut of the overall take.

After crossing the border, traffic picked up again, and they continued south on route 45 for some time, moving down through the cluttered city until they reached a two-lane road that would carry them west. They turned right and drove into the empty desert, the white sun beating down on the rented Toyota, nothing but shrub-punctuated sand and rocks on either side of them, rattlesnakes stretched across the faded asphalt.

■ Coop turned onto Avenida Hidalgo about eleven o'clock, drove the Toyota through La Paz until he hit the north end of town, and made a left onto Calle Santa Lucia. He drove slowly, checking the place out. James had been arrested here, and since he and James were a scout sniper team, since he'd worked as James's spotter in Afghanistan, he found himself instinctively noting the landscape as if reconnoitering enemy territory. Here was a blind alley. Here was a good place from which to shoot, offering protection and a 180-degree view of the surrounding area. Here was an old church with only one entrance, boarded-up windows, and thick walls, a good place to hole up if facing more enemies than you could handle; they might come in but you'd pick them off as they did.

There was no good reason for this. La Paz was a mid-sized desert town in Mexico with little that might distinguish it from any other desert town, but on instinct he filed the information away. He simply couldn't turn off that part of his brain.

"Do you know where you're going?" Pilar said.

Coop's iPhone map indicated that they should have reached the jail already, that they'd passed it a quarter mile back, but since they hadn't, he'd have to go old school and ask for directions. "No," he said, "but I'm about to find out."

He pulled the car into a strip mall and brought it to an angled stop at the front of the building. Looked at the various businesses lined up in front of him. A couple restaurants, a bar, a dry-cleaning place, and a convenience store. Someone in one of those joints would be able to tell them how to get to the jail. He pushed open the door, stepped outside, and slammed himself into a wall of heat. Sweat beaded on his skin.

He walked toward the convenience store.

◼ They arrived at La Paz City Jail visitors' entrance about twenty minutes later. Eleven other cars were already parked in front of them. Visiting hours, according to a sign on the front of the guard station, were twelve to one Monday, Thursday, and Saturday, and the gates were open from eleven fifty until twelve ten on those days. Any car not let through at that point wouldn't be let through at all. They waited, their air-conditioned vehicle motionless, a chain of cars extending behind them, new links constantly latching to the back of the line.

Finally, the gate guard began letting vehicles through one at a time. The line moved forward and they moved with it. When they reached the guard station, Coop handed the guard all four IDs. The guard noted their names, recorded their license plate number and its origin, and waved them through.

Coop drove them onto the jailhouse grounds. It was five past noon.

They rolled along tire ruts in the sand to a large dirt parking lot.

Once Coop brought the car to a stop, they stepped out into the heat and walked to the back of yet another line, this one human in form, a couple dozen people standing and sweating under the sun's glare. The line led toward a cinder block building. A guard with a clipboard stood by the door. Above his head was a sign telling them that the door closed at twelve thirty; anybody still outside at that point would remain outside. The line progressed as people were processed and allowed through. After about twenty minutes, with visiting hour almost half over, they reached the guard.

He asked who they were visiting.

"James Murphy," Pilar said.

The guard looked at the clipboard, flipping through the pages. Finally he said, "James Murphy can have no visitors."

"Why not?"

"He is in the infirmary."

Coop felt a ball of dread plunk into his gut like a lead fishing weight, splashing acid up into his throat. He swallowed, glanced at Pilar, and saw her face blanch.

"Is he gonna be okay?"

"You think I'm a doctor?"

"What happened?"

The guard shrugged and looked past them to the next person in line, ending the conversation. James was in the infirmary and they had no idea what had happened other than he was injured, which could mean anything from a bad hangnail to a cracked skull.

Maybe he'd be okay; maybe he wouldn't.

"What do we do now?" Pilar said.

"Let's see if we can find a hotel in La Paz," Coop said. "I'm not leaving Mexico until I know what the hell is going on here."

5

Juan Jesus Gonzales folded the wad of cash Rocha had given him without bothering to count it and shoved it into his uniform's right hip pocket. He looked at the man standing across from him in that bloodstained seersucker suit, black hair neatly trimmed, eyes bright as lanterns. Finally, Juan Jesus spoke: "It will be taken care of."

"What did I say?"

"You said he is to be hurt."

"But."

Juan Jesus paused a moment as he thought about what Rocha expected of him. He knew he must say the right thing. Rocha appeared calm on the surface, like a lake on a windless day, and he might have been calm, but he could turn violent with shocking suddenness. Things were happening beneath the glassy surface that you couldn't see, a frenzy of violence down in the darkness. "But not killed," he said.

"That last part is important. Do you understand?"

"Yes, sir."

"Make sure the man you hire understands as well."

"Yes, sir."

"Have it done tomorrow. On the yard."

"Yes, sir."

"Okay." Rocha stepped outside. Juan Jesus watched the door swing shut behind him, pinching the light that slanted in through the doorway, and as it latched, cutting it off.

Relief washed over him. Rocha paid well, but being around him made Juan Jesus nervous, made his chest feel tight with the fear that he'd do something wrong, or something Rocha perceived as wrong, and face violent consequences. That fear made him think of his wife and his one-year-old daughter, made him think about their lives without him.

If he died today, his little girl wouldn't even remember him.

He exhaled in a sigh, turned, and walked with Miguel, the other guard, stumbling along beside him. They walked in silence for a while, but as they got to the break room, Miguel said, "Why did he give you the money and not me?"

"I guess he trusts me."

"Didn't *sound* like he trusted you."

"Trusts me more than he trusts you."

"It's bullshit. Like I don't need money?"

"Take it up with him next time you two sit down for a heart-to-heart."

"Very funny."

Juan Jesus pulled out the fold of cash Rocha had given him, peeled off a hundred-dollar bill, and handed it to Miguel. He slipped the rest back into his pocket and told Miguel he had to take care of business now, so why didn't he go back to what he'd been doing before Rocha had showed up. Miguel left, and once he was gone, Juan Jesus walked to his locker. He unlocked the padlock, pulled open the blue metal door, pushed aside his lunch bag, which was on the top shelf, and from behind it grabbed a shiv he'd confiscated from an inmate last week.

The same inmate slit someone's throat in the cafeteria two days later.

If someone in jail wanted a weapon, he'd find a way to make or procure one. Earlier this year, an inmate even managed to get a gun in. His brother shoved a PSA .25 Baby Browning into a Nerf football and threw it over the fences. Guards hadn't seen it happen. The next day he shot three members of a gang that'd been threatening him. Might as well hand them *all* guns and be done with it. Let them kill each other. It'd save time and money in the long run.

He slipped the shiv into his uniform pocket, leaned down, and grabbed four packs of Marlboros. They traded better in jails and prisons than any other brand, so he always had a few cartons on hand. He slammed the locker shut, threaded the padlock, and snapped it into place. Walked out of the break room and made his way to Block D, one of the three long-term wings in the jail, cell 24.

A bespectacled man in his late forties sat at the desk on the other side of the bars reading *La Luz Que Regresa* by Salvador Elizondo in the early morning light that poured in through the window. He was thin and clean-shaven with short gray hair. His lenses were thick, wedged into black plastic frames. He was nearsighted but even behind the glass, his eyes looked big as boiled eggs. If he weren't a brutal murderer, he might have been a librarian.

He didn't have a name. Or rather, nobody knew his name. He'd been arrested while in the midst of disemboweling a prostitute, his tenth victim that police knew about, but refused to identify himself to police. His fingerprints had been burned off with acid. So he was called Fulanito, which meant "so-and-so," making him as nonexistent as a man could be nowadays. He never had visitors, had no friends, and wasn't a member of a gang, though he'd been here four years, in a kind of purgatory, waiting until his identity was discovered so he could face trial. But nobody messed with him. Nobody dared to.

His crimes were severe enough that, after his conviction, he'd almost certainly be moved to a federal prison. But since that trial would never happen, he'd instead remain here until he died, never facing judgment other than God's.

He looked up at Juan Jesus, keeping his place in the book with an index finger, and said, "How may I help you?"

"I have a job for you."

"What kind of job?"

Juan Jesus removed the shiv from his pocket and held it out to Fulanito through the bars. The man took it, examined it a moment, and set it down on the desk.

"Who is this job for?"

"Does it matter?"

"I'd like to know."

"Alejandro Rocha."

"Ah. Payment?"

Juan Jesus held out the cigarettes, but Fulanito only blinked, refusing to take them.

"I require a full carton of cigarettes for such a job."

"You're not supposed to kill him."

Fulanito raised an eyebrow.

"This man needs to understand that if Rocha wanted to, he *could* have him killed."

"I see." He took the cigarettes.

"It needs to happen tomorrow. On the yard."

"The white-bread American brought in yesterday?"

Juan Jesus nodded.

"Anything else?"

"Try not to cause any permanent damage."

"Not a problem. Now, if that's it, I'd like to get back to my book."

◾ The lights came on in the cell block at eight o'clock. James, who'd been in bed, staring at the ceiling, sat up and slipped his Pumas on. The cell doors unlatched and rusting hinges creaked as they fell open. He walked to his barred door and looked out into the corridor. Prisoners stepped from their cells and lined up. He followed their lead and stepped out of his cell. The man behind him muttered an insult in Spanish, but he ignored it. The last thing he wanted to do in his current situation was make enemies. He'd fight if he had to, but he'd neither start one nor be goaded into one. He had no friends here, which meant everybody was a potential enemy, and it was best to make as few as possible.

After all the inmates were lined up in the corridor, two guards led them to the cafeteria, a large room lined with pressed-wood tables and benches. Guards stood in each corner, pepper spray and saps tucked into their belts, eyes scanning.

James followed the line to the back of the cafeteria. Several prisoners stood on the other side of a long stainless steel serving counter. He picked up a damp tray and plastic utensils—a fork and a spoon and a butter knife—and slid his tray along the front of the counter while those on the other side used ice cream scoops to slop thin oatmeal, eggs scrambled with stale corn chips, and burned refried beans onto his tray's various compartments. As he reached the end of the counter someone tossed two mold-covered tortillas onto his tray.

He picked up a half-pint carton of expired milk and turned to face the room.

Against the far wall he saw a table at which only two people were sitting. He walked to the table and sat with his back to the wall. He wanted to be able to face the room and the men in it. You didn't turn your back to a roomful of killers and rapists.

He looked down at his food. It smelled sour, just a little bit off. He peeled the mold away from the edge of one of his tortillas, spooned beans into it. He was very hungry. This was his first meal since breakfast the day before, and breakfast had consisted of nothing more than a Snickers, but the smell in here, the smell coming off what he'd been served, made him nauseous. He took a bite, chewed. The tortilla tasted like mold. The beans tasted like the burnt black film at the bottom of a pot left on the stove too long.

But while they tasted bad, they also reminded him of fishing trips he used to go on with his dad. They'd head out on Friday night, after his father was done at the car dealership, and make their way to one of the few good fishing rivers they could reach before dark. Find a nice spot and set up their tents. Dad would start a campfire and they'd cook beans in a thin metal pan and hot dogs skewered on wire coat hangers. Share a six-pack of Pabst and talk in the quiet darkness. He'd once told Dad about a recent breakup he'd gone through.

"Did you love her?"

"I don't know."

"Then you didn't. You'd know if you did. It wouldn't be a question. So let her go. You'll probably end up being with a lot of women in your lifetime, and most of them you'll have to let go. You want to leave them better off than you found them, if you can, but mostly they don't matter in the long run. Until you find the one who does. What matters is how you feel when you're out in the middle of nowhere with nobody but yourself to keep you company. How you feel in the darkness with the crickets chirping around you and not a single other human within earshot. People are never fully themselves when they're in the company of others. They try to be the person they think others want them to be. But you want to be able to sit alone on the river's edge and feel peace. That's how you know, no matter what else happens, that you'll be okay. Everybody's life is cluttered with so much white noise—work, car payments and electric bills, obligations to friends and lovers, goddamn idiot television— that they forget themselves. They grind out their existence without stopping to reflect. You don't want to be like that, James. You don't want your soul to fill with the static of an un-tuned television. No matter what else is going on in your life, you need to be able to find occasional quiet moments. You need to find—" Dad burped, took a swallow of his beer, and laughed at himself. "You get my point. You need to let her go and move on. Your hot dog is burning."

In the morning, they got up with the sunrise, put on their wading boots, and walked out into the water. They liked to fly-fish, so they generally stood about twenty or thirty yards from one another, which they did on this morning too, their lines whipping and twirling over their heads in large flowing arcs. Though they both fished for white bass, James used a nine-foot, seven-weight rod with a fast tip while Dad used his soft-tip trout rod.

On this morning, James tied a white and gray clouser on the end of his line. Stood with the river flowing around his calves, the only sounds in his ears the water rushing around him and the gentle whistle of his fly rod whipping back and forth, and he emptied his mind and moved rhythmically, listening to himself from the inside, and he felt peace, and despite his recent breakup—and how he'd been feeling about it—he knew he'd be okay.

For just a moment, sitting in this jailhouse cafeteria, he felt that peace again—and all because of burnt refried beans with an aftertaste like cigarette ash.

The static in his soul went silent.

Then he looked up, suddenly overwhelmed by the feeling he was being watched. Several of the other inmates were glancing at him between bites of food. But that didn't concern him. He was new here. They'd want to know what he was about. Whether he was hard enough to survive. Whether he might be of some value in one way or another.

But there was one man, a thin guy in thick black-framed glasses, who was sitting still as stone three tables down, laced-together hands resting on the wood surface in front of him, staring at James with eyes big as Ping-Pong balls, and that man *did* concern him. His face was expressionless. Nothing about him to indicate he might be dangerous. But there was a malevolence about him. Nothing James could pinpoint, nothing he could put his finger on, but there all the same. Hanging all around him like a dense fog. If humanity could be looked at as a single organism, this man would be a cancer cell.

James would have to be wary, would have to be ready.

He continued to eat, keeping his own face placid.

But while he ate, he dropped both his plastic knife and his fork to the polished concrete floor. Let them lie there while he continued to eat with his spoon. After several minutes, he reached down to scratch his ankle. Shoved the plastic utensils into his shoe. Sat up again. Ate some more, the food settling like hot stones in his gut. He wanted to come across as a man without a care in the world. The men in here were animals. Dangerous. And he was one of them, the same kind of man, so he knew they could sense weakness—a slight limp, a nervous look in the eye, beads of sweat on the forehead—and as soon as they did, they'd attack. It wasn't their fault. It wasn't anybody's fault. Hungry animals didn't walk away from easy meat.

But there was one hungry animal, in particular, that concerned him.

He glanced at the bespectacled man. The man stared back, smiled a humorless smile, and raised his hand in a friendly wave.

James took another bite.

■ Later, in his cell, he melted the plastic utensils together. Stood on the desk chair, broke the light bulb, and used the heat from the burning filament. It took a while, but finally the black plastic softened and sagged like hot wax. He twisted the two pieces together. It burned his fingertips, but he didn't care. If an attack came, and he believed one would, he needed to be prepared. After the two pieces had become one, he dipped the malformed hunk of plastic into the toilet to cool it. He sat on his cot and worked to sharpen it into a weapon, filing it against the cinder block wall.

It took about an hour.

■ James stood in the yard, back against a chain-link fence, sun beating down on him. Not a cloud in sight, just pure blue—like a stretched bolt of raw denim—and that white sun melting the world below. Sweat beaded and rolled down his face.

He had his hands clasped behind his back, plastic utensil shiv tucked up into his sleeve.

He watched the other men in the yard, at least a hundred in all, maybe a quarter of the population. Sitting on bleachers doing nothing. Playing soccer, feet kicking up orange dust that swirled and twisted around their calves. Lifting weights. Playing basketball on a dirt court with a rusted hoop nailed to a plywood backboard. He watched them warily, waiting for something to happen, just like he'd done yesterday. Nothing had happened then, and perhaps nothing would happen now, but he needed to be ready. It was the only way he had a chance. If he let himself forget, if his mind drifted, that was the exact moment someone would choose to attack.

He was watching the entire yard but his real focus was on the basketball game. A three-on-three half-court battle full of shoving and shit-talk, violent blocks and panicked scrambles for knocked-away balls.

Several men stood on the sidelines, waiting for their turn to play. One of them was the man he had noticed in the cafeteria yesterday. He had seen him several times since. He stood stiff, and rather than watching the game, he appeared to be watching James. Looking right past the game and the dust swirling through the air.

One of the players threw a brick and it bounced off the side of the rim toward James. Came flying at him, this brown leather ball, covered in dust, underinflated. Hit the dirt, bounced left, hit again, bounced right, and rolled.

He put out his foot and stopped the ball.

When he looked up again, he saw the man in the black-framed glasses walking toward him. Brisk, efficient movements, friendly face.

James didn't believe the benevolent expression, the man had been staring him down for two days now, so he readied himself.

When the guy arrived, he bent down, sat on his haunches, and grabbed the ball from under the Puma that'd brought it to a stop.

"Thank you," the man said. "My game's next and I'm hoping I get a chance to play before we all have to—"

He came up while he talked and suddenly he was swinging his arm. James saw the blur of movement. Something in the mother-fucker's hand. He brought his left arm up to block the blow while letting the shiv slip from his right sleeve. It dropped into his palm and he swung it around toward the soft meat of the lower back.

The man spun himself toward James, rolling inside the strike, and elbowed James in the stomach. It was such a quick, efficient, and unexpected move that James didn't have time to prepare for it. The air rushed out of him. He started to double over, stepping backward, pressed against the fence. But as he bent at the waist, he saw the other man preparing another swing, ready to bring it down on his back like a hammer blow, so he lunged forward like a bull, pushing off the fence, slamming his head into the gut, and the two men fell to the dirt, his attacker on his back.

Dust flew up around them, twisting and swirling on the motion-disturbed air.

Other men in the yard began to shout.

James swung again, putting his shiv into the motherfucker's left side, just under the ribs. It slid in with almost no resistance, but James grunted from the force of his swing. He *thought* that was why he grunted. But then he felt a deep pain in his left arm and warm, sticky liquid running down his chest. He looked down and saw a shiv jutting from his jumpsuit like a coat hook. Blood spreading out around it.

He tried to stand, succeeded, and looked down at the bespectacled man in the dirt below him. James was breathing hard, and in pain, but he said, "I bet that didn't go the way you planned."

There was shouting to his right.

He turned to see guards rushing at him, their saps drawn.

He held up his empty hands. "It's over," he said.

One of the guards whacked him in the leg with a stick and he dropped to his knees. Another whacked him in the back of the head.

6

Gael Morales stepped out of Alejandro Rocha's house and into the desert heat. He walked past the suited guards standing on either side of the front door, made his way down the stairs, and along the cobblestone driveway to the garage. Leaning on its kickstand behind one of Rocha's cars—a red Tesla he almost never touched—was the 1969 Honda CL350 Gael had spent a month converting into a café racer, though, he had to admit, it wasn't much for speed. If he was on a good downslope, he might be able to do the ton, but horizontal he couldn't hit anything above ninety-five. He could have spent the same on a used Ninja 636, had fewer mechanical issues and more speed, but there was something to be said for style. Ninjas were ugly bikes. There was also something to be said for getting your hands dirty, and older bikes tended to be easier to work on. When he had the time, he'd put in a new exhaust system and re-jet the carbs, which he believed would get the bike to top a hundred. It still wouldn't be as fast as a Ninja 636, or handle as well for that matter, but if speed and handling were all that mattered, nobody would drive a classic car.

Gael was wearing sneakers, cuffed 527s, and a gray Original Penguin Buffalo Pete T-shirt. He also had a backpack strapped over his shoulders. Within the backpack, a folder into which he'd slipped several pieces of evidence he intended to leave at the dead drop for George Rankin.

He pulled his matte gray Bell helmet off the handlebars and slipped it over his head. Clipped the chin strap. Footed the stand out of the way. Two kicks later the motor was rumbling and he was off, rolling down the cobblestone driveway toward the wrought-iron gate, toeing the bike into second. The gate swung open and he rode through it, making a left onto Calle la Armonia and heading south until a bend in the street turned him west. He took it to Avenida Hidalgo, where he made another left, heading south again. Finally he came to the main road and made his third left.

If he rode straight for another thirty or so miles he'd be in Juarez, but he had no intention of doing that. Instead, he cruised through the desert at fifty miles per hour for less than five miles, passing the brown and green and yellow streaks of desert shrubbery.

When he reached the dead drop, he brought the bike to a stop on the sandy shoulder of the road. He squinted back over his shoulder and saw nothing but desert and the ribbon of asphalt twisting through it, wavering behind heat vapors. He didn't believe anybody suspected anything but it was best to be careful. If Alejandro Rocha found out he was DEA, he'd be dead within the hour. Every day he lived with that knowledge. Went to bed with it and woke up with it. Part of the job you didn't like to think about. But you had to, or you might forget to be cautious, which would lead to the very thing you feared.

He got off the bike, walked to what appeared to be a desert stone, and picked it up. It wasn't actually a stone but a cast plastic container made to resemble one. He flipped it over and opened a hatch in its bottom. Pulled out a cell phone zip-locked inside a sandwich bag, removed the phone from the bag, turned it on, and waited for it to boot up. Once it had, he called Special Agent George Rankin, his stateside man on this undercover operation.

While the phone rang in his ear, he lit a Camel, took a deep drag, and spat a fleck of tobacco off the end of his tongue.

"George Rankin."

"Gael."

"What's the news?"

"Got some paperwork for you at the dead drop."

"What kind?"

"Bank transfers, phone records, that kind of thing."

"No shit?"

"Yeah."

"That's good news. Anything else?"

"I'm hoping the bank information might get us somewhere."

"Laundering money, sure, which we can nail him on if it all lines up, but we really need a solid international drug trafficking case."

"I'm working on it."

"I know you are."

"Think I might be getting somewhere too."

"In what way?"

"Hard to put my finger on it. More a feeling than anything."

"A feeling's better than nothing."

"Rocha's starting to trust me, for one thing. Also, there's a couple girls I'm pretty sure want out of the life. Might be able to work one of them, get her to flip."

"Be careful with that."

"You don't need to tell me; it's *my* ass on the line."

"Is it worth the risk?"

"These girls have a broader view of Rocha's organization than anybody else. They know drug routes, stateside dealers. Might not be the safest way to pin this motherfucker down, but it's gotta be the most efficient."

"Hard evidence is better than a talker, though; evidence won't get scared and back out. Or get itself murdered."

"I'm going at it from all angles. I want Rocha pinned in. Besides, a talker might lead us to hard evidence. You know that."

"I understand." Rankin was silent for a long time. Finally he said, "You hanging in there?"

"I'm fine."

"Gael—are you really?"

George Rankin was a good guy but Gael hated when he got that tone. He wanted the conversation to stay on business. Someone asked you how you were doing, it made you think about it, and that was something he didn't want to do. He'd left his wife back home in El Paso and he missed her. They'd only been married eight months now and hadn't seen each other or talked for six of them. He might leave a widow behind, might never smell her hair or hear her laugh again. He wanted to be shut off from those kinds of thoughts, wanted to be the person he was pretending to be until he could be himself again. It made it easier. You couldn't keep one foot in each life and function. You had to dedicate yourself fully to what you were doing. Otherwise you hesitated. You made mistakes.

"I'm fine," he said again.

"Good."

"Listen," Gael said, "I gotta go. I'll call if I get anything else. Meantime, pick up the shit at the dead drop, see if you can pull anything out of it."

"Talk to you later."

Gael hung up the phone, powered it down, slipped it back into the sandwich bag, and shoved it into the dead-drop rock. Next in was the paperwork, which he removed from his backpack and folded in half. He shut the rock's hatch, clipped it shut, and set it back down on the desert sand. Walked to his bike, kicking his footprints away as he went, and looked back at the rock over his shoulder.

It was just a rock again.

He straddled the Honda, stomped it to life.

■ George Rankin, feeling guilty, shoved his cell phone into the right hip pocket of his slacks. Leaned back in his desk chair, sitting in his cubicle in the DEA's Intelligence Center in El Paso, Texas—which was located on Fort Bliss—paperwork spread out in front of him. He might have been sitting in a large but low-rent law firm. Cheap desks and office chairs in each cubicle. Outdated computers on the desks. Pictures of family members thumbtacked to the cubicle walls. Men and women in cheap suits talking on phones and banging away at computer keyboards with crumbs from dozens of working lunches stuck between the keys.

George had a picture of his thirteen-year-old daughter thumbtacked to the gray fabric wall to his left. He got to see her every other weekend unless a case made it impossible. Happened at least half a dozen times a year, and he felt bad every time. Meghan was used to it, but that only made him feel worse. She was so accustomed to being disappointed, it no longer came as a surprise. He'd call on Friday afternoon, she'd pick up, and the first words out of her mouth were, "It's okay, Dad. I'll see you in two weeks."

Like a punch in the gut every time.

But that wasn't making him feel guilty at the moment. He wasn't thinking about his daughter at all. This wasn't his weekend to have her. He was thinking about Gael Castillo Jimenez and his wife Sarah, who was seven months pregnant while Gael was in Mexico on a dangerous undercover assignment, no idea he was soon to be a father.

George thought about that every time he talked to Gael on the phone, and wanted to tell him, but knew he couldn't. The man needed to stay focused.

Sarah had said this herself when George spoke with her over lunch three months back. "You can't tell Gael. I understood the job when I married him and I won't have you distracting him from doing it." She said this while eating a foot-long cold cut trio at Subway, her already large belly resting on her lap like a medicine ball, her eyes serious, and he'd known she was right in her desire to keep this from Gael. But that didn't stop George from being concerned, and it didn't stop his guilt.

He also felt pressured to get this case wrapped up before Sarah's due date, which was rushing up quick, but couldn't let Gael feel that pressure, not even on a subconscious level. The man needed to make smart decisions that would keep him alive. Which meant he couldn't know Sarah was two months away from giving him a son.

He'd spoken at Gael's wedding, was supposed to be his friend, and even though not telling him was the best thing for him right now, it didn't make him feel one damn bit better about it. This was news he would tell his friend in any situation but this one.

In any situation but this one he wouldn't have to. Sarah would have done it already.

While he was thinking about this, Francis Waters leaned over the cubicle wall they shared and looked down at him, arm resting on the barrier between them. George glanced up, felt what he usually felt when he looked at the guy—mild distaste—and said:

"What's up, Francis?"

"That call about the Rocha case?"

"Yeah."

"How's it going?"

George shrugged. "I'd hoped to have more at this point."

"What *do* you have?"

"Not much."

"Maybe you got the wrong man undercover."

"No, he's doing what he can."

"Who do you have down there?"

"You wanna know that, ask Ellison."

"You don't trust me?"

George Rankin didn't trust him, but he wouldn't have told anybody. You tell one person, you might as well tell the entire office, and this he wouldn't do. The organization worked hard to keep case information need-to-know, and when agents went undercover, they were "transferred" to another field office first. The only people who knew where they really were, other than the deputy chief and the chief, were the individual agents supervising each case.

But all of that aside, George thought they had a leak, someone drip-feeding Rocha information. He might have been wrong, but wasn't about to bet against his own gut, especially not with Gael's life. If Rocha found out Gael was DEA, Gael was dead, buried in the desert, and never heard from again, and because it happened in Mexico, they'd be unable to do a damn thing about it. He said none of this, only:

"I don't talk about ongoing investigations, Francis."

"Just wanted to know how it was going."

George stood up. "I gotta go talk to Ellison."

He stepped out of his cubicle, walked down the carpeted aisle to the back of the room—passing a dozen cubicles along the way, people in half of them talking on the phone, snatches of conversation floating through the air—and knocked on Ellison's closed door.

When Horace Ellison first transferred here from Chicago, as the new chief of intelligence, he'd stood at the front of this room and given a speech about how his door was always open, but that was strictly metaphorical language. George had never seen the damn thing open unless someone was stepping through it, after which it was immediately closed again, slammed shut with a bang.

From the other side of the door: "What?"

"George Rankin, sir, about the Rocha case."

"Come on in."

George pushed open the door, stepped into Ellison's office, and closed the door behind him. The office was white-walled and tidy, with not a picture in sight. To the left of the desk, a bookshelf stuffed with books on drug law, DEA procedure, and so on. The desk itself bare except for an in-box and an out-box. The in-box empty, the out-box full.

Ellison looked up from the three-year-old iMac on his desk. He was about fifty, with a half-halo of thin gray hair hooked over his ears with sideburns, the top of his head polished-chrome bald. Brown eyes. Lips like a wide-mouthed bass. He wore tailored suits but they still hung off his shoulders oddly, never appearing to fit. His tie was knotted with a neat, if asymmetrical half-Windsor.

"What's going on, Rankin?"

George told Ellison about his latest phone call from Gael, told him that Gael had gotten his hands on some paperwork that might prove useful, told him he was thinking about trying to flip one of the girls who worked for Rocha.

"I think it might be too dangerous."

"Hard to know," Ellison said. "He's in the middle of it, probably has a better picture of the situation than either of us."

"I'm just worried he's putting himself in danger to make the case."

Ellison leaned back in the chair. "He put himself in danger the moment he went undercover, Rankin. I know you two are friends, but you have to trust he knows what he's doing, because he does. He's good at his job."

"I know. You're right."

"Why don't you go pick up whatever he left at the dead drop and replace his phone with a charged one. Maybe we can start to make a real case."

George nodded. "Yes, sir."

He turned to step out of the office.

"Don't forget to shut the door behind you."

■ Gael Morales stopped at El Pollo Loco on Santa Lucia, pushed through the fingerprinted glass door, and dug into his Levi's for the order sheet he'd scribbled on. He reached the counter, and after the woman in front of him had paid, read from the list. He paid with one of Rocha's credit cards, signed, and wrapped the receipt around the card before slipping them both into his wallet. Rocha demanded receipts for everything. You bought a pencil with his credit card, he wanted verification of purchase and proof you used the pencil to write work-related shit. This meant he kept neat books—and neat records were incriminating records—but so far Gael had failed to locate them.

When his order came up, he shoved the food into his backpack and headed out into the bright day.

He kicked his bike to life, twisted the throttle, wondered to himself how much longer he'd be stuck in this world of drugs and violence. But he decided it didn't matter. Once this case was over, he'd be on another. Again and again he'd be in this world, or a version of this world, working with men who would murder kids over seventy-eight bucks stolen from a cash register. He wouldn't be out of it until he retired, and even after he *was* out of it, he doubted it would be out of him. When you became part of something, it became part of you.

He had a wife back home, a newly built house with three bedrooms, a late-model CR-V parked in the driveway, but he couldn't even wear his wedding band. He'd slipped it into a blue Tacori box and stuck it in his sock drawer six months ago, before leaving for Mexico, before he'd even gotten used to wearing it. He couldn't pet his dogs, Truman and Paul. Couldn't feel his wife Sarah's heart beating against the palm of his hand. Couldn't wake to the sounds of her shuffling around in the kitchen downstairs. That wasn't the life he was living, and when he began living it again, would it feel different?

What would Sarah think of him if he told her he'd hit a kid with a van, dragged him to Rocha's backyard, and watched as Rocha put a bullet through his head? What would she think of him if he told her he'd wrapped the kid in plastic and driven him out to the desert, and with Diego Blanco at his side, dug a shallow grave and dumped him into it? What would she think if he told her the others things he'd done—much worse than that?

Would she decide he wasn't the man she thought he was?

She might, and she'd be right: he wasn't *only* that man. He was at least one other person besides. But he wouldn't tell her. She'd never know that he had another man living inside him, a man capable of things she'd never understand, a man capable of things *he* didn't understand.

He toed the bike into first, rode out to the street, and kicking through the gears quickly, made his way east toward Alejandro Rocha's estate.

Back home in El Paso, he was Gael Castillo Jimenez, a good man living in a suburban neighborhood, the kind of guy who'd bring a twelve-pack of imported beer and several sirloins to a backyard barbecue, a guy who laughed at dumb jokes and held his wife's hand in public, but he wasn't in El Paso. He was in La Paz, Mexico, and here he was Gael Morales. He didn't have a wife here, he didn't have dreams of future children, and there was no ethical center within him that might prevent any action he chose to take.

He wondered what other horrible things he'd have to do before this was finished, but he supposed it didn't really matter. If something was expected of him, he'd do it.

7

Alejandro Rocha was walking along the verge of his swimming pool, pacing from one end to the other with an iPhone to his ear, when he heard the sliding door shudder open. He glanced toward the house, watched Gael Morales step outside with an avocado burrito from El Pollo Loco and a beer from the fridge, one in each hand.

"Just set them on a table, please."

Gael nodded and put down the burrito and the beer.

"Thanks."

"Anything else?"

"No, just take care of the girls."

"Sure."

Gael headed back inside. Kid hadn't been with the organization long, but Alejandro liked him. He did what he was supposed to do, didn't ask questions, and didn't mouth off around town. That was a rare combination in this business. Didn't speak well for capitalism—and Alejandro thought of himself as the apotheosis of capitalist success—but when you started dealing in illegal merchandise, even good pay wouldn't necessarily buy you good men. You ended up with the dregs of society, men willing to take big risks for big money, and that did him very little good. He ran a careful business, his biggest risk the necessity of trusting the people he hired, but he thought the risk with Gael would be minimal.

Soon it would be time to have him step up.

A voice from the other end of the line: "*¿Bueno?*"

In Spanish, Alejandro said, "Do you know how long I've been on hold?"

"I apologize, Alejandro."

"*Señor Rocha, pendejo.* We're not friends."

"*Lo siento.* How can I help you?"

"James Murphy."

"What about him?"

"How's he doing?"

"He was stabbed in the shoulder, a painful but minor injury, and should recover without any lasting damage."

"Do me a favor and cut off any mind-altering medications you have him on."

"He'll be in a lot of pain if—"

"Give him some fucking aspirin. I'm gonna pay a visit and I want him coherent for the conversation. *¿Entiendes?*"

"Yes, sir."

He hung up his cell phone, slipped it into his pocket, and walked to the table on which his lunch was waiting. Sat down on the edge of the chair beside it. Picked up his beer and took a swallow. It was warm after only five minutes in the sun, but he took another swallow before unwrapping his burrito. As soon as he was done with lunch he'd drive out to the jail. He thought his second conversation with James Murphy would be quite a bit different from the first.

In fact, he was sure of it.

◘ James lay on a bed in the infirmary, his wrists cuffed to it, his ankles shackled. He stared at the ceiling. His shoulder throbbed. His head felt heavy, and thoughts were slow in coming, as if his skull had been stuffed with cloth through which they must filter. He looked left. The man who'd attacked him was two beds over, oxygen being fed into his nostrils, a beeping monitor at his bedside. His wrists and ankles were shackled as well.

James thought the nameless son of a bitch was asleep, his eyes closed behind the thick lenses of his glasses, but he must have felt James looking at him because he opened his eyes and turned his head.

He smiled a toothy smile, spoke in English: "Next time I'll kill you."

"Good luck with that."

"I don't need luck."

"Last attack didn't turn out too well for you."

"I was told you weren't to be killed, which rather limited my options."

"You couldn't have killed me if you wanted to."

"That's where you're wrong, *bolillo*. Killing you would be a trivial matter. A guard opens your cell while you sleep. I step inside, knife-punch your carotid. You bleed out before you even know what's happened. I'd be surprised if you lived another week, and after what you did to me, I'll make certain that I'm the one to end you."

He turned away and closed his eyes.

James thought about what he'd said. Probably believed every word. But so long as he had information Rocha wanted—so long as Rocha *believed* he had information—he thought he was safe. The man had said it himself. You don't burn a book you have yet to read, but sometimes you need to break its spine to get to the information you want. But James would give Rocha nothing despite this nameless motherfucker trying to break him. Because the implication was that once you'd gotten the information, there was no reason *not* to burn your book, and James didn't want to be murdered in a Mexican jail.

He was two years from the end of his most recent contract with the Marine Corps, after which he intended to leave. He'd join the FBI or CIA if they'd have him—they'd certainly be able to make use of a man with his particular skill set and education—turn in his camouflage for a three-piece suit. Worst case, he'd join the police department in Austin.

Buy Pilar a house someplace so they could start their life in earnest. He'd be thirty then and she'd be twenty-six, a good time to start a family. She'd go off the pill and they'd spend a few months having fun with each other, trying to make it happen.

But first he had to survive in this jail, get the charges dropped, and kill Rocha, the man responsible for his sister's death—though he didn't know how any of that might be accomplished.

He closed his eyes and felt the pain crash through his body in waves, one after the other, eroding his tolerance. He tried to ignore it, tried to empty his head of all thought.

He inhaled, exhaled.

But the static in his soul wouldn't go silent.

Have hope when life is hopeless, and if reality doesn't match the dreams in your head, you work to change reality.

Inhale, exhale.

Think nothing.

But as soon as he managed to empty his mind, images flashed across the walls of his skull. The sight of his sister dead in the morgue. Her cold lips. Her still hand. The chipped polish on her fingernails.

Rocha lined up in his sights. A finger squeezing a trigger. Rocha's head kicking back. Rocha dropping to his knees and falling forward like a felled tree.

Some deaths must be paid for, and the cost of a life was another life.

■ Alejandro Rocha walked through the corridors, his pace brisk, his footfalls echoing through the empty spaces. The corridors were dimly lit, walled with bare cinder block, nothing to distinguish one from another, but he turned left and right through them, moving from one to another, knowing exactly where he was headed.

Finally he arrived at the infirmary, pushed open the door, and stepped into the room. It was only ten feet deep but at least sixty feet wide, filled with beds, a chain of them lined up side by side, blue curtains hanging from rusting steel rods between them, the curtains all drawn back. Most of the beds were empty, with sheets taut and pillows in place, but four of them were occupied by men injured in the yard or in their cells.

Alejandro walked to the bed in which James Murphy lay with his eyes closed and looked down at him. His face was expressionless, seemed to hold the peace of sleep, but only a moment after he looked down at them the eyes opened. They looked up at Alejandro but the face remained expressionless. Neither man said anything for a long time.

Finally Alejandro spoke: "He lives."

"I'll still be living long after you've been buried."

"Said the man shackled to a bed. I could strangle you to death right now. The only reason you're alive is I've *allowed* you to live."

"You want a thank-you?"

"I want understanding."

"I understand you're a cunt who has other people do his dirty work for him."

Alejandro slapped James Murphy across the face. The man's utter lack of respect made Alejandro want to gouge out one of his eyes and show it to him, and for a moment he considered it, but he hadn't gotten where he was by thoughtlessly acting on his emotions. Each decision he made was a considered one. It was how he survived in a dangerous business.

He released his anger in a sigh and when next he spoke, his voice was calm, free of all emotion: "Let me be clear. I intend to visit you on Tuesday. We'll sit down together and we'll talk, but if you don't tell me what I want to hear, you'll die on Wednesday. I'd kill you today, but I expect you haven't experienced enough here to fully understand the situation you're in."

"You won't kill me if I have information you want."

"That's where you're wrong. If you were a man of importance, if you were a man who had information I *needed*, someone would be trying to get you out to make sure I never got that information. But you've been here three days now and no one seems to care. If you're disposable to the person or people who hired you, you're disposable to me. I'm giving you until Tuesday only because I'm curious. Do you understand me?"

"I do."

"Do you *believe* me?"

"I do."

"Are you going to talk?"

"I thought I *was* talking."

"We'll see how you feel on Tuesday, when death is impending. I'm tired of wasting my time with you."

Alejandro turned to walk away.

"Before you go—"

He turned back, raised an eyebrow. Maybe the son of a bitch would tip today after all. He was curious to see what spilled out.

"I have this itch behind my left ear."

Alejandro walked to the door, stepped through, and slammed it shut behind him. Motherfucker wouldn't think it was funny come Wednesday. Motherfucker wouldn't be capable of thinking anything at all.

◼ James watched Rocha leave before he dropped his head to the pillow. His shoulder throbbed with radiating pain. He asked himself whether he believed Rocha *really* intended to kill him if he didn't talk, and decided he did, but he still wouldn't say anything. The man would kill him whether he talked or not, so he might as well keep his mouth shut. Let him wonder.

But if he wanted to live he'd have to do more than that. He'd have to find a way out of this place. Problem was, he didn't know where to begin. For now he was stuck here, waiting to be killed, and unless something changed before Wednesday, that was exactly what would happen.

8

They were sitting at a table in La Casa de Dora, a small Mexican restaurant just off Santa Lucia. It was past eight o'clock Saturday evening, but the place was still hot. The sun outside was low, glaring at the world from the west, but not yet blocked by the horizon.

Coop couldn't imagine working a kitchen in that heat, probably twenty degrees hotter than here in the dining room, and he was drenched in sweat, his T-shirt dark with moisture, fabric sticking to his chest and back, sweat running down his rib cage from his dripping armpits. He sat across from Normal and Bogart, with Pilar to his left. She'd been quiet since they visited the jail and found out James was in the infirmary. Her responses were monosyllabic, her face expressionless.

A cast-iron skillet sat in the middle of the table, loaded with chicken, shrimp, steak, green peppers, and onions. It smelled strongly of cumin. Beside the skillet were small bowls of grated cheese, guacamole, and sour cream. Also, a nearly empty pitcher of beer.

Coop picked up his glass, the surface covered in condensation, and took a swallow.

"I'm staying until I have a chance to talk to James," he said. "I decided before we left the jail. Hell, I decided before we *visited* the jail. You guys want to get back to El Paso, I understand, but I can't abandon him here. At the very least I have to meet with him, find out what the hell is going on. I'll take it from there, but I'm not going back to Fort Bliss on Monday."

"You aren't fuckin' around with unauthorized leave," Normal said. "You'll end up in the brig, you don't show up Monday."

"He's my partner in the field, he's my partner here. I can't leave him to rot. I might be court-martialed when I get back home, might spend some time behind bars, but James is behind bars right now. We don't know why. We don't know for how long. But we all agree he didn't do what he's accused of doing." He took another swallow of beer. "But like I said, I understand if you guys wanna go back."

Coop assumed Pilar would stay. She had no reason to return to El Paso if James wasn't there. She'd only sit in their apartment, waiting to find out what was happening, everything in the place reminding her of the man who wasn't there but should be. The men sitting across from him, however, he wasn't sure about.

Neither of them said anything for a long time. They only looked at one another, communicating silently.

Finally Bogart turned to look at Coop again.

"We're staying," he said. "Marines don't abandon their brothers."

"Good," Coop said. "I might need your help."

"For what?" Normal said.

"I don't know."

"What if he did it?"

Coop turned to look at Pilar as she sat with slumped shoulders, her expression one of deep worry, her hands clenched together in her lap.

"He didn't," Coop said.

"You don't know that."

"Of course I do—and so do you."

"Even if he's cleared of the drug charges, they can nail him for the guns, and that's enough to keep him behind bars for years. What if he tells us to go back to El Paso and forget about him?"

"First of all, we don't know whether the guns were his or not, and we won't know until we have a chance to talk to him. Second, he doesn't get to make that call."

Pilar's eyes had a faraway look. Lost in thought. Maybe she was thinking about what she knew and what she didn't know about James, about her future with him, about what her future would look like *without* him. A place in her life that had once been filled was now an empty hollow, like the lot where a razed house once stood.

Coop could read it on her face.

When James first met Pilar in Jacksonville, North Carolina, near where they were going through scout sniper school at Camp Lejeune, he'd been at Dirty Deeds Bar & Laundry doing a load of civilian clothes and flirting with a bartender named Katie who he thought was annoying but had a hard-on for. Pilar was doing laundry too, and she needed his dryer, which he'd had clothes sitting in for half an hour. She got frustrated waiting for him to empty the machine, so she'd done it herself, folding his clothes. He'd found them in a neat stack, a note on top telling him:

You owe me a drink, motherfucker.
I'm not your mother and I don't fold clothes for free.
Pilar

He found her, bought the drink, and promptly forgot about Katie.

Later, when James was telling Coop about her, he'd said, "I'm gonna marry her. Just you wait. Get ready to be my best man."

At the time, Coop thought it was the alcohol talking, but he didn't think that anymore. Sometimes people met, and like puzzle pieces, they fit together. That was the case with James and Pilar. He envied them. He was thirty years old now, two years older than James, and had never felt anything like love, though he'd been looking for it.

He met women he liked, dated them, slept with them, sometimes even had relationships with them, but like never turned into love. His heart never opened. He didn't know why, didn't want it to be so, but that's how it was. He had more love for James Murphy than he'd ever had for a woman.

"Okay," Pilar said finally, pulling Coop from his thoughts.

"Okay what?"

"You're right. James doesn't get to make that call. We'll do what we need to do. I don't want to live my life without him."

◼ Gael parked the Honda in front of his building and walked up the concrete steps to his small bachelor apartment. He unlocked the front door and pushed his way inside.

He lived in a two-floor stucco building off Calle de Plata, as did all of Rocha's men. None of the bills came to him. They all went to Rocha, including the phone bills, both cellular and landline. Which meant Rocha knew every call dialed or received, both the number and duration. The man had full trust in no one, not even Diego Blanco, which explained how he'd survived in this business as long as he had while others had been decapitated, disappeared, or both.

Gael flipped the light switch by the door and the lamp on the nightstand left of the bed flashed to life, spilling its sixty watts across the single-room apartment. It was furnished with a queen-size bed, headboard against the left wall; a green-clothed La-Z-Boy Peyton recliner pushed against the back wall; and a few tables. Several books were stacked on the end table off the right arm of the chair, a few more on the nightstand, and dozens more on the floor. To the right, a small kitchenette. A mini-fridge, a short counter, and on the counter a two-burner electric hot plate and a toaster. Three fiberboard cabinets hung on the wall above the counter. The walls were painted white, and before he'd moved in, had been unblemished by art of any kind. But it had been so impersonal that he'd felt terribly lonely here, so he ordered a couple prints that might make the space his. Van Gogh's *Café Terrace at Night* hung above the La-Z-Boy and a Vivian Maier photograph of a girl in a car hung above the bed. He'd like to have a picture of Sarah on display somewhere but it was too risky. He wasn't supposed to have anything here that might give Rocha a clue as to his real identity, and while it was unlikely a single picture of Sarah could connect him to his other life, it was best to be safe.

But it was hard to cut yourself off from life completely. He had a Polaroid of Sarah slipped between his mattress and box spring. There she was in a tank top and shorts, her body tanned, her hair pulled back into a ponytail, standing in front of the Grand Canyon. Every once in a while, when he was feeling particularly low, he pulled it out and looked at it.

He didn't do that now, however. He walked to the mini-fridge, grabbed a bottle of Sierra Nevada, and headed to the La-Z-Boy recliner. Sat down and turned on the table lamp to his right. Took a swallow, grabbed a book, and lit one of his Camels. Tried to read while he smoked, but only managed to go over the same sentence fifteen times, retaining not a single word of it.

His mind kept turning to thoughts of Danielle Preston. She was one of the girls Alejandro kept around the house, maybe twenty-five years old, very pretty in a conventional kind of way.

He liked women who had an air of Eastern European exoticness about them, like Sarah did, despite her plain-Jane name. In truth, he liked his women to *be* Sarah. She was the only woman he thought about. She was the woman he loved and so, in his mind, she represented every woman, and he measured every woman against her.

They all came up wanting.

But Dani was smart and funny and open in a way most drug addicts weren't. The other girls Rocha kept around the house walled themselves off, always detached, both from their surroundings and from themselves. Dani was different. She was a junkie, as several of the women were, and about that he couldn't kid himself, but she was self-aware and talked often about cleaning up. She smoked heroin rather than shooting it, and she did it in order to maintain. She wasn't, or didn't appear to be, hunting for the feeling she'd gotten from her first high. She knew what she was and wanted to change.

To Gael's mind, that meant she might prove useful. If he could promise her protection and rehabilitation, she might give him something in return. Information at the very least. Maybe testimony. She'd know talking was dangerous but she might also believe the benefits outweighed the risks. He hoped so, but he wouldn't know for sure until after he approached her, and once he did there was no going back. She could refuse to speak, or decide to run, or tell Rocha about the request. In the best of those scenarios, the situation would be as it was now, except she'd have something on them; in the worst, he'd be dead. But if she did talk, she'd be able to give him information that would lead to more hard evidence. She'd be able to provide names and dates and locations, and each of those gave the DEA another angle. She might even agree to testify.

He butted out his cigarette, finished his beer, and got to his feet. Set his book down and shut off the table lamp. Walked to the kitchenette and tossed the empty bottle into the bin under the counter. Pulled open the refrigerator and looked at a bowl of tuna salad he'd made a few days ago. Thought about grabbing a fork and eating some, but decided against it. Closed the fridge, walked to his bed, and slipped his clothes off, tossing them on the floor in a pile. Pulled back the blanket and lay down on the wrinkled sheet. Stared at the ceiling.

Tomorrow he'd talk to Dani and by the end of the conversation he'd know that either his case against Rocha was stronger or his life was in danger. It was a risk, but he thought it was a risk worth taking.

He leaned over and shut off the bedside lamp. The white ceiling turned gray. He lay on his back and looked up at it. He was tired, but his mind continued to turn over on itself. He wouldn't be able to sleep feeling how he felt. He closed his eyes and projected images of Sarah onto the backs of his eyelids. He thought about the day he'd be able to see her again.

◼ Pilar and the others had rooms on the second floor of Hotel Amigo. She lay in bed now, hugging a pillow, listening to the TV in Normal's room. She couldn't tell what he was watching, the voices muted by the wall, but it sounded like some sort of action movie. Lots of yelling and what sounded like gunfire.

Pilar put the pillow she'd been hugging over her head to block the noise. She closed her eyes and thought about James in jail. Thought about the drugs found in his trunk. About his sister's overdose. About the guns and what he might have been doing with them. But maybe they'd been planted too. She didn't believe it—but maybe.

James loved Layla as much as one person could love another. Before he left for Afghanistan, they talked at least twice a week on the phone, their conversations sometimes lasting an hour. Pilar would lie in bed, watching television, listening to James talk to his sister. In truth, it made her jealous. James spoke to Layla the way she wished he'd speak to her. Every thought that entered his head during those conversations left his mouth. He laughed a lot. He offered advice and friendship.

Pilar loved James, and she knew he loved her, but she'd been jealous of the relationship he had with his sister.

But now that Layla was dead, Pilar felt petty for that jealousy. She felt stupid for not understanding the hollow Layla's absence would leave in his heart. With his sister gone, the hole might be filled by something corrosive.

Had she been a better girlfriend she'd have sensed the hollow in his heart and tried to fill it with her love. She'd have been able to stop him from coming to Mexico and doing what he'd come here to do—whatever that had been.

It was too late for that. But it wasn't too late to do something.

She wanted James out of jail. She wanted the two of them to have another chance at finding happiness together.

9

James spent most of Sunday in the infirmary. He woke up at six o'clock to a nurse pushing meds and asking how he felt. His right hand was uncuffed for breakfast at nine o'clock and he spooned food into his mouth. His hand was cuffed again and he lay there staring at the ceiling. To his right lay a man who had attempted suicide the night before—he was dragged in at around two o'clock in the morning, protesting, saying they should let him die—his wrists stitched and bandaged with gauze. He'd been crying intermittently for the last several hours, gasping and sobbing, and James thought that if he were free he might be tempted to hold a pillow over the man's face just to shut him up. Instead, because he was cuffed, and because he had nothing better to do, he turned to look at him.

Man about forty: pockmarked face, high cheekbones, large ear-lobes, Native American features, black hair clipped close to the head, bright brown eyes. Something about him made James think he wasn't a man of the city. Maybe grew up in a wattle and daub house in southern Mexico, spent his days farming.

"You speak English?"

The man turned to look at him with red eyes that glistened with tears. "Yes."

"Why'd you do it?"

"What?"

"Your wrists."

The man said nothing for a long time. He wiped at his eyes. He coughed into the side of his fist. Finally he spoke: "My daughter."

"What about her?"

"She's dead. Nine years old."

"What happened?"

"Anti-Zapatistas nailed shut schoolhouse door and burned to ground. Three people dead—my daughter, another girl, their teacher. She was all I had."

Though James didn't have children, he wanted them, and he couldn't imagine outliving a son or daughter. Small coffins were heartbreaking even when empty; what they represented was enough to make them heartbreaking.

The only time he'd come close to failing in Afghanistan was when a child suicide bomber had been his target. Eight or nine years old. Kid running with an IED toward a group of Marines entering a village to capture an al-Qaeda cell. If James hadn't pulled the trigger, the kid would still be dead—and twelve Marines would have been injured or killed as well—but it was hard to do what he had to do. Hard to line the face up in his sights and squeeze his trigger. He still saw the young face in his dreams, filled with innocence despite the murder cradled like a baby in his arms.

He thought about his sister. The person he loved most in the world. The fact that she was dead. The fact that Alejandro Rocha was still alive.

"You can't kill yourself."

"Why not?"

"Because no one else can bring your sister . . ." He paused, blinked, corrected himself. "Your daughter—no one else can bring your daughter justice."

The man shook his head. "There is no such thing. If there was, she wouldn't be dead."

James was silent for a long moment before he spoke. Finally he said, "Sometimes you have to *create* the justice."

But the man wasn't interested in conversation. He turned away, looked toward an empty wall, said, "Leave me be."

So James lay in silence, the hands of the clock on the wall making their way slowly around its numbered face. Ten o'clock gave way to eleven, which gave way to twelve and one, the hours dropping off the world like dead leaves.

Lunch arrived. He ate in silence.

He looked to his left, to the man who'd stabbed him, as he smeared his rolled tortilla into a scoop of refried beans. He must have felt James watching him because he turned his head and made eye contact. A subtle smile touched his lips.

"Another day closer to death," the man said.

"For both of us."

"Perhaps. But you can be certain it will find you first."

The doctor came to check on him at around five o'clock. He was a haggard-looking man in his late fifties, hair turning gray, mustache a reddish color that, from a distance, made him look as though he had a rash on his upper lip. Wore blue scrubs and red Crocs with white tube socks. Name badge clipped to his shirt.

The doctor had a guard take the handcuffs off James and checked him thoroughly, heart rate, blood pressure, and so on. Leaned in close and said James was okay to go back to his cell if he wanted to, but he'd recommend staying out of the general population if he didn't want to face another attack.

But the infirmary had no windows and one door, which only led deeper into the jail; if he wanted to find a way out of this place he couldn't do it from here.

"Thanks, but I'd just as soon leave."

Doc looked concerned, unhappy with the decision James had made, but after a sigh he nodded. "Okay. I'll put in the order."

It was another four hours before two guards came to collect him.

They took the handcuffs off his wrists, unshackled his ankles, and walked him through the jailhouse corridors to his cell. He stepped into the small room. The barred door clanked shut behind him. He walked to the window at the back of the cell and inhaled the cool night air of the desert. Looked up at the stars and the bone moon in the bruise-purple sky.

He wondered if maybe his sister was looking down on him.

He walked to his cot and sat down. Tomorrow was Monday. Alejandro Rocha had told him he would die on Wednesday unless he talked. He had two days to figure a way out of this mess. But the more he thought about it the more impossible it seemed.

But still, that hope. He couldn't let it go.

10

Coop woke up Monday morning with a knot in his stomach. At first he didn't know why, head too cloudy with sleep to make sense of what he was feeling. Then he remembered. This was the first time in twelve years as a Marine he wasn't reporting for duty. His first unauthorized absence. He told himself his superiors would understand he was neglecting one duty in order to fulfill a higher one, but he didn't believe it. If you were a Marine, you were a cog and expected always to function as a cog. Your real life didn't matter. Obligations outside the Marine Corps didn't matter. Your feelings didn't matter. Nothing mattered but showing up on time and doing what you were told to do. This was why it was called duty, and it was what he'd signed up for.

But though the corps might not recognize it, this *was* more important.

Marines didn't abandon their brothers.

He sat up on the edge of his bed and stared a moment at the wall. He looked at the digital clock on the nightstand even though he already knew the approximate time. This was when he awoke almost every morning whether he had an alarm set or not. The clock's red numbers told him it was 5:59. He blinked. Now it was 6:00. The alarm sounded. He reached out and slapped the bar on the top of the clock, silencing it. Grabbed a pack of Newports from beside the clock, flipped the top of the box, brought it to his mouth, pinched a filter between his teeth, and dragged a cigarette out of the pack. Lit it and inhaled the smoke deep into his lungs. Exhaled through his nostrils, watching the smoke swirl on the still air, watching it twist in a beam of light coming in between the panels of the drab yellow curtain.

He sat doing nothing but smoking for five minutes, allowing his mind to catch up to reality, to absorb his surroundings.

Once he'd smoked the cigarette down to his fingertips he dropped it into a Pepsi can on the nightstand. The liquid within killed the ember with a hiss and a small ribbon of smoke drifted out. He got to his feet and padded across the brown carpet to the bathroom, turned on the shower, and waited for the water to get hot. Took a leak while he waited, then kicked his underwear away. Stepped into the tub and let the water splash against his chest.

When he was done in the bathroom—showered and shaved—he tossed his duffel bag onto his unmade bed, opened it, and pulled out clothes. He got dressed, putting on cargo shorts and a New York Knicks shirt before he slipped his Nikes on. He smoked a second cigarette and looked at the clock. It was a quarter to seven.

They wouldn't be able to see James for hours, but there was no way he could sit in this room and wait. He got to his feet, put his cigarettes, wallet, and keys into his pockets, walked to the door, unlocked it, and stepped out into the empty corridor.

◼ Normal woke to the sound of someone banging on his door. He opened his eyes and found himself staring at the pillow his face was smashed into. He rolled onto his back and looked at the cracked ceiling. His eyes stung and his head felt as though it'd been stuffed with newspaper.

After the others had gone to bed last night, he'd headed out to

Los Parados, a dive bar just across the street. He'd only had three beers and a Johnnie Walker Black, but for some reason the drinks hit him hard. He'd stumbled back to the hotel and stripped off his clothes as he walked to bed, leaving a trail of fabric on the stained carpet. He'd fallen atop the comforter, and lying on his side with the room spinning around him, passed out.

He sat up now, neck aching, and scratched at his right bicep. A few years ago, while home on leave in Louisville, he'd gotten a tattoo of an eagle in black and gray, USMC above the bird and SEMPER FI below it, and anytime he got even a mild sunburn, the tattoo would itch like a motherfucker. As it did now. He'd tried to get in with his regular tattooist, Rodney at Twisted Images, but the guy was booked out a month, so he'd found another street shop near Fern Creek, which he now regretted. His skin didn't react well to the cheap ink they'd used.

More banging at the door.

"Hold on—Jesus *fuck*."

He stood up, wearing nothing but white briefs, and stumbled to the door. He unlatched the chain and twisted the dead bolt out of its socket. Pulled open the door. Blinked at Coop, who stood on the other side of the doorway, looking at him.

"What time is it?"

"Almost seven."

"What do you want?"

"Get dressed, we're going to breakfast."

"Who's *we*?"

"You and me. I couldn't sit around in my room all morning."

"I was sleeping."

"Well, now you're not. Get dressed."

"Hold on."

Normal turned around, leaving the door open, and followed the trail of clothes that led to his bed, picking them up and putting them on as he went: black Bonnie "Prince" Billy T-shirt he'd cut the sleeves off of, paint-stained cutoff shorts, black socks, Emericas. He sat on the mattress to tie his shoelaces and found himself sitting there, staring at his feet, spacing out. Thinking nothing at all.

"Dude."

"What? Oh."

Normal got to his feet, grabbed his wallet and his cell phone, and headed for the door. Stepped through and closed it behind him.

"Where we going?"

"I don't know. Figured we'd find something."

They made their way outside, pushing into the warm desert morning—sun glaring down at them, the sky a sheet of bright blue with not a cloud in it—and started walking. Normal had a headache, a mild hangover throbbing behind his eyes.

He remembered going to Mag Bar when he lived in Louisville, back in his early twenties, chatting with Beenee Overstreet, who was usually tending bar when he strolled in, and easily consuming twice what he'd had last night. He'd wake up the next morning to get ready for work—he was a short order cook at his dad's diner on Baxter Avenue—and be fine. Getting older was no fun. He was thirty-one but felt the same as he had when he was thirteen and seeing his first girlfriend. Kids looked at him and saw a man, sometimes called him sir, but he was still that boy inside. Still confused by sex, women, and the world. It was strange to him. He wanted to skateboard, drink Red Stripe beer, and sleep in on weekends, like he'd done when growing up, but somehow he'd become a man without realizing it, and he had responsibilities to both the government and people, and a bad right knee, and bills he needed to pay.

Despite the fact he loved it, he'd only skateboarded twice in the last five years. Last time he went home, he took one of his boards out to Louisville Extreme Park, but after an hour he drove home, his knee throbbing, sat on the couch, and watched golf with his dad.

He hawked up a loogie and spat into the street. Coop lit a cigarette and smoked while they walked. They didn't talk.

A few blocks north of Hotel Amigo they found a McDonald's, and after Coop had finished his Newport and dropped his butt into an ashtray by the door, they stepped inside.

Normal knew people who would never go into a fast-food place while in a foreign country. They wanted to eat how the locals ate, they said, without ever considering that locals might eat at Mc-Donald's. He thought fast-food joints were where you really saw the differences between cultures.

He and Coop walked to the counter and scanned the menu. After a couple minutes, they ordered their food.

When their order was ready, Normal grabbed the tray. He and Coop walked to a table by a window. They sat down across from one another, grabbed what food they'd ordered. Normal forked scrambled eggs into his mouth.

He glanced up at Coop. "Do you think we'll get to see James today?"

"I hope so."

"We all hope so. What do you *think*?"

"I think we'll get to see him. I'm worried what we'll find out."

"What do you mean?"

"I'm afraid he did it."

"You told Pilar—"

"I know what I told her, and I believed it at the time. I still don't think it's something he would normally do, but we don't know why he was here. If he thought it was something he had to do, if Layla got herself into debt before she died, put her family in danger . . . I don't know. I'm just saying, I've had time to think and been able to imagine scenarios in which he might do something he normally wouldn't do. So I'm worried he did it. Even if he didn't have the drugs, even if those were planted, I'm almost certain the guns *were* his. I know he owns a SIG."

"What if he did do it—what if those five kilograms of cocaine were his?"

"I don't know. I guess it doesn't change the situation much."

"Then don't worry about it."

"Might change the way I think about it him."

"After what we all did in Afghanistan, who gives a fuck about a little cocaine?"

"We were in a war, Normal, regular rules of civilization don't apply."

Normal ate his breakfast, but noticed that Coop didn't touch his. He only sipped his coffee until it was cold and then pushed it aside.

◼ James was sitting in the jailhouse cafeteria eating his own breakfast. He was alone at the table, back to the wall, watching others go through the service line and find places to sit. Watching them eat. Food was slopped onto their trays with ice cream scoops by other dull-eyed prisoners; tattoo-knuckled fingers wrapping around plastic utensils; feet shuffling across the dirty floor; gold teeth chewing on food. The man who'd attacked him in the yard sat down three tables over, forked egg into a tortilla, folded the tortilla in half, and took a bite. Looked at James while he ate, face expressionless.

While he was watching the guy, another man sat across from James. His wrists were bandaged: the man whose daughter was killed in the schoolhouse, the man he'd spoken to in the infirmary.

"I never told you my name," the man said.

"I never told you mine."

"Pedro."

"James."

"Who did you lose?"

For a moment James didn't reply. Didn't know if he wanted to. But looking across the table at the man—his wide brown eyes so filled with empathy—he decided he might as well.

"My sister."

"I'm sorry. Were you close?"

"Not close enough."

"You plan to seek vengeance." It wasn't a question.

"What makes you say that?"

"The things you said in the infirmary."

"I do—if I can."

"Why would you be unable to?"

"I may be killed before I have the chance."

Pedro thought about this. His eyes had a faraway look, briefly, before shifting toward James again. There was kindness in them. "Someone here wishes to kill you?"

"Someone here works for someone who wishes me dead. Which is about the same."

"Who?"

James nodded in the direction of the man who'd attacked him.

Pedro glanced over his shoulder. Quickly, subtly.

"The man with no name," he said. "Is he the one who put you in the infirmary?"

"Yeah."

"You put him in the infirmary too."

"I read the bible."

Pedro smiled subtly. "An eye for an eye."

"That's the verse I was thinking of."

"Will you tell me who he works for?"

"Alejandro Rocha."

"I've heard of him."

"Many people have—yet he avoids prison."

"He knows who to pay. His heroin has hurt many people in Chiapas. Is he the one you wish to kill?"

James nodded.

"I will help you to stay alive."

"I don't think you want to get involved in—"

"What else do I have to live for?"

James didn't have an answer to this. The man had tried to kill himself, so he wasn't only not afraid to die but welcomed death. That didn't mean, however, that James wanted the man to die for him. He had his own battles to fight. After a long silence he said as much.

Pedro waved away the comment. "I'm far from home and don't know if I'll ever return. I might never be able to find justice for my daughter, but I can help you find justice for your sister by helping you to stay alive."

James opened his mouth to protest.

"You cannot talk me out of this."

■ They were on the road by nine thirty. It was early—the gates wouldn't open for almost two and a half hours—but Coop figured the sooner they got there, the better their chances of seeing James. He wanted them at or near the front of the line. So they drove west through the desert, toward the jail and the crescent of low gray hills that surrounded it.

Pilar didn't normally smoke, but asked Coop for one of his Newports. He handed her his pack and she slipped out a cigarette, lit it, and stared out the window taking long drags. The cigarette shook between her fingers. She didn't say so—she didn't say much of anything—but he knew she was thinking about James, worrying over his situation.

They were the fourth car to arrive. Coop pulled up behind a green Pinto sedan, shoved the transmission into park, turned up the radio. They listened to The Fall's *Grotesque* while waiting, running through the disc more than once.

Though they waited for a long time, there was almost no talk. They sat in silence, everyone in his or her own world, thinking about James and what might follow their conversation with him, if they got to talk.

Coop smoked cigarette after cigarette, looking through the windshield, listening to the music thumping through the speakers.

Pilar gazed out the passenger window to the desert and the jail growing from its sands like some sort of tumor. When inmates were in the yard, she scanned the faces, but because of her silence, Coop assumed she didn't see James. He didn't see James either.

Bogart pulled a deck of cards from his right hip pocket and began practicing silently, without patter. Double lifts, triple lifts, snap changes, swivel cut flourishes, and so on. During his time in Afghanistan, because he'd wanted to fill the empty hours, he'd gotten into close-up card magic, and seemed to practice it whenever he had a few empty minutes. He'd done some tricks for Coop, maybe two dozen in total, and it was impressive how good he'd gotten.

Bogart's manner made the tricks even more impressive than they were. He moved and talked slowly, had a stoner's laugh—people thought he was a pothead long before he ever touched weed—so you assumed he'd be incapable of the sort of sleight of hand and misdirection that good card tricks required. That was ridiculous, of course. The man could hit a target from a thousand yards, which meant he knew both subtle movement and precision, but he *seemed* incapable of such things. He also seemed astounded by how the tricks came out, part of the audience despite the fact he was performing, which made the card tricks feel like something more than they were.

Normal watched Bogart, popped his knuckles, looked out the window, shifted in his seat, scratched the Willie Nelson tattoo on his leg, popped his neck, rolled a quarter over the back of his knuckles, hummed to the songs he liked, sang to "New Face in Hell" and "The Container Drivers," opened his window, closed his window, and generally acted like an impatient child.

Finally the guard station's window slid open and the guard began to check identification and let cars into the visitor parking lot.

■ They were told at the door only one of them could meet with James. They walked into a waiting room. The room was lined with chairs, six of them occupied by those who'd entered before them. They talked and decided that Pilar should be the one to speak with James. She was closer to him than anybody, which meant they'd probably get more out of him if she went in.

That was important.

■ James was lying on his cot, staring at the ceiling and thinking about his fate, when he heard footsteps coming toward him. Two sets of footsteps, which grew louder as they drew near. They stopped in front of his cell. His cell door unlatched. He sat up and looked. Two guards looked back. They wore crisp uniforms, pepper spray and saps and handcuffs tucked into their belts, their faces expressionless.

One of them said, "You have a visitor."

James got to his feet and walked out of his cell. Trudged down the corridor, one guard in front of him and the other behind. They stopped at five other cells on the block, collected five other prisoners. Wended through cinder block–walled corridors, left and right, right and left, until they reached the visiting room.

The prisoners were led through a door.

The room was about eighty feet wide and thirty feet deep, no windows, guards in each corner and at the midpoint on each wall. The room itself was filled with small round tables, two chairs at each of them. The tables were wood, with graffiti scratched into them.

James scanned the faces of the people sitting in the chairs and saw Pilar. She was hunch-shouldered, fingers laced together in front of her, looking down at nothing in particular. Her eyes had a far-away look, short black hair hanging down to her jawline, dark skin flawless. Her brown eyes, even now, flickered with the light of what-ever was sparking in her mind. She was wearing blue eye shadow. Lips the color of a cabernet sauvignon and pursed slightly. She was wearing a faded gray scoop-neck T-shirt that said BROOKLYN.

He hadn't known who he was going to find here, but despite the fact he didn't want Pilar to see him in jail—in a jumpsuit, face need-ing to be shaved, eyes tired—he was glad it was her. It might be the last time they had a chance to talk. It was Monday. If every-thing went how it had been going, and he still had no idea what might change his circumstances, he'd be dead by Wednesday. Noth-ing of a legal nature could be accomplished by then, and after thinking about it long and hard, he wasn't sure much of an illegal nature could be accomplished by then either.

He walked to the table at which Pilar was sitting. She looked up as he neared, saw him, and smiled. She stood up and hugged him, her arms wrapped tight around his middle.

A guard shouted at them in Spanish to separate, no hugging, but James continued to hold her for a moment anyway. Inhaled her scent, a combination of soap, lotion, deodorant, and clean sweat. Felt her back warm under his palms. Felt her hair against his cheek. He wished he could fall asleep holding her, his face in her neck. He wished he could feel the rhythm of her slow breathing, his palm on her breast while he dreamed.

Finally he let her go and they sat down across from one another.

"I'm glad you came." He reached across the table and took her hand in his. Waited for one of the guards to say something, but none of them did.

"I had to see you. You look a little ragged."

"I feel a little ragged. I'm sorry I left the way I did."

"I understand."

"I don't know that you do under—"

"You weren't going to the funeral, you were coming to Mexico. Whatever you intended to do here, you intended to do alone. Given that you're in jail, I can assume you were trying to protect me. You were wrong and stupid to do whatever you did, and I wish you hadn't done it, but I think your heart was in the right place."

"I guess you do understand."

"I understand that part."

"What don't you understand?"

"Everything else. What the hell were you *doing* here, James?"

"You don't want to know."

"Did it have something to do with your sister?"

"Yes."

"I do want to know. I liked Layla. She's the only person in your family I've met."

Layla had come to visit them in North Carolina three years earlier, stayed with them for a week. While James spent his days at Camp Lejeune, Pilar and Layla had Mario Kart battles, went shopping, ate several lunches, and talked about everything. They'd become friends, and through that friendship, Pilar told James, she'd begun to understand him better.

James knew what appealed to Pilar about her: she was smart and funny and seemed not to give a fuck, which made her *real*. So many people pretended to be something else (James himself did this). Layla let it all hang out, emotions and opinions alike. She'd been mercurial, possibly a bit unstable, but somehow she'd made even that aspect of her personality charming.

"I know. She liked you too. She told me I should marry you."

Pilar held up her left hand and wiggled her fingers. "You didn't listen to her."

"If I get out of this, I plan to." He paused a moment in thought. "If you let me."

"I won't be able to help you get out of this if you don't tell me what you were doing here, if you don't tell me what happened."

"You won't be able to help me anyway."

"Did you have cocaine in your trunk?"

"No."

"So it was planted?"

"Yes. But can we talk about something else?"

"No. It's the most important thing happening in your life. Which means it's the most important thing happening in *my* life. You might think you're protecting me from this, but you're not. If something's happening to you, it affects me, whether you like it or not. I won't put my head in the sand about this. Tell me what's going on, James. Were the guns yours?"

James thought about it for a long time, thought about how much he should tell her. It was true he wanted to protect her from the situation, but what she'd said was also true. There was no way to do that, no way to keep her outside of it. So he'd tell her what had happened and why—and he'd tell her what was happening now.

"Yes," he said, "the guns were mine. Do you remember when I mentioned a man named Alejandro Rocha?"

"I do," she said.

He told her everything.

■ Coop was sitting in the waiting room between Bogart and Normal when Pilar stepped through the door. She looked like she was in shock, face expressionless but eyes wide and staring. She walked jerkily, as if she were a wind-up toy.

Coop got to his feet, stepped toward her, and said, "What happened?"

She blinked, raised her head to look at him. "What?"

"What happened?"

"Let's get out of here," she said. "I need a drink."

11

Gael Morales walked up the steps that led to the second floor and made his way down a long hallway, feet thudding against the polished hardwood floor. He reached the fourth door on the left, tapped it with his knuckles, and waited. After a short time the doorknob rattled, turned, and was pulled open from the other side. Danielle Preston, a pretty Midwestern woman in her mid-twenties, stood facing him. She wore sweatpants, the fabric visibly thin, and a fitted Armani Exchange T-shirt. She smiled when she saw him and stepped to the left, welcoming him inside with her body language if not her words.

"Hey, Gael, what's up?"

He looked past her a moment to the bedroom, to the posters thumbtacked on the white walls, to the unmade queen-size bed, to the shoes piled next to it, to the pair of 501s thrown over a desk chair, to the flat-screen television sitting on the dresser, the volume low, the screen flashing frames from a Roman Polanski film.

"The Tenant?"

"It's my third favorite movie."

"What are the first two?"

"*Brazil* and *There Will Be Blood*. Daniel Day-Lewis makes me tingly."

"So you like happy movies, then."

Dani laughed. It lit up her eyes and made her more than pretty, made her beautiful, but only a moment after it began the laughter stopped and the light died. "I was gonna go to film school before I got involved in all this." She swept her right hand out, like a real estate agent displaying the room to a prospective buyer, but she didn't mean the room.

"You're young. You could still go to film school."

"In eleven years I could also run for president, but I don't think it's gonna happen."

"I'm not sure those two things are equivalent."

"From where I'm standing they are. But you didn't come here to talk about my discarded ambitions. Come in if you want."

Gael hesitated a moment, then stepped into Dani's bedroom. She closed the door behind him. It latched with a metal click. He had yet to say anything to her but he still felt vulnerable. What he intended to do here was dangerous, bordering on stupid, and for a moment he thought about leaving the situation as it was.

He liked Dani, but she was a junkie, and junkies couldn't be trusted. That old saying was true: an alcoholic will steal your wallet and feel guilty about it; a junkie will steal your wallet and help you look for it. He glanced toward the television, watched as Trelkovsky pulled a tooth from a hole in his apartment's wall.

Dani walked to the unmade bed and sat down.

After a moment he said, "I want to talk to you about something."

"I assumed as much."

"I know you're not happy with this life."

"I'm paid well for an easy, if dangerous, job. I have no complaints. What I'm not happy with is myself. I never thought this was who I'd be." She laughed through her nose, but there was no humor in it. "I used to have dreams."

"What if I told you, you don't have to be who you've become?"

"I—I don't know. Depends on what you mean by that."

Gael exhaled in a sigh. Never before during an undercover operation had he revealed himself as a DEA agent. He'd been found out once, and that had almost ended in his getting killed with the claw end of a hammer. His instinct for self-preservation made him resist giving himself up even now, but if he hoped to make this case, he thought it necessary. The paperwork might lead somewhere—he hoped like hell it did—but he couldn't count on that alone. He needed more, and in order to get it, he'd have to talk.

It was best, he thought, if he just came out with it.

He built himself up, readied himself, and blurted:

"I'm an undercover DEA agent."

She laughed. "Yeah, okay, Gael. I'm the financial director of the Lollipop Guild."

He turned and looked at her, his expression deadpan. "Dani, I'm an undercover DEA agent."

Something about his expression, or the tone of his voice, made her stop laughing at once. Her mouth snapped shut, teeth clacking. She looked at him in silence for a long time.

"Is this some kind of test Alejandro set up?"

"No. I don't work for Alejandro. Not really."

"You're DEA?"

"I am."

"Don't fuck with me, Gael. I'm serious."

"So am I."

"Were you the one talking to Layla?"

"Nobody from the DEA was talking with Layla."

"Yes, they were."

"Who?"

"She didn't say."

"How do you know?"

"She told me. A few days before she died, she told me she'd been approached by the DEA, asked me what she should do."

"What did you tell her?"

Dani was silent for a moment. Her eyes went dull as she turned her focus inward, thinking about what had happened. Finally she looked at him again, her focus external once more. "I was worried about her. She'd lost a lot of weight. She was depressed. Looked unhealthy. I told her she should talk to the DEA if they could get her out of here. But that was a mistake. I'd take it back if I could. She'd be alive if she hadn't agreed to meet with them."

"Layla died of an overdose."

"How?"

"What do you mean?"

"How did she die of an overdose, Gael? How *could* she?"

"She ran away, found a connection in El Paso, and she overdosed."

"She didn't run away."

"What do you mean, she didn't run away?"

"She left to meet with her man from the DEA and never came back. If she'd been running, she would have taken her personal belongings and some clothes, but until Alejandro had it cleaned out, her room looked like she was still living there."

"She didn't want to be weighed down. She wanted to get away."

"We're not prisoners here, Gael. I could pack my bags and walk out tomorrow. Alejandro would have Diego drive me stateside and drop me off at a bus station. Probably give me a couple hundred bucks for the journey."

"Why don't you?"

"You know why. Same reason Layla didn't."

She was right. Rocha's girls weren't in prison. They could do what they liked. Or would have been able to if they weren't leashed by drugs. If Layla had run, she wouldn't have had any reason to leave behind everything she owned. Gael should have realized that on his own, should have sensed that something wasn't right about the way Layla died.

Now he had revealed himself, and because of Layla's death, Dani would almost certainly refuse to speak to him. But that wasn't even the most important issue.

There were two possibilities for the man who'd approached Layla.

Either he was someone who worked for Rocha testing loyalties or he was an actual DEA agent—and also working for Rocha by testing loyalties.

Both situations were bad, but the latter might be devastating for both the case and for him, because if there was interference from someone inside the DEA, that interference would be coming from someone with access to all sorts of inside knowledge.

But he could think about the consequences of that later. He pushed those thoughts to the back of his mind and looked at Dani. "I don't know who Layla talked to," he said, "but it wasn't me. I'll have to find out who it was, and I *will* find out, but right now I want to talk to you about Rocha and his cartel—if you're willing."

"Talking got Layla killed."

"Talking to someone on Rocha's payroll got her killed."

"*You're* on his payroll."

"I'm undercover."

"I know you say it wasn't, but as far as I know it might have been you she talked to. If I talk to you, I could end up dead too."

"Look at me, Dani," Gael said. She looked him in the eyes. "I'm exactly what I say I am. If Layla was your friend—and since she confided in you, I assume she was—you must want some kind of justice for her. Rocha killed her, or someone who works for him did, and the only way we can get justice, the only way we can take Rocha down, is if you talk to me. I know, despite what I say, that you'll be taking a risk. But I'm taking a risk too. If you tell Rocha what I've told you, he'll kill me, and he won't do it with an overdose. He'll shoot me in the head and bury me in the desert. My body will never be found. My wife, who's not involved in any of this shit, will never know what happened to me. So you need to understand that we're in the same situation. You might not be certain you can trust me, but I'm not certain I can trust you either. I'm talking to you because I *believe* that I can. If you believe you can trust me too, I urge you to talk. If you do, the information you provide might prove invaluable even if you don't testify when we put our case together. But if you *do* testify, the DEA will put you through rehab. We'll give you a new identity and set you up in a new life. You'll be able to go to film school—or do whatever else you want to do. I know you want to get out of this life. Talking to me can be your way out."

Gael stopped his speech, but continued to look Dani in the eyes, and as he did, as he watched her face and waited for her response, he wondered how similar his pitch was to the one that Layla had heard, the one that got her killed.

Dani didn't respond for a long time. She stared back at him for a moment, then dropped her head, looking down at her hands. She popped her knuckles, one by one. After what felt to Gael like a long time, she finally spoke:

"Okay—what do you want to know?"

■ She told him everything she knew. Told him about the tunnel leading from the church to a feed shed on an ostrich farm across the border. Told him about heroin deliveries to Chicago, Los Angeles, and New York. Told him the names of the men she'd delivered to and to whom she'd probably deliver again.

She told him these things and more.

But when she was done, she said, "You use that information how you want, use it to nail Rocha if you can, but I won't testify."

"If you don't testify, we can't protect you."

"If I don't testify, I won't need you to. Build your case with what I've given you."

Gael opened his mouth to say something, but before he could she shook her head. "Don't insult me, Gael; don't talk to me like I'm stupid. I like you and I wanna keep liking you."

"Okay," he said.

He stepped out of the room.

12

Diego Blanco knocked on Alejandro's bedroom door.

"Come in."

He pushed open the door and found Alejandro standing naked by the bed, a pair of boxer briefs gripped in his fist. He'd just showered after a swim and was getting dressed for an afternoon meeting, and though usually Diego would go with him, he had a meeting of his own to get to. Alejandro glanced over at Diego and stepped into his underwear.

"What is it?"

"Just letting you know I'm heading to El Paso."

Alejandro picked up a pair of pants from the bed and slipped into them, squeezed the button through the eye, and zipped up. He threaded a belt through the loops. "Let me know how it goes."

"I always do."

"I know." A pause. "Before you go, let me ask you something."

"What is it?"

"What do you think of Gael Morales?"

Diego liked Gael but didn't want to put himself out on a limb when Alejandro was the one holding the chainsaw, so he only shrugged and said, "He seems okay."

"You've spent more time with him than I have. Worked shoulder to shoulder."

"He's done good work."

"Do you trust him?"

"Did he do something?"

Alejandro slipped into a button-down and stitched the front together, dexterous fingers working quickly. "No. I've been thinking about giving him more responsibility. I wanted to know what your feelings were." He shrugged himself into an off-white Ralph Lauren seersucker sport coat with navy pinstripes.

"He hasn't been here that long but—"

"If you were in a life-or-death situation, would you trust him to have your back?"

Diego thought about it for a moment and—after weighing the risk: this was tantamount to vouching for the man, which might make him responsible if something went bad—he decided to answer honestly. "Yes," he said, "without hesitation."

Alejandro nodded. "Good. Thank you."

◼ Francis Waters was already sitting at an outside table, looking at the Circle K on the other side of the parking lot, when Diego brought the car to a stop in front of Ripe Eatery. He shoved the transmission into park, killed the engine, and with the key ring dangling from an index finger, pushed his way out of the car and into the heat. Sweat immediately began to bead on his face and head. He pocketed the car key, raised a hand at Waters, and made his way to the table where the man was sitting. Pulled out a green plastic chair and sat down himself, tonguing a wooden toothpick from one corner of his mouth to the other.

Waters sipped his coffee. "Afternoon."

Diego grunted his greeting and set a thick white envelope on the table.

"I was waiting for you to order. Know what you want?"

"Not yet."

He picked up a menu, browsed it, and decided on the chicken-fried chicken. Looked up, waved at the server and, when she walked over, ordered his lunch. Francis Waters ordered the grape steak salad, which surprised Diego not at all. He seemed like the kind of asshole who'd order salad for lunch.

Diego glanced at the table and saw the envelope was gone. Waters had, at some point, slipped it away. Five thousand dollars. Every two weeks he received a similar envelope. In Diego's opinion, the man was overpaid, but Diego's opinion didn't matter. Alejandro thought he was worth the expense, so that was that.

He pulled the toothpick from his mouth, snapped it in half, and set it on the table.

"Did you find out anything more about the undercover agent?"

"No," Waters said. "I tried but Rankin's an untrusting mother-fucker."

"You can't work around that?"

"Not without raising suspicions."

"How much does the DEA pay you?"

"About sixty-seven after taxes."

"How much does Alejandro pay you?"

"A hundred and twenty."

"A hundred and thirty. There's fifty-two weeks a year, not forty-eight, so a hundred and thirty. Tax fucking free."

"I get your point, but if I don't stay with the DEA, I'm useless to Alejandro. I collect what information I can without jeopardizing my position. That way I can *remain* useful."

There might be truth in the man's words, but more than that, there was justification for cowardice. Francis Waters was unwilling to stick his neck out despite what Alejandro paid him. It only made Diego dislike him more than he already did. Waters was useful, but there was something distasteful about a man who worked both sides, talking out of both corners of his mouth. He was a man whose loyalties couldn't be trusted. His *real* loyalty would always be to himself, which meant he'd do whatever was expedient in the moment.

Diego might be a drug dealer and a murderer, but he owned what he was. He was one of the bad guys and didn't pretend he was anything else, didn't rationalize his actions.

But, unlike Francis Waters, he reasonably could have. He'd gotten into this so he'd have money to raise his daughters, but he didn't pretend he was noble. He was a bad man who sometimes did good things, and he was as loyal to Alejandro as he was to his girls. His junkie ex-wife was useless. She might be dead for all he knew. He raised his girls because that was his obligation, and he did what he did for Alejandro because that was what he'd signed up to do. An electrician wasn't noble; he was a man doing a job.

The same was true of him.

"What'd you find out about James Murphy?"

"He's a Marine Corps sergeant, part of a scout sniper platoon currently stationed at Fort Bliss after a year in Afghanistan. His little sister used to work for Alejandro."

Their food arrived. Diego looked up at the pretty server and smiled. "Thank you."

"No problem, handsome."

Diego watched her walk away—she had a fine backside— and after she was gone, turned back to Waters. "Used to work for Alejandro? Who was she?"

"Layla."

Diego thought about this, then said, "Does he know she was murdered?"

"No way he could. El Paso police don't. There wasn't even a thorough investigation. She's just another dead junkie. No point in wasting police resources. But my guess is he blames Alejandro for her overdose."

"Is there any reason to think he isn't here on his own?"

"No."

"Should Alejandro be worried about him?"

"He's not a carpenter. He's a Marine Corps sniper. A trained assassin. This isn't a guy you want on your bad side."

"So . . . yes."

Waters forked a bite of salad into his mouth.

"I'll let Alejandro know. Who's next on your list of girls?"

"Danielle Preston."

"Good," Diego said. "She's supposed to make a run to Los Angeles in three days, which means she gets a shopping trip to buy clothes. The girls love that shit. Approach her tomorrow afternoon."

"Any reason to suspect she might turn?"

"No. But there was no reason to suspect Layla might turn either. Until she did. It's why we do this."

"I'll take care of it. Will you be with her?"

"I don't think so. It'll probably be another one of Alejandro's men. Guy named Gael Morales."

"He'll know what to do about it?"

"I don't know. Just see what Danielle does and call me. We'll take it from there."

Waters nodded.

■ George Rankin sat in an unmarked black sedan parked at a gas station some distance from the table where Diego Blanco and Francis Waters were talking. He had a parabolic dish aimed at them, recording their conversation, and was taking pictures using a 500mm lens, but while he was getting good shots, there was a too much traffic to get consistent audio. Westwind Drive sat between George and the restaurant, and every couple minutes a new patch of cars would rumble through. Still, he heard enough to understand the nature of the conversation, and to pick up a few specifics.

He'd been second-guessing himself while tailing Francis Waters earlier, second-guessing himself and thinking he was being an asshole for doing this to another DEA agent, but he was glad he'd listened to his gut and ignored his brain, glad he'd been suspicious of the man's questions about his case and the way he'd asked them, because while he'd known Francis Waters was crooked, or suspected it, the fact he was putting Gael Castillo Jimenez in harm's way meant something must be done about it. In truth, it made him want to murder Francis Waters where he sat. George could, without any guilt, do to him what Rocha would do to Gael if he ever discovered he was a narc. Walk up to him at the restaurant, put the barrel of his weapon against the motherfucker's temple, and squeeze the trigger.

But while he might be capable of killing Francis Waters, he wouldn't do it.

Instead, he'd nail him to the fucking wall with evidence. He'd make the man do time in prison with men he'd put there, men he'd testified against, and let *them* kill him. Because based on what George had heard of the conversation, Francis Waters was involved in at least one murder. Someone named Layla was dead and he'd had something to do with it. Layla. The little sister of a Marine Corps sergeant named James Murphy.

He needed to find out who these people were and how they were connected to Rocha.

He started the engine, shoved his car into gear, and pulled out into the street.

He wondered how long he had before Francis Waters did something to ruin his case or get Gael killed. There'd be no way to find out until it was too late. But he did know one thing. He had to work fast. He needed Gael out of Mexico as soon as possible. If Francis Waters saw Gael, he'd recognize him, and all the precautions would prove pointless.

Gael had been in Mexico for six months, and every day he'd been in danger, every day at risk of being discovered, but now George knew how much danger he'd been in, and he wanted him out of there.

But not before they put their case together.

13

They were sitting at a table in Los Parados, the dive bar across the street from Hotel Amigo. The table was streaked with moisture and had the musty stink of a dirty bar towel. Coop had bought them all drinks: three fingers of whisky sat on the table in front of him while Pilar had a screwdriver and Bogart and Normal each had a bottle of beer. Everybody was in a pensive mood, the table quiet but tense with things unsaid. Normal took a swallow from the neck of his brown bottle and set it back down on the table. He looked at it for a long moment. Finally he spoke: "James might never drink another beer."

Coop said, "Come Wednesday, he might be done with breathing," but when he saw the look on Pilar's face, he regretted it.

"Don't talk like that," she said.

"He's just telling the truth." This from Bogart, who must have smoked a joint when he went to the bathroom a few minutes ago. His eyes were bloodshot. "Unless we can figure out something to do about it, James is gonna end up dead."

Pilar's eyes welled with tears. She wiped at them with the heels of her hands, looking to Coop like a little girl, and his heart broke for her, but he didn't know how to make it better. Neither for her nor for James. The situation was impossible.

"He's not gonna die," Pilar said, her voice steady.

Coop took a mouthful of whisky, strained it through his teeth to swish it around his gums, tilted his head back, and swallowed. He looked at the ceiling for a moment, then closed his eyes. He understood Pilar's refusal to accept the situation, but she was wrong. James was going to die. The day after tomorrow he was a dead man. He'd be shanked in the cafeteria or the yard. He'd have his throat slit in his cell while he slept. A guard would shoot him and claim he'd tried to escape. Something would happen and though Coop didn't know what, he knew the result: James in a coffin in a dark suit.

He opened his eyes and looked from one face to the other, pale moons in the dim light of the bar, and after a moment he said: "We have to break him out."

"Have you lost your fucking mind?"

"If we don't, he's dead."

"You *have* lost your fucking mind."

"Do you have a better solution?"

"There *is* no solution."

"I just gave you one."

"Bullshit."

"It's the beginning of one," Pilar said.

"What does that even *mean*?"

"We save his life, get him out of jail, and with him safe, we can work to prove his innocence."

"He's *not* innocent," Normal said.

"Those drugs weren't his."

"The guns *were*."

"He was seeking justice," Coop said.

"Vigilante justice ain't exactly legal."

"It wasn't justice, anyway," Bogart said. "It was vengeance."

"Thank you," Normal said.

"They're the same fucking thing." Coop had been thinking

about this since he'd found out what James had been doing. They'd worked together in Afghanistan, and together they'd killed people, but the decision to do so hadn't been theirs. They'd followed orders, which had made it acceptable. They weren't responsible for these deaths. They were only tools. They were the weapons the United States government was using.

This was different. James had made a decision that someone must die and had gone about trying to make that death happen. If he had succeeded, he'd be a murderer.

Except he wasn't killing some random person. He had a specific target and his target was himself a murderer. The man who, as far as James was concerned, had killed his baby sister. So while it might be murder, it was also justice, even if it was vengeance too.

"They're the same thing," he said again.

"Not in the eyes of the law."

"He's not being charged with attempted murder."

"Doesn't mean he don't wanna kill someone," Normal said.

"Point is, if we don't break him out, he's a dead man. I think he'd rather be on the run than in the grave."

"If we *do* break him out, we'll end up where he is."

"Not if we don't get caught," Bogart said.

Normal turned to look at him, and Coop could see the feeling of betrayal floating behind his eyes. Bogart was his partner and was supposed to side with him in arguments such as these, even if he didn't agree.

"If Bogart was in jail," Coop said, "would you just let him die?"

"Of course not, but—"

"But what?"

Normal was silent a moment. He sipped his beer. He looked to the corner of the dark bar and stared at nothing in particular, a far-away look in his eyes. Finally he turned back to Coop and said, "If we *were* to break him out, how would we do it?"

"I don't know."

"Well, there you go."

"We do it when he's in the yard," Pilar said. "It's the only way."

"What's your plan?"

Pilar told them, and when she was finished, she looked from face to face expectantly. Coop put his hand on her shoulder and said, "You know I'm in."

"I'm in," Bogart said.

Normal was silent. He took a swallow from his beer bottle. He scratched the Marine Corps tattoo on his bicep.

"Fuck it," he said. "I'm in too."

14

The next morning, Tuesday, George Rankin walked across stained gray carpet to Lou Billingham's office, florescent lights humming in the ceiling overhead, the low drone of work chatter all around. He knocked on the thick wooden door. Billingham, deputy chief of intelligence, worked directly under Horace Ellison. Ellison's office windows were dark, which meant he wasn't in yet, otherwise George would talk to him. But the man didn't show up until seven fifty every morning, and that was still twelve minutes off.

"Come in."

He pushed open the door to find Lou Billingham behind his desk eating a bagel with cream cheese and lox. He had gray hair and a pockmarked, though clean-shaven, face. Brown eyes that always looked tired. A sag in his neck like a turkey wattle. He took a sip from a coffee mug with WORLD'S BEST GRANDDAD written across it. It was hard to imagine Billingham being any kind of granddad, much less the world's best; he struck George as the kind of guy who'd push kids away with a broomstick.

"Rankin."

"Sir."

"Cup of home-brewed coffee? Got a thermos full and you can bet your ass it's better than that slop in the break room."

"No, thank you, sir."

"Then how can I help you?"

"Ellison isn't in yet or I'd have asked him, but have we got anything back on that bank account information Gael got us? Or the phone records?"

"We got a name but we haven't been able to connect it to a birth certificate, or anything other than an Illinois driver's license and a Citibank Visa card with a two thousand dollar limit, and of course, the bank account itself."

"Wouldn't he need a social security number for the bank account and the credit card?"

"Yeah, we're still waiting on the SSA to get back to us."

"What about the phone records?"

"People are going through the numbers, seeing what they can pin down."

"What's the name?"

"First name Mulligan. I can't remember the last name offhand, but I'll get you Xeroxes of everything that came in."

"Mulligan like in golf?"

"Just like."

"Think it's a real person's name?"

Billingham shrugged. "Look at the dumb shit some of these actors name their kids and it doesn't seem impossible."

"Did we get an address from the driver's license?"

"We did. It's a bar in Chicago. Nobody lives there, and best as we can tell, nobody there knows anybody named Mulligan—and it's not exactly a forgettable name."

"Will you keep me updated on anything new?"

"It's your case."

"Thank you." George paused, opened his mouth to speak again, but hesitated.

Billingham let him dangle a moment before he said, "What is it?"

"We have a problem."

"What kind of problem?"

George told Billingham about Francis Waters asking after the Rocha case; told him about yesterday's meeting with Diego Blanco; told him what he thought these things added up to: "The son of a bitch is crooked, sir."

Billingham sipped his coffee. "Do we have anything solid?"

"Just the recording and the pictures."

"We'll need more than that."

"The recording is pretty incriminating."

"You've never said anything that might seem incriminating if taken out of context? We can't have agents afraid to do their job, Rankin, and sometimes doing your job means talking to bad guys about bad things. You know that."

"It's not his case."

Billingham shrugged. "Maybe he's taken an interest."

"He could be putting Gael's life in danger, sir."

"We can't go after a DEA agent with a single recorded conversation, Rankin, especially if we don't know the motives behind that conversation."

"Best scenario, he's working a case he's not authorized to work and endangering the whole operation. I don't want to sit on this and—"

"You're not sitting on anything. You've told me. If you really think he's crooked, stay on him, try to get something we can use. That's the end of our conversation on that matter. Do you have anything else?"

"No, sir."

■ George flipped through the paperwork they'd gathered so far. The phone records looked like a dead end unless they happened to arrest people with corresponding cells in their pockets. They'd managed to connect several numbers to local businesses, but George would bet green money that those calls were legitimate. Otherwise Rocha talked to people using burners or to people with cell phones he paid for. The bank account information was a different story. The wire transfers were going from accounts in Alejandro Rocha's name into an account belonging to a man named Mulligan Shoibli. The one record they had was for a transfer in the amount of five hundred thousand dollars. The DEA had subpoenaed records from both banks, but they were in the Cayman Islands, which meant they'd never get them.

For two hours, George sat at his desk and with both his computer and telephone, tried to build a man out of fog. But Mulligan Shoibli never solidified, never took on shape or form. No fingerprints in any database. No address other than that bar in Chicago where no one knew him. No pictures on file. No Facebook page. No LinkedIn account. Not even an abandoned Myspace page or a comment on a three-year-old *New York Times* article. The man was a ghost.

There was something about Chicago floating just under the surface of his consciousness, but George didn't know what it was, and didn't know if it would be useful when it finally breached the surface of his mind. Such unconscious connections were useless almost as often as they were useful. You looked for patterns and sometimes saw them where they either didn't exist or weren't relevant.

But still: Chicago. He let it lay there below the surface and hoped it floated up at some point, like a bloated corpse.

George moved on to James Murphy and his sister Layla, working under the assumption that they shared a last name. Layla Murphy didn't have an arrest record, but her death had been page-nine news in Austin, Texas, two days after her body was discovered.

EL PASO—Layla Murphy, daughter of well-known local car dealer Brian Murphy and sister of Marine Corps Sergeant James Murphy, recipient of the Silver Star Medal for distinguished service in Afghanistan, was found dead Friday morning of an apparent drug overdose. Two boys, whose names have been withheld by police due to their status as minors, found her body while walking to school in northeast El Paso.

An autopsy revealed that Ms. Murphy had died of "fatal

respiratory depression" due to heroin use. El Paso Police Department spokesperson Michael Samonek said in a statement yesterday that there was "no reason to suspect foul play." Ms. Murphy's family were aware that she had a drug problem and had attempted to convince her to enter a recovery program.

Barbara Allan-Murphy, the decedent's mother, asks that those considering cards or flowers instead send a small donation to the Austin Recovery Drug and Alcohol Treatment Center.

There was more on James Murphy, who'd been an offensive guard for the Aggies up until six years ago. He'd declined to enter the draft when he became eligible and instead joined the Marine Corps as a private after graduation. There was a big write-up about this decision, as many thought he might be a third- or fourth-round pick. Local man turns his back on millions in order to serve his country. Even though a middling offensive guard with fourth-round prospects probably wasn't turning his back on millions, there was something admirable about walking away from what might have been a four hundred thousand dollar salary in order to pick up a weapon and maybe get yourself killed in a desert country for fourteen hundred bucks a month. George also found a piece from two years ago about Murphy being awarded the Silver Star Medal. What exactly he'd done was kept vague, but Silver Stars weren't Chiclets; they didn't hand them out to just anybody.

Finally, an item about James Murphy being arrested in La Paz, Mexico, last Wednesday. A young man with NFL prospects who chose duty over cash wasn't the kind of person to end up arrested with five kilograms of cocaine, a pistol, and a sniper rifle in his car. Especially not when he'd only been back in the states for a month. He wasn't the kind of person to end up arrested for anything, except maybe an on-leave DUI, a charge that would probably never be filed.

The arrest stunk.

Not that he hadn't been up to something. According to the news item, a rifle of the type found by La Paz police in James Murphy's car had gone missing from Fort Bliss, and though they didn't have that weapon now to match serial numbers, chances were good that when they did, it would turn out Murphy had taken the thing. Though he didn't like to admit it, this made George admire the guy. It meant James Murphy had gone to Mexico to find justice for his sister. He had either known Layla was murdered—as yesterday's conversation between Diego Blanco and Francis Waters had made clear—or he'd blamed Alejandro Rocha for her overdose. Either way, he'd been acting out of love.

If La Paz police had nailed James Murphy for the guns alone, George might have bought the arrest as legitimate. Might have thought Murphy was the victim of nothing more than bad luck. Wrong place, wrong time. That kind of deal. But he didn't believe the drugs. His guess was that Rocha's men had seen James Murphy watching his estate and Rocha decided to have him locked up until he knew what his motives were. He owned the police force. It would have taken nothing more than a phone call to make it happen.

What George needed to know now was how involved Layla had been in Rocha's operation, how much James Murphy knew about it, and if he knew a significant amount, whether he'd be willing to testify. About the last question he had some doubt. James Murphy, based on the evidence at hand, wanted Rocha buried, and he'd be hard to bury if he was locked away in prison. He might refuse to testify to keep Rocha out of jail and therefore accessible by bullet. George could understand this, part of him would even approve of the murder, but he was a man of the law, which meant he couldn't allow it.

While George worked, while he thought about the situation, he also listened to Francis Waters through their shared cubicle wall. Mostly he was quiet. There were a few telephone conversations early on, two business calls and one personal, the latter being an argument with his third wife, Lydia. For an hour after that, George heard only the tapping of fingers on a keyboard.

George had stopped paying attention, concentrating on his work, when Francis Waters got a call on his cell phone.

"Yeah," he said, answering the call. This one word was followed by a long silence. When Francis Waters finally spoke again, he said, "I'm on my way." He got to his feet, grabbed his suit coat from the back of his chair, shrugged into it, and strode across the gray carpet to the door.

George hesitated only a moment, locked his computer, and pushed away from the desk. He didn't know where Francis Waters was going, but he intended to follow him there.

15

Coop drove his rented Toyota toward the jail, the desert sun floating just over the eastern horizon behind him, its light shining into
the rear window and bouncing off the mirrors. Normal sat in the
passenger seat, looking out at the desert, eating jalapeño pork rinds.
He had a plastic grocery bag filled with snacks sitting on the floorboard by his feet. The sound of his chewing was already irritating
Coop and they'd only left the convenience store five minutes ago.

"How long you think we're gonna have to sit out here?"

"Until we get the information we need."

"How long you think *that'll* be?"

"I don't know, Normal. If I knew enough to tell you that, we
wouldn't need to come out here in the first place."

As they approached a road sign telling them the jail was five kilo-
meters away, Normal rolled his window down, hawked up a loogie,
and spat. Coop heard the mucus thwack against the sign. Normal
said, "Got it," put another pork rind into his mouth, and rolled up
the window.

They continued west, driving into the wavering distance. As the road curved around the low crescent of brown hills that surrounded the jail, the buildings, fences, and guard towers came into view, gray and forbidding. But that might have been Coop's mind. He knew what they were planning, knew the dangers involved, which meant he knew the likelihood of something going wrong was greater than the likelihood of things going well.

He cut the car right, turning the wheel hand over hand, leaving the asphalt for the bumpy desert sands. Weaved his way around any rocks or boulders he saw, but let the car rumble over desert shrubbery, listening to the push-broom sweep they made as they brushed against the vehicle's undercarriage.

Normal squinted toward the hills and when Coop brought the car to a stop, he said, "I'm gonna go for a walk."

"Reconnoiter?"

"Yeah. I also need to piss."

"All right. I'll do my thing here."

Normal shoved his pork rinds into the grocery bag, pushed open the passenger door, and stepped out into the sun. He slammed the door shut. Coop watched him as he walked toward the hills, then turned his attention to the jail. The yard was quiet, empty of people, the guard towers uninhabited hunting blinds, but already friends and relatives of the imprisoned were arriving and parking outside the fences, walking to the yard and looking in, waiting to see those inside.

The presence of vehicles besides theirs, and of people besides them, would make their own presence less noticeable, less worrisome, which was a good thing. If theirs was the only vehicle out here it would be suspicious, so Coop was glad for their presence, but he was also concerned. If there were too many cars here tomorrow, they might be an issue, might stand as a wall between James and escape.

Unfortunately, there was nothing to be done about it. The situation would be what it would be. They'd have to assess, act in the moment, and hope things turned out okay.

Given their current plan, Coop figured they had maybe a 50 percent chance of success, which wasn't terrible. But he didn't want to think about the consequences of failure. Neither for James nor for the rest of them.

He picked up a bottle of Pepsi from his cup holder, unscrewed the cap, and took a swallow. He squinted toward the empty jail-house yard.

■ Normal walked along the base of the hills, looking back and forth between those great mounds of dirt and the jailhouse yard, gauging distance and angle. He squinted toward the sun and tried to envision its movement throughout the day. Its arc across the blue. If they were going to do anything from this side of the jail, it'd be best to do it before the sun reached its apex, with it behind them, blinding the guards in their towers. Anything after three o'clock in the afternoon and shooters on the hill would be looking *into* the sun, which—while also being dangerous—would make them damn near useless. Their scopes would reflect the sun for the towered guards, making targets of them.

It should be done before noon, if at all possible.

He stopped at a desert shrub and unzipped his fly. Pissed into the sand behind it, trying to write his name, but he only managed NORM before he ran out of liquid. He continued walking, looking between the jail and the hills.

When he reached a hill he liked he began hiking his way up, kicking sand even as it slid out from under his Emericas, using rocks as footholds whenever possible.

There were two large boulders in the side of the hill near its crest and he squatted behind each of them to be sure they'd work. The view was good from each. They didn't offer ideal protection, but this hill was almost a thousand yards from any of the guard towers and he doubted the guys who manned them would be able to make thousand-yard shots on anything even approaching a regular basis. They weren't sharpshooters; they were used to watching inmates within a hundred-yard radius and the last time they'd fired their weapons was almost certainly on the range. But sometimes it didn't matter who was squeezing the trigger; the more bullets you fired in a general direction, the better your chances of getting lucky once, and a guard getting lucky meant either Bogart or Normal getting dead.

Still, these were the best positions available, and they'd probably suffice. Getting back down would be the real danger—at least it would be if they descended the front of the hill. They wouldn't be exposed for long, but if someone was shooting at them, it would feel like an eternity. He walked to the top of the hill and looked down the backside.

After a moment's consideration, he decided it wouldn't work. Things needed to happen fast if they expected to get away. Going down the back of the hill would eat up a lot of time. The descent itself wouldn't be much slower. It was the pickup that concerned him. Their position would be inconvenient, the getaway vehicle having to hook around the hills to reach them, adding at least a quarter mile to the distance it must travel, and the time that took might be the difference between a clean getaway and being caught.

They needed to get in and out in a hurry.

He and Bogart would just have to risk going down the front of the hill and hope that the sun blinded the motherfuckers who might otherwise kill them.

■ For the next several hours, Coop and Normal sat in the rented Toyota and watched the jail. Coop with a notepad resting on his leg and a ballpoint pen in hand, making note of when the guards went to the towers, how many guards were stationed in the yard, when prisoners were let out, and how many at a time.

Though the car was parked some distance from the jail, he thought he saw James standing near the fences at one point, around eleven o'clock, talking to another man, a dark-skinned Hispanic guy maybe six inches shorter than James himself.

The sun moved across the sky.

Wispy clouds like masses of cotton balls drifted through the blue.

Normal talked and pulled snacks from the grocery bag and pissed two more times outside the car. It was like being on a road trip with a child.

But finally the time came when Coop believed they'd gathered as much information as they could. He put down his notepad and his pen. He grabbed the shifter, thumbed the button, and shoved the car into gear. He pulled his foot off the brake pedal and pressed it against the gas. The tires spun, kicking up dirt, and they turned toward the road.

"Thank God," Normal said.

"I hope Bogart and Pilar have good news for us when we get back to the hotel."

"They'd better," Normal said, "or James is dead for sure."

16

James was sitting on his cot with shoulders slumped, staring at the wall opposite and thinking about how there was no way out of this, when two guards walked down the corridor to his cell, their footfalls echoing against the cinder block walls, and told him to stand up, *cabrón*. He got to his feet. One of the guards unlocked his cell door and told him to step out. He did, and they marched him through the corridors. They didn't tell him what this was about and he didn't ask. He already knew.

After five minutes—being led through the labyrinth like a rat—he arrived at a door. One of the guards opened the door. The other guard pushed him through, then shut and locked it behind him.

Rocha was sitting on a metal folding chair at a steel table. The corner of his mouth was turned up in a smirk. His eyes sparkled.

"Have a seat."

"I'd prefer to stand."

"*Please* sit."

"Only because you asked so nicely." James sat down across from

Rocha. He laced his fingers together and rested his hands on the table. The steel was cool against his skin.

"I'm beginning to find our conversations boring, Mr. Murphy."

"Beginning to? I guess your threshold for boredom is higher than mine."

"Then time in jail must be torture."

"Not really. *You* bore me, solitude I can live with."

"You must be glad this is our last conversation."

"I wish that were true."

"I assure you it is—unless you intend to spend the afterlife haunting me."

"I'm not dying tomorrow."

"Denial never did anyone any good, Mr. Murphy. Tell you what." Rocha reached under his seersucker sport coat and removed a revolver. He held it up a moment before resting it on the table, keeping his fingers wrapped around it, index finger tapping the outside of the trigger guard. "There's one thing you can do to avoid dying tomorrow."

"Die today?"

"A possibility but not a requirement."

Rocha lifted the revolver again, clicked out the cylinder, let six bullets fall into the palm of his left hand. He pocketed five of them, put one back into the cylinder, and spun it like a roulette wheel. Eventually it clicked to a stop.

He set it back down on the table and pushed it toward James.

"I've done some research on you, Mr. Murphy."

"Have you?"

Rocha nodded. "I know who you are and I know what you have against me. Your sister Layla was once in my employ but, sadly, overdosed a couple weeks ago. I can only assume that you blame me for this. If I were in your position, I might blame me too. You want the world to make sense. You want justice. I get it. But nobody's to blame for your sister's death but your sister. That might be a hard reality to face, but unless you do face it, you'll end up dead."

"You introduced her to this life, and it was this life that killed her."

Rocha was silent for a long moment. He let out a sigh. "So there's nothing I can say to make you change your mind about this."

"No."

"Fair enough, but as I said, you can still walk away from this. *If* you walk away from this. I know I've been portrayed in the media as some kind of animal, but I'm a businessman first, and a smart businessman doesn't take unnecessary risks. There's risk in keeping you alive, but there's also risk in killing you. It's a matter of weighing each decision against the benefits. So here's what I'm willing to do. If you agree to walk away from this after today, to walk away from me, we'll play a game, giving us each a nearly seventeen percent chance of death. That six-chambered revolver holds a single bullet. Put it to your temple and pull the trigger. If you live, I let you live. I'll put it to my temple and pull the trigger. If I live, you let *me* live. We walk away and never look over our shoulders again, never look back, but this is contingent on you *agreeing* to walk away. You strike me as an honest man, so I'll take your word for it. I understand your motives now, and I'm sympathetic to a degree, despite your hatred being aimed in my direction, so I'm inclined to let you live if you can look me in the eye and say you won't try to harm me."

"Then why the game—especially if you aren't inclined to take unnecessary risks?"

A faint smile touched Rocha's lips. "Because if you kill yourself, I won't have to worry about you anymore."

"And if you kill yourself?"

Rocha shrugged. "*All* my worries will be over. I am not *eager* to die, Mr. Murphy, but the prospect doesn't frighten me."

"You're not afraid of hell?"

Rocha laughed. "We're not children anymore, Mr. Murphy. Let's put away childish beliefs."

"What about the charges?"

"Dropped."

James reached out for the revolver, but Rocha grabbed his wrist. "Do you agree you won't shoot me with it?"

"I do."

Rocha removed his hand. James picked up the revolver, flipped out the cylinder to make certain there was only a single bullet loaded, and snapped the cylinder back into place. He spun the cylinder and put the revolver to his temple while looking Rocha in the eyes. Thought about the fact that this man was responsible for his sister's death. He wanted to kill him right here and now. Wanted to squeeze this trigger as many times as it took to push a bullet through the son of a bitch's forehead. If he did this, it would be the first time he'd killed with emotion, with murder in his heart, and he knew that would change him. But he didn't care. His heart was full of love for his sister and equal to that love was the hatred he felt for the motherfucker who'd taken her from him.

But now was not the time.

If he killed Rocha here, he'd be dead himself within the next five minutes. If that.

He still had hope that he could walk away from this.

He squeezed the trigger. The hammer dropped with a loud click. He pulled the gun away from his head and set it down on the table. Pushed it toward Rocha.

"Maybe you should have gone first," he said.

"Why is that?"

"I had a sixteen-point-six percent chance of putting a bullet through my head. *You* have a twenty percent chance."

"In fact, I have a zero percent chance." Rocha picked up the gun and aimed it at James. "You do, in fact, strike me as an honest man. But people change their minds all the time. Today's truth is tomorrow's lie." He squeezed the trigger—click. "Because of this, I'm not at all inclined to let you live." Another squeeze of the trigger, another rotation of the cylinder—click. "This would be true even if you weren't a trained killer. Which you are." Click. "Where are we now? Two chambers left. Fifty-fifty chance that this next pull is the one that kills you."

James said nothing, only looked at the man sitting across from him, waiting for the squeeze—click.

"You don't seem worried, Mr. Murphy."

"I'm not."

Click.

Rocha laughed. "You removed the bullet."

James raised his right hand, the .38 round pinched between index finger and thumb. "I'm not one to take unnecessary risks either."

"You know I have more where that came from."

"Try and load them—see what happens."

"No need." Rocha got to his feet. "You'll be taken care of tomorrow, and I won't have to get my hands dirty." He slid the revolver away. "Enjoy your souvenir." Rocha walked to the door and knocked. A moment later James heard a dead bolt retract. The door was opened from the outside. Rocha stepped through it.

James rolled the bullet between his fingers, thinking he might have his way out of here, if he played it right.

All he needed now was a gun.

17

Gael Morales backed Rocha's BMW 650i out of the garage, vermillion red leather cushioning him as the car purred out into the sun. He slid the shifter into drive, turned the wheel, and rolled toward the gate. Danielle Preston and a girl named Monica sat in the backseat. He skipped through the discs in the changer while he drove. Finally found one he liked, the Stones' *Some Girls*, and turned up the volume as "Miss You" kicked off the album. He tried not to think about Sarah, fifty miles away but a world apart, living alone in their house, grocery shopping for one, lying alone in their queen-size bed and watching bad reality television, laughing at something and glancing toward the place he should be to see if he was laughing too, to see if he'd looked up from his book at the sound of rising voices and caught whatever ridiculous thing was happening on TV, finding the bed empty beside her.

Yes, that was exactly what he tried not to think about.

They approached the estate's wrought-iron gate. He squeezed the brake pedal to slow the car as the gate swung open with a creak of dry hinges. Once the gate had swung its arc, he pulled out into the street, headed north for three blocks, made a left, and cruised along, stopping at two red lights before he reached his destination.

The department store sat on the north side of the sun-faded asphalt, the parking lot on the west end of the building about three quarters full, cars twinkling beneath the hot sun, reflecting its white light.

Gael pulled into a driveway and rolled through the parking lot until he found a spot near the back of the lot between a Ford Escape and a Mazda 3. He backed into it so he'd be able to watch the department store and shoved the shifter into park. Leaned left and pulled his wallet from the back pocket of his 527s. Removed one of Alejandro Rocha's credit cards. Handed it to Danielle Preston, and said, "You girls have five thousand pesos each to spend on clothes, no more, and I need the receipt."

"Okay, *Dad*." Danielle smiled at him in the rearview mirror.

Monica, however, was less than pleased. "Five thousand?"

"Five thousand. If you spend a penny more, I'll return everything you bought."

"Whatever."

The girls pushed out of the car. Gael watched as they walked across the faded asphalt to the department store, weaving between cars, the sun throwing its light and heat down on them.

Once they pushed into the store, Gael lighted a Camel and leaned the seat back. He'd probably be out here for an hour or two before the girls finished their shopping. Maybe he'd try to catch a nap. He hadn't slept well last night.

He was worried about what might come next, so his mind kept folding back in on itself as he worried over the situation he was in, over the variables and what the consequences of each might be. All night this had happened.

He finished his cigarette and flicked it out the window.

■ Francis Waters, parked on the street, watched in his side-view mirror as Gael Castillo Jimenez pulled into the department store driveway. He wasn't here to identify the DEA agent working undercover. He was here to test the loyalties of Danielle Preston. But dumb luck had accomplished what questions and sneaking through George Rankin's paperwork had not.

Francis didn't recognize the man at first, maybe because he hadn't been expecting him, maybe because he'd never spoken to him, only seen him around the office, but after a moment it clicked in his mind: an image of the man walking from the kitchen at work with a coffee mug in hand, nodding at Francis as he shuffled by.

He pulled his second cell phone, a prepaid burner, from his pocket. Dialed Diego Blanco and put the phone to his ear. Listened to it ring and waited.

"Francis."

"You oughta get down here."

"What is it?"

"I found your undercover DEA agent."

"Who is it?"

"I don't know what you know him as, but his real name is Gael Castillo Jimenez."

A long pause before Diego spoke. "You're sure?"

"I am."

"What about Danielle?"

"I don't know yet."

"Find out. I'll be right there."

The line went dead. Francis slipped the phone into his pocket, killed the engine, and with the key ring hanging from his hooked finger, pushed out of the car.

He walked toward the department store.

◾ Danielle Preston was standing at a shirt rack, sliding through hangers, picking up blouses that caught her eye, when a bad feeling shuddered through her body, raising the hair on the back of her neck and arms. She stopped what she was doing and looked around. About fifteen feet behind her stood a man in a well-tailored, well-made suit and expensive shoes. He had dark wavy hair dusted with gray at the temples. He was watching her, his hands in his pockets.

There was a bulge under his left armpit that almost had to be a holstered weapon.

Until this moment, she'd been glad Gael had stayed outside, glad she had brief freedom, time away from the life she'd been living, but now she wished more than anything that he was here with her, standing by her side.

The man raised a hand in greeting.

Without thinking, she raised her own.

He walked toward her. His face was friendly and open. He had kind eyes. But she didn't believe the face. She believed her own assessment, believed the hair on the back of her neck and arms. This was the dirty cop who'd either killed Layla or gotten her killed.

"Danielle Preston," he said.

"Do I know you?"

"Not yet." He held out an identification card with his left hand. In the top right corner, a picture of the man. In the top left corner, the emblem of the Drug Enforcement Administration, below which were words identifying him as Special Agent Francis Waters, working out of the El Paso, Texas, Intelligence Division. He held out his right hand and she shook it. His touch was cool and dry, his hand soft and powdery, like wood to which fine-grain sandpaper had been applied. He looked her in the eyes while they shook, looked for far too long, making her uncomfortable. She dropped her gaze and pulled her hand away.

"Sorry to approach you like this," Francis Waters said, "but I needed to do it while you were alone. This was my only opportunity."

"I don't know what interest the DEA would have in me."

"You work for Alejandro Rocha."

"I *live* with Alejandro Rocha."

"Still, you must have seen things."

"I don't know what you mean."

"He runs a drug cartel. He's murdered people. You've lived with him for three years."

"I don't know what you're talking about, but if you have evidence, you should arrest him."

"Don't insult my intelligence."

"As far as I know, he runs a few businesses in town. He's a businessman."

"We've been watching him. We know what he is."

Danielle shrugged. "Then you know more than I do."

There was a long moment of silence during which Danielle could see the gears turning behind the man's eyes, then he said, "Gael already told me what you told him. We're working this case together. He wanted me to talk to you in a place he was sure wasn't bugged. Rocha can be paranoid and we wanted to make sure you were safe."

"Gael wouldn't—" She stopped herself, but knew it was too late. She'd just revealed to a dirty cop that she *had* been talking to Gael. He'd been fishing and he'd caught her.

Francis Waters smiled. "Gael wouldn't what?"

"Gael wouldn't be involved with the DEA."

"I don't think that's what you were saying."

"This conversation is over. Now excuse me, I have to use the bathroom."

Danielle turned away from Francis Waters and started for the back of the store, where she'd seen the ladies' room. She didn't run—she didn't want to draw attention to herself—but her pace was brisk. She looked over her shoulder while she walked. Francis Waters was there, following her, hands in pockets. He walked casually, but kept pace, making sure he could see her at all times.

She thought about Gael parked in the lot next to the store, thought about getting to him, but didn't know if that was a good idea. She liked Gael—she *had* liked him—and she'd trusted him, but maybe she'd been wrong to like him, and even more wrong to trust him. Maybe this man and Gael *were* working together. If so, she'd be running into the arms of a man who might kill her.

She had to find a way out of La Paz. She didn't know how she was going to do it but knew she must if she hoped to survive. She had one of Rocha's credit cards, but if she used it, he'd be able to track her purchases, follow her by using the trail of expenses. She'd have to make a large cash withdrawal and then toss it.

After that, she could make her way out of Mexico.

If she stayed hidden for long enough, he might start to believe she wasn't a threat. He might eventually forget about her. She could work some kind of under-the-table job, as a waitress at a place that didn't mind her working for tips alone, and disappear for a while. It wouldn't be a good life, but she could survive, and that was the important thing.

But first things first.

She pushed her way into the ladies' room and walked across the tile floor to one of the toilets; she stepped into the stall and locked the door behind her. It was small, the walls painted blue, a toilet paper dispenser to her left, a steel receptacle for tampons and sanitary napkins to her right, the toilet directly in front of her with pee on the seat because some dumb bitch had hovered while urinating rather than sitting down.

And above the toilet, a small window: her way out of this mess, if she was lucky.

She stood on the toilet seat and pushed the window open. Punched out the screen. Pulled herself up by the windowsill, and grunting, began to slide her way out into the hot day.

■ Francis Waters pulled a Glock 17 from his shoulder holster and pushed into the ladies' room. The Glock 17 wasn't his service weapon but one he'd stolen from the evidence room. It was always good to have a weapon on hand that couldn't be traced back to you. If he ended up having to kill Danielle Preston himself, he could wipe the weapon clean and dump it.

"Danielle?"

She didn't respond but he heard grunting from behind the only stall door that was closed. He drew back his right leg and kicked. The cheap aluminum lock snapped and the door swung open. Slammed against the left wall and bounced back. He saw feet slip through the window above the toilet. Heard a thud and a grunt. Feet pounding against asphalt.

He jumped onto the toilet and looked out the window.

Saw Danielle Preston running through the parking lot on the north end of the department store, making her way toward Calle de Plata.

He cursed under his breath, jumped off the toilet, and hurried out of the bathroom. Made his way through the stock room to the back doors and pushed out into the day. Ran after Danielle, telling her to fucking stop or he'd shoot, but she didn't fucking stop.

If anything, she ran faster.

■ Gael Morales lit another cigarette and blew smoke out the side of his mouth. Watched it drift through the cracked window and break apart as the hot desert breeze caught it. Looked at his watch. Only twenty minutes had passed since Danielle and Monica disappeared into the department store.

Gael saw movement in his rearview mirror. He looked up at it, but by the time he did, whatever he'd seen back there was gone. The window was empty of movement.

The passenger door swung open.

Diego Blanco sat down, looked at him, his expression unreadable. He tongue-shifted a toothpick from one corner of his mouth to the other. He had a pistol in his right hand. Gael, however, was unarmed.

"What are you doing here?"

"I think you know what I'm doing here, *pendejo*."

"Afraid not." But, of course, he *did* know. Diego Blanco had found out who and what he was. Gael didn't know how, but how didn't matter. Unless he could extract himself from this situation, he was about to die.

"You aren't stupid. You know what this is."

"I don't."

Diego Blanco aimed his weapon. "Get out of the car," he said. "I don't want to ruin Alejandro's upholstery with a stain like you."

Gael thought about going for the weapon, but there was no way he'd reach it before Diego squeezed the trigger. He didn't know if his moment would come, but he knew this wasn't it.

He pushed open the driver's-side door.

18

Bogart and Pilar took a cab to a pawnshop in the heart of the slums. The streets were punctuated by potholes, the buildings crumbling. Stray dogs with their rib cages showing like tarp-covered roof beams wandered about. Even the air felt depleted here, oxygen poor.

Guns were illegal in Mexico—or nearly illegal, as you had to get approval for weapons from the Defense Ministry—but Bogart thought that if they were careful about how they approached the subject, there was some chance they'd get taken to a back room where weapons were available.

His dad owned half a dozen pawnshops in Florida, and he'd worked at two of them, which meant he'd heard stories. Most pawn-brokers were careful about the law. Quick cash usually wasn't worth the price you eventually paid for it. But this place was surrounded on all sides by people without enough change to make a Mason jar rattle, which might mean trading in illegal contraband just to stay in business. Guns, passports, that sort of thing.

Bogart hoped so.

They could cross the border and pick up some rifles at Walmart, but he didn't want any of their names attached to weapons used in a prison break. What they were doing was risky enough without autographing their crime.

The cab pulled into the cracked-asphalt parking lot.

Bogart asked the driver to keep the meter running while they were inside. He and Pilar stepped out of the car. He looked toward the two-story building with its crumbling stucco walls and a sun-faded asphalt-shingle roof. It had been painted gray. The stucco in the corners of the building was gone, revealing the chicken wire it was supposed to cling to. Graffiti had been spray painted across the walls. The dust-filmed windows were filled with throwaway garage-sale items: cheap beginner guitars with bent necks, old boom boxes with broken tape decks, used vacuum cleaners with missing belts, ancient TVs, stacks of paperback novels and CDs from the 1980s, old Motorola cell phones, a few lamps with stained or torn shades, chipped plate sets, rusting flatware, a leather chair with a duct-taped tear in the seat cushion.

Bogart and Pilar walked toward the front door. He pulled on the handle, but the door was locked. He thumbed the buzzer.

The door unlocked with a hum and a click as the electric dead bolt retracted.

He pulled it open and stepped inside. Pilar followed.

The floor was covered in ancient green carpet leopard-spotted with stains. Metal garage shelves lined the floor, filled with various cheap items. A drum kit sat in the corner. Guitars, electric and acoustic, bass and six-string, sat on stands to the right. A five-gallon bucket filled with fishing rods and umbrellas. Glass display counters about three feet off the back walls, lining the northwest corner, each filled with bracelets, cuff links, earrings, necklaces, and watches, none of which looked to be worth much.

A Mexican man, maybe five six, a hundred and fifty pounds, stood at the back of the shop with both palms flat on one of the glass cases. He watched them enter with tired eyes, but didn't so much as nod a greeting.

After picking up a few random items and putting them down

again—a tackle box, a windup flashlight/radio, a banjo with two missing strings—Bogart wandered toward the man, looking into the glass cases as if interested in something within them.

In heavily accented, throaty English, the man said: "Can I help you find something?"

"I'm not sure," Bogart said.

"Why is that?"

"Well, I'm looking for something specific."

"Then *be* specific, I might have exactly what you want."

"My girlfriend and I bought a house on the east end of town and we come across rattlesnakes sometimes. Other desert animals too."

"So . . ."

"I'm looking for something that'll let me take care of the snakes without getting too close. Don't wanna get bit—or even risk getting bit."

"I see. What kind of money are you willing to spend?"

"Let me see," Bogart said. He reached into his pocket and pulled out the cash he and the others had contributed to the gun fund, about eighteen hundred dollars, but because several of the bills were fives and tens, and because the cash was a rubber-banded fold, it looked like more. He held up the wad of cash and said, "I'll spend this."

The man looked from Bogart to the money in his right hand. Bogart could see the thoughts passing like shadows behind his eyes. He was asking himself if he should trust this stranger who walked through his front door with a wad of cash in his hand. Bogart knew better than to say anything. Anything he said at this point would be as likely to get them kicked out of the store as it was to get them what they wanted. He had to wait, let the man come to his own decision, and hope it was the right one.

Finally, the man's eyes shifted from the money to Bogart. "I think I might have something could help you."

"Yeah?"

The man nodded. "But I keep such items in the back."

He led them through a narrow wooden door to the stockroom,

which held shelves full of tagged and dated items. They walked through an aisle between shelves to the back of the stockroom where a locked metal cabinet stood to the right of a door leading outside. The back door was gray. There was a small box on the hinge-side of the door frame, about the size of a cigarette lighter, probably part of an alarm system. The cabinet itself was green, dented in several places, rusted where the paint had chipped away. Its doors were held shut by a padlock. The pawnbroker pulled his keys from his pocket and let them hang from his finger while he turned to face them. He hesitated a moment, then said:

"Before I unlock the cabinet, I need to be certain—are you looking for what I think you are looking for?"

"I'm almost certain I am."

"Okay." He turned back to the cabinet, flipped through the keys on his ring, keyed open the padlock, and pulled open the doors. The rusty hinges squeaked.

Inside, resting on their butts, stood about a dozen rifles and shotguns, as well as several boxes of ammunition. A few pistols and revolvers lay on a shelf at the top of the cabinet.

"For your needs," the man said, "I would suggest a long-barrel shotgun, which will keep the pattern relatively tight for a good distance. This way you don't have to get too close to your snakes in order to take care of them—but you also don't have to be a sharpshooter. Take this weapon, for instance." The man picked up a Mossberg with a thirty-inch barrel. "Pump-action. Five-shot tube. Good at up to fifty meters." He pumped the weapon and lowered the barrel, aiming it at Bogart's chest. "At this range, it would put a hole through you the size of a tea saucer." He smiled. His right eyetooth was capped in gold. "Drop your money and walk away."

"Now, wait a minute."

"I can shoot you right now and say you tried to rob me. Shoot you both, put guns in your hands, and call the police. You make up your own minds, though, lose a little money or lose your lives *and* your money. It doesn't matter to me."

Bogart held out the money and took a step forward.

"Don't move. Just drop it on the floor."

Bogart dropped it.

"Now walk away."

"I was just looking to—"

"You come into my store as a stranger, tell me lies about rattle-snakes, and think I'll sell you a gun? You're lucky to be walking away with your life. Get out of here."

Bogart and Pilar backed away—now without any money and still no guns.

19

Gael Morales stepped out of the car and into the sun. The heat seemed to have weight to it, so thick and heavy it was pushing down on him. He looked over his shoulder. Diego got out of the passenger side, aiming his gun over the roof of the BMW, and keeping his barrel trained, walked around the trunk. Gael watched him approach, asking himself how he might get out of this mess, but he had no answer.

"Put your hands in the air and keep them there."

Gael did as he was told.

"Turn around. Don't fucking look at me."

Gael straightened his head. Found himself squinting at the department store in front of him, and the sea of cars that lay between him and the building, this aluminum and steel and fiberglass ocean of red and blue and yellow and black. It was midday. People were around. He watched a woman glance toward him and then hurry to her car. Diego would have no hesitation about shooting him here. He could put a bullet in the back of Gael's head, throw his body into the bed of his truck, and drive away, and even if there were witnesses, they would remain silent. No one would speak against Rocha or his men for fear of losing their own lives, and truth was, they were wise to remain silent. Talking would do nothing but get them killed too.

"Get on your knees."

Gael dropped to his knees, which popped simultaneously as they hit the ground. The asphalt was hot through the fabric of his Levi's. Loose pebbles poking through the fabric, digging into his skin. The barrel of Diego's gun pushed against the back of Gael's head. He could feel it against the base of his skull. When Diego squeezed his trigger, the bullet would sever Gael's spinal column.

He was going to die and there was nothing he could do about it. Sarah, after less than a year of marriage, was going to be a widow, and she wouldn't even know it. He'd simply vanish. She'd hold out hope, for months or years living in a state of paralysis, her life on pause, unable to move on because there was no body, and if there wasn't a body, maybe he was still out there somewhere.

Only he wouldn't be out there somewhere.

He'd be three or four feet beneath the surface of the desert sand.

Coyotes might discover his body, scatter his bones across the desert floor, but that didn't mean he'd be discovered anytime soon. Diego would take him deep into the desert, thirty or so miles southwest of La Paz, and the next closest town, Ascension, was still another twenty or more miles away. He'd be buried in the emptiness between those towns, surrounded by nothing.

Even if his body or part of his body—a femur or his left hand or part of his skull—was discovered, it was likely to be discovered by drug traffickers. Ascension was controlled by the Sinaloa cartel and La Paz by Rocha.

Several years back, the entire police force in Ascension quit for fear of being murdered by the cartel, leaving the town of five thousand without any law enforcement, and it was now patrolled by soldiers who might or might not be getting paid by the cartel to look the other way, but even if they weren't, it didn't matter. La Paz sat in the desert between Ascension and Juarez, and the road connecting the three cities was used to move drugs.

Drug traffickers weren't likely to go to the police if they discovered his body.

He was going to die here and Sarah wouldn't know she was a widow for years. If ever.

Thinking of her alive but in stasis was worse, to his mind, than his own death. This was his job and he knew the risks, knew death might happen, but he loved Sarah and wanted her to be happy—with or without him—and it was impossible to find happiness when your life consisted of waiting, waiting for your husband to return from the field, waiting to find out whether he was alive or dead.

"Just get it over with," he said.

"I trusted you."

"You sound betrayed."

"I *feel* betrayed."

"It was my job to make you trust me. It wasn't personal."

"It was personal to *me*."

Gael closed his eyes and waited for the bullet.

But the bullet didn't come. Instead he heard George Rankin's voice: "Diego, you drop the fucking gun and turn around or I'll shoot you in the back right here."

◾ Danielle Preston ran west along a two-lane strip of faded asphalt. She glanced over her shoulder and saw Francis Waters coming after her. He shouted at her to stop, damn you, but stopping would only ensure she died a little bit sooner than if she continued to run.

After about a quarter mile, pain already knifing into her side, she reached Avenida Hidalgo, and chest heaving, came to a brief stop. She didn't know where to go or what to do. For a moment, she considered giving up, succumbing to her fate—at least then it would be over—but she pushed that thought away. She didn't want to die, she wanted out of this situation, and death wasn't an escape but a result of the mess she was in.

She thought about the church at the north end of town, the tunnel beneath it that led to the United States. If she could cross the border, she might be able to hitchhike into El Paso, go to the police there, tell them who and what she was and hope they'd protect her. Or she could hitchhike west, make her way to California, and hide out in Fresno for a year or two.

Either way, the tunnel was her only option at this point.

She turned right, heading north, and ran toward the church at the end of the road. She saw it up ahead, freshly painted white, the large crucified Jesus at the top of the spire backed by clear blue sky.

She glanced over her shoulder again and saw Francis Waters running after her, the distance between them cut in half, and because his legs were longer, he was gaining on her with every step he took.

Finally she reached the gravel parking lot, the stones grinding beneath her feet as she ran across it, and headed up the stairs to the large double doors.

She grabbed one of the door handles, thumbed the paddle, and as she pulled open the door, she could hear feet crunching into the gravel behind her. She stepped inside, shut the door, and turned the dead bolt.

The handle rattled behind her.

"Unlock this door, you fucking bitch."

"Fuck you," she said, lungs aching. She turned to face the room even as the man who would kill her slammed his shoulder against the door. Colored light beamed in through the stained-glass windows, projecting biblical images on the walls.

There was a tunnel under the church, a tunnel that would take her to safety, but she had no idea where it was. Nor did she know how long she had to find it before Francis Waters made his way inside. Sooner or later, he'd find a way in. She only hoped she was gone when he did.

◼ Gael Morales heard Diego's pistol clack against the faded asphalt.

"Turn around and pick it up, Gael. You put your fucking hands in the air, Blanco, and keep them there. If you even fucking twitch, you're dead."

Gael turned around and for a moment found himself looking directly into Diego's eyes. They glared back with hatred. Part of him felt a strange, unexpected sadness. Diego was a drug smuggler and a murderer but that wasn't all he was. He was a father, had three daughters, and until today, he'd been a friend.

Gael had eaten meals at Diego's apartment, his daughters sitting with them, and they'd discussed the difficulty of being a single working father. How Diego had gone through half a dozen babysitters over the last few years. How his work schedule and his schedule as a parent often contradicted one another, making him miss soccer practice or band recital. Though their friendship had been based on a lie, Gael hadn't pretended to be Diego's friend. He'd *been* his friend.

In order to work undercover, you had to become the person you were pretending to be. You had to find those aspects of your personality that would make that person real and push them to the front while simultaneously forcing everything else back.

It made you realize that you were no better than the people you were trying to imprison. You were capable of everything they did. The only difference was that you'd repressed those dark parts of your personality while they had—for whatever reason—embraced them.

Gael leaned down and picked up the pistol, a Smith & Wesson M&P. He stepped back, taking himself out of Diego's reach, and raised the weapon, aiming it at the man's face. Over Diego's shoulder, he watched as George Rankin holstered his own weapon and pulled out a pair of handcuffs. He walked up behind Diego, snapped one of the cuffs around his right wrist, and yanked his arm behind his back, twisting it hard.

"You're not killing anybody today, motherfucker."

George pulled the left arm back and cuffed it.

Diego smiled a malevolent smile. "There's always tomorrow, Gael Castillo Jimenez. You'll get yours. I'm a patient man."

20

Francis Waters walked the perimeter of the church, feet moving from gravel to sand as he left the driveway and headed around to the back, shoes kicking up clouds of dust that swirled around his ankles. A rattlesnake lay stretched across a boulder jutting from the earth some ten yards to his right. Brown shrubs dotted the landscape between here and the tar-papered border fences. If Danielle Preston found the tunnel and made it stateside, he was fucked. He might be able to convince whoever she talked to that she was a lying junkie bitch but what he needed to do was make sure she was incapable of talking at all.

The stained-glass windows were out of reach. The back door rattled it in its frame but refused to open. When he reached the front of the building again, he walked up the stairs and banged on the front door.

"Let me in, you stupid bitch, or I'll fucking kill you twice."

No answer.

He reached into his pocket, pulled out his disposable cell phone. He called Diego, put the phone to his ear, and listened to it ring.

The call went to voice mail. Francis waited for the beep, and when it came he said:

"Danielle's at the fucking church and she's locked me out. If she finds her way down, we're fucked. Get over here."

He thumbed the red button, slid the phone into the right hip pocket of his slacks.

He banged on the door with the side of his fist, slammed his shoulder against it.

◼ George Rankin was walking a handcuffed Diego Blanco to his car when the cell phone in Blanco's pocket began to ring. George yanked back on the other man's shirt collar like a horse's reins, stopping him, and retrieved the phone. He looked at the display: an El Paso number but no name. He shoved the phone into his own pocket and continued to guide Blanco toward the street where his car was parked. By the time they reached it, the cell phone chimed with a new voice mail. George pulled open the back door of the car and shoved Diego into it.

"I hope you like prison food."

He slammed the car door shut, pulled the cell phone from his pocket, and listened to the voice mail. *"Danielle's at the fucking church and she's locked me out. If she finds her way down, we're fucked. Get over here."*

George looked toward Gael Castillo Jimenez. He'd followed them down toward the street and stood now, smoking a cigarette, watching them from the department store driveway.

George held up the cell phone. "You need to hear this."

◼ Francis Waters heard the car approaching and looked over his shoulder. A black sedan came tearing down the street toward the church and for a brief moment Francis felt relief. Diego was on the way. They'd get inside and kill this bitch and . . .

But the car coming toward him wasn't Diego's.

The car coming toward him looked like . . .

It tore into the gravel parking lot and he saw the faces behind the windshield, George Rankin driving, Gael Castillo Jimenez in the front passenger seat. The car came to a locked-brake stop, the tires kicking up gravel as it slid across the blanket of stones.

Francis jumped off the stairs and began running around the side of the church even as car doors opened and men stepped out. He didn't know what he was going to do, but he couldn't let George Rankin take him in. He might end up in prison with people he'd put there, and if he did, he wouldn't last a week.

He ran to the back of the church, and gun in hand, waited with his back to the wall. His hearted thudded against his rib cage. Scattered thoughts swirled through his head like hurricane debris. He was fucked.

"Come out, Francis," George Rankin shouted. "There's nowhere to run."

Francis was silent for a long time, trying to think of a way out of this. George was right that there was nowhere to run, and if it turned into a shootout, he was likely to get himself killed. There were two of them. They could easily pinch him, circling the church from both sides, and the church was his only shield. Open desert surrounded it.

Francis holstered his weapon and stepped out from behind the building. He walked toward the parking lot. George and Gael were both standing in the gravel with guns gripped in their fists. He smiled at them and said:

"I didn't realize it was you, George. What are you guys doing here?"

"Cut the shit, Francis."

"I don't know what you're talking about. I know I shouldn't have been working the case independently, but I tracked one of the bitches who works for Alejandro to the church here. I think there's an underground tunnel somewhere on the premises that leads across the border. She's still in there unless she made it out the other side already."

George raised his weapon. "Walk on over here, Francis."

"I don't like that you've got your weapon trained on me."

"I don't like that you're in Alejandro Rocha's pocket."

"Now hold on, there's been some kind of misunderstanding. I'll admit I shouldn't have been working the case, but I was trying to help out. I'm not in any motherfucker's *pocket.*"

"I need you to start walking toward me."

"I'm not gonna do that if you have a gun on me, George. I'm not one of the fucking bad guys and I won't be treated like one."

"If you don't wanna be treated like a bad guy, you shouldn't work for bad men."

"How many times do I have to say—"

"You need to shut the fuck up, Francis."

"This is a misunderstanding, George."

"Yeah—it's you misunderstanding the situation. Shut your mouth and walk toward me."

"I'm not gonna do that."

George looked at Gael and said, "I've got another set of cuffs in the glove box. Mind grabbing them and taking care of this?"

Gael nodded, walked to the sedan, and pulled open the front passenger door. He leaned into the car a moment. Francis watched him and considered his options. He could either continue with his story—which wasn't working—or cop to what he'd been doing and agree to talk. If he did the latter, he might at least be able to make a deal, get a reduced sentence served on a protective wing. All time was hard time, but at least he'd have a chance.

After three years of working for Rocha, he had plenty of information to trade. Like the fact that he wasn't working for Rocha at all. Mulligan Shoibli was the true head of the cartel, and though that wasn't the man's real name, Francis thought he knew what his real name was. He'd done some digging on his own just so he'd be able to cover his ass. It looked like that digging might pay off, allow him to push someone else into the hole to keep himself out of it.

Gael walked toward him with handcuffs gripped in one fist and a pistol in the other.

Francis swallowed, but his mouth was dry, his throat only clicking. He didn't want to go to prison, reduced sentence or not. He wouldn't be able to handle prison, and even if he ended up on a protective wing, there'd still be ways to get to him. He knew of other people being protected in prison who'd still ended up dead. Sharpened toothbrushes in their carotids. There was no such thing as complete safety in prison.

Gael tucked the pistol into the back of his Levi's while he walked. Francis watched him as he reached up for his raised right hand, moving to slap a cuff around the wrist.

There still might be a way out of this.

He'd have to disappear afterward, but that would be better than prison.

As Gael reached for him, Francis grabbed the man's arm and twisted, turning him around, and with his other hand, reached down and pulled the weapon from the back of his Levi's. He put it to Gael's head and said:

"You're not taking me in, George."

"You let him go, Francis. You're crossing a line you can't step back from."

"I crossed that line a long time ago, George."

21

Normal ran his fingers through his hair and cursed under his breath. He was sitting on the edge of the unmade bed in Coop's room, shoulders slumped, looking down at his Emericas. Black suede shoes with two white stripes on either side. The suede on the outside of his left toe box had been sanded away by grip tape when he'd last been skateboarding.

He looked up at Bogart, who was sitting at a table by the window, across from Coop, nervously doing one riffle shuffle after another with a deck of Bicycle playing cards. Looked to Pilar, still standing by the door. She blinked, her face expressionless.

"What the fuck are we gonna do now? It doesn't matter that your uncle agreed to set us up with a vehicle, Pilar; we can't do the job without guns."

Bogart set the cards down on the table. "We know that, Normal."

"I know you know it, but what the fuck are we gonna *do*?"

"I'm not sure, Normal." Bogart paused a moment. "I'm too upset to think." He reached into his pocket and pulled out a prescription pill bottle and a pack of Zig-Zags. He broke a bud into one of the papers, licked it, and rolled it tight. He put it between his lips and put a flame to the end of his joint. Inhaled and held the smoke in his lungs. Exhaled.

He did all this in a silent room.

Finally, Coop spoke: "We're gonna break into the pawnshop."

"We're gonna what?"

"We already paid for those fucking guns. We'll just be collecting what's ours."

"Make sense to me," Bogart said before taking another hit from his joint. He tapped his ash into a Pepsi can sitting on the table.

"I was drinking that," Coop said.

"Sorry. I'll get you another one from the machine in a minute. Pilar?"

"Makes sense to me too."

"So now we gotta rob a pawnshop before we break our friend out of jail?"

"We're not gonna rob it," Coop said.

"Then what the fuck are we gonna do?" Normal said.

"Burglarize it."

"Oh, great, that makes it better. Thanks for the clarification."

"Do you have a better suggestion?" Pilar said.

"No, but maybe on the way home, since we'll have guns anyway, we can stick up a gas station or something. You know, just to round out the fucking day."

"That's not a bad idea," Coop said.

Normal looked at him in silence for a long time. Coop stared back, his expression blank.

"Are you fucking—"

"Yes, Normal, I'm fucking kidding."

"That's not funny."

Bogart said, "The look on your face, man—it *was* kinda funny."

"Oh, fuck you."

"Fuck *you*."

"Fuck me? Motherfucker, we're supposed to be in a partnership.

You've been going along with Coop and Pilar ever since this started, undermining everything I had to say."

"James is in jail, Normal, and unless he gets out tomorrow he's gonna die there."

"That doesn't mean we have to get *ourselves* killed too. He baked that shit cake, he can eat it. You people are out of your goddamn minds. Every day brings some kind of new crazy bullshit, and I've been going along with it but, goddamn it, I'm supposed to be the crazy one here. You motherfuckers live on Mars."

"I never do this," Bogart said. "But have a hit."

Normal looked at the proffered joint, got to his feet, and walked to the table. Took the joint and put it to his lips. Inhaled, held it, exhaled. He was going for a second draw when Bogart grabbed his wrist with one hand and took the joint with the other.

"I said have a hit, Normal, not two hits. Shit."

"Are you in or out?" Coop said.

Normal ran his fingers through his hair. Sighed. Cracked his knuckles one after the other. Finally, he spoke: "Fuck it, I'm in."

"Okay, good," Coop said. "You were at the pawnshop, Bogart. What do we need to know?"

Bogart tapped his ash into the Pepsi can.

22

Gael Morales could feel the cool metal of the gun barrel against his left temple and the pain of his right shoulder being twisted near its breaking point, but still couldn't believe he'd gotten himself into this situation. He should have anticipated it and been able to stop Francis before it got to this point. But he hadn't thought the man would be desperate enough to pull this kind of shit. Francis Waters might be crooked but he was still law enforcement and had to know this situation almost never played itself out well.

Gael looked across the gravel driveway to George Rankin, who was holding his gun steady as stone, no shake in his hands at all, but his eyes were darting quickly from Gael to Francis and back again.

"Calm down, George, it's fine. Francis doesn't want a murder charge against him."

"I don't give a fuck about a murder charge. I go to jail for a week, I might as well get the death penalty, because I'm dead and we all know it. I won't be locked up."

"You kill me, you won't make it out of an interrogation room alive."

"You know if you shoot him, it's over for you," George said.

"I'll only shoot him if I have to."

"Can you ease up on my shoulder a little?"

"Shut up." But Francis did ease up on his shoulder some and the pain subsided. It was still there, throbbing, moving through his body in waves, but it wasn't as sharp as it had been.

"What's your plan, Francis?" George said.

"My plan is to leave."

"How are you gonna do that?"

"Gael is gonna drive me out of here."

"Then what?"

"Then I'm not standing here with a gun aimed at my face, what do you think?"

"I think it's a shitty plan."

"I'm not real interested in your opinion of my plan, George."

"You should be."

"Why's that?"

"Because I'm the one who can save your life. You get into that car—and I won't make it easy for you—you'll be dead within thirty minutes. I know exactly what it leads to, and that's you in a shallow grave."

"You have no fucking idea what I'm doing or where I'm going once I leave this place, which means you have no fucking idea what happens. So cut the shit, Uri Geller."

"But he does know, Francis."

"Bullshit."

"Do you want to explain it to him or do you want me to?" George said.

"I'll do it," Gael said. "I'm just standing around anyway." But instead of explaining the situation to Francis he said, "Bullets come right out the end of that gun, you know. You don't have to push the barrel *through* my fucking skull."

"Shut the fuck up." But he pulled back.

"Thank you. Now let me explain what happens if you make it to the car and have me drive you away from here."

"I'm all ears."

"What happens is, you have me drive you to Rocha's estate. You and Diego will tell him what happened and offer me up. He'll kill me. That's a given. I'm undercover DEA and I know too much about his operation. But what you don't seem to realize is that he'll kill you too, because you know more than I do. He'll be worried that the cops will catch up with you and that if they do, you'll spill like a toddler's milk glass." Gael gave him a few moments to think that through before he went on. Once he believed it had sunk in, he continued.

"Now you're thinking that through, and it's making sense to you, so you've decided you can't go to Rocha's estate. You're thinking, fine, I'll get into the back of the car, kick Diego out—if I'm not going to the estate, Diego's dead weight—and have Gael drive me south. You'll get to Mexico City and take a flight from there to Costa Rica where your brother has a vacation home. He isn't there right now and you can hole up for a while and decide what to do next.

"Problem is, the DEA knows that's what you're thinking. George is standing right in front of you. Rocha will probably know that's what you're thinking too. Question is, who gets to you first?"

"I'm not going to Costa Rica." His voice sounded weak.

"No, you're not. But the only reason you're not is because I just told you what happens if you do. Let me tell you this too. What you're thinking of doing now doesn't work out any better for you. So why don't you put the gun down? There's no good outcome for you. But there are better and worse outcomes. Cooperating now will lead to one of the best of the bad."

Francis was silent for a long time, thinking through the situation. Finally, he dropped his weapon to the gravel.

Gael turned around, shoved Francis against the wall of the church, and slapped handcuffs around his wrists. He paused a moment. This idiot would have had no problem killing him. He was supposed to be a good guy but he'd have triggered a bullet through Gael's temple without hesitation if he thought it would save his own ass. Gael grabbed the back of Francis's hair, pulled back, and slammed his forehead into the wall.

It bounced back with a ripe-melon thud.

"That's for putting a gun on me, you dumb shit."

He led Francis to the black sedan and put him into the back of the car next to Diego. He slammed the door, looked at George, and said:

"Let's get Danielle Preston out of that church."

"How did you know he'd go to Costa Rica?"

"I heard him talking to Sylvia in the break room about his brother's vacation home once."

"What if you'd been wrong?"

Gael shrugged. "I wasn't."

■ Danielle was sitting on the stage, staring blankly down the length of the center aisle to the back of the church, thinking she was a dead woman. She knew there was a tunnel that led across the border, but she'd been unable to find it. Any minute now men would break down the door and kill her. She was trying to find some sort of acceptance, since death couldn't be avoided, but she wasn't able to. She wanted to live. She wanted to leave Rocha behind and live like normal people lived. It was too bad she'd never have that opportunity. She'd waited too long and now she was going to die. She wanted to cry, but couldn't. The shock of reality—the reality of this situation she'd put herself in—made it impossible. She felt almost numb.

A knock on the front door.

A voice: "Danielle, it's me. Diego Blanco and Francis Waters are handcuffed in the back of a DEA vehicle. You're safe now."

She looked toward the door and wanted to believe what she'd heard. Gael might be lying, and if he was and she stepped out the front door, she'd be shot as soon as the sunlight hit her face. But despite this, she felt hope. She'd trusted Gael once and wanted to trust him again.

Anyway, she couldn't hide in here forever.

She looked toward one of the stained-glass windows. Jesus in a white robe, a halo of light hovering above his head. She'd never been religious, but the image of Jesus had always made her feel calm, and as she looked at that stained-glass window, she felt peace seep into her pores and find a home in her chest.

She got to her feet and walked down the aisle. She reached the front doors and twisted the dead bolt. It retracted with a clack. She grabbed the handle and thumbed the paddle and pulled. Bright light slanted into the church, a dark man-shaped silhouette partially blocking it. Her eyes adjusted and she saw Gael take on form and definition. He reached out his hand to her.

"Let's get out of here. You're safe now."

She took his hand.

■ The three of them stood in the gravel driveway. Gael lit a Camel and took a deep drag, smoke filling his lungs. He exhaled through his nostrils. His hand shook as it pulled the cigarette away from his lips, but he tried to hide it.

"What are you gonna do now?" George said.

"We're gonna act like nothing happened."

"What if Rocha knows?"

Gael shrugged. "Then we're dead. But I don't think he does. Only way he would is if Diego told him and, knowing Diego, I think he'd want to handle the situation himself."

"You sure that's the best decision?"

"No. But it's the decision I've made."

George stood silent a moment before he said, "You want a ride back to the department store?"

"We'll walk," Danielle said.

"Okay. I'll take care of these two." He nodded toward the sedan.

"What are you gonna do with them?"

"Francis is going to jail. I haven't decided what I'm gonna do with Blanco yet. He needs to be in prison too, but he's a Mexican citizen in Mexico, and even if he weren't, we don't want his arrest to get back to Rocha. I might hole him up in the Juarez safe house for a while."

Gael nodded. "Okay. We're gonna head back to the department store. Danielle has to finish her shopping."

He turned and started walking south. Danielle followed.

"Gael."

He stopped, looked over his shoulder.

"You okay?"

"What do you mean?"

"You've had guns aimed at your head twice today."

Gael shrugged. "Nobody pulled a trigger."

23

James Murphy pulled open the desk drawer in his cell and removed the pen casing and the rubber band and the spring. He set
them on the desk next to the bullet he'd taken from Rocha's gun,
and for a long time, stood motionless, looking down at the four
items sitting in a neat row. These were the primary items he had to
work with. Perhaps he could find other useful gun parts in his
cell—he'd have to—but sitting before him were his barrel and his
firing mechanism, assuming he could figure out a way to make
them work.

He picked up the metal pen casing and the bullet. Unscrewed
the two halves of the pen casing and slid the bullet into the longer
half of the casing. It fit snugly, which was good, but he'd need to
reinforce the barrel if he didn't want the thing exploding in his hand.
The aluminum was thin and wouldn't handle the force of the bullet's
explosion.

He pulled open the desk drawer again, removed the pad of paper, and set it down. Stared at the blue lines running across the yellow paper. Thinking about how he could make this work. How he

could turn these items into a deadly weapon. One that wouldn't also kill him when he fired it.

After a moment, he sat down in the chair.

This is what you have to work with, James, so make *it work.*

He began to rip sheets of paper out of the notebook, one by one, and then to tear those sheets into thin strips. Once the notebook was empty of paper, only the cardboard backing sitting on the desk undamaged, he got to his feet, carried the pile of strips to his toilet, and dropped them into the water.

While they soaked, he went back to the desk. He bent the pen casing against the desk's edge, working to break off the tapered end. Once he had a good bend in it, he twisted it back and forth until it snapped away. With that done, he reshaped the barrel so that the bullet's progress wouldn't be hindered by the bent end. He slipped the bullet into both ends of the barrel to make sure it would be able to travel through cleanly, but then decided the barrel was too short, so he broke the end of the other half as well, and screwed the two pieces together. This gave him about four inches of cylindrical aluminum to work with.

Finally he began to form a handle for his weapon from the cardboard backing of the notebook, folding it into thirds lengthwise and putting a seam into the middle of this nearly three-inch wide handle. He cradled the pen casing in its fold.

Now he had something shaped like a gun—sort of.

He walked to the toilet and began pulling out the strips of paper one by one, wrapping them around both the barrel and the handle, crossing the strips back and forth over one another so that when they dried—if they dried before he needed his weapon—they'd add strength to the whole thing and hold it together.

After about ten minutes of careful wrapping, he was done.

The weapon looked like shit and he still had to devise some sort of firing mechanism, but with a little luck, it would do what he needed it to do when he needed it done.

He set the weapon on the windowsill to dry, and while the sun shone down on it, walked to his cot and lay down.

Tomorrow he was either going to escape or die trying. Probably the latter. His plan, if it could be called that, didn't amount to much. But if he stayed in jail, he would die anyway. Maybe not tomorrow—he thought he could fight off anyone who came after him for a while—but soon. If they kept coming after him, there'd come a time when he wasn't ready, and they'd manage to finish him.

He'd be damned if he was going to sit around and wait for that to happen. There were things that needed doing and the only way to do them was to first get out. Rocha had to pay for what he'd done to Layla. He had turned a beautiful, happy girl into a junkie, and then he'd killed her. Maybe not in a straightforward way. But that didn't matter. If you hand a suicide case a pistol, you're responsible for what happens next; if you provide a junkie with junk and they overdose, you're responsible for what happens next—especially if you're the one who made her a junkie to begin with.

James wanted Rocha dead. *Needed* him dead. Needed him to pay not only for what he'd done to Layla but for what he'd done to every girl like Layla—and for every girl who'd become her in the future.

If Rocha remained alive, it would happen to someone else.

Somewhere—in Augusta or Kankakee or San Francisco—was a beautiful girl living her life oblivious to the fact that circumstances would put her in Rocha's path and that their meeting would lead to her death.

James knew what it felt like to lose someone. He knew what it felt like to think about all the lost years. Layla had been twenty-four, at the very beginning of her life, when everything was stolen from her. She'd never meet the man she might have married and he'd never have the opportunity to meet her. The children she'd wanted would never be born, never nurse at her breast. She'd never get to feel them fall asleep in her arms, never get to kiss their soft cheeks or know what it was like to love something—to love someone—you had created. She'd never celebrate a tenth wedding anniversary—or a first. Never get to watch her husband become an old man. Never get to experience the ups and downs of life as a wife and mother. She'd never get to watch her kids leave for university and feel both sad and proud.

Rocha had killed not only Layla but in so doing had erased every moment she might have lived. Every child she might have mothered.

How many other Laylas had there been before her? How many might there be after her if James didn't do something to stop it?

Thinking about this made him think too, about what he'd done in Afghanistan. While he'd been there, he'd only thought about doing the job with which he'd been tasked. He'd felt separate from his actions, numb to them. But now, every trigger pull carried with it a burden. The burden of knowing that in taking eleven lives, he might have also destroyed countless others. At the time, he'd only thought about the immediate consequences. He was killing one person to save dozens of others. But the consequences of each trigger pull didn't stop when the bullet hit. The consequences—like ripples from a lakeside stone throw—would travel outward for years.

Now that he'd lost someone he loved, he understood that.

After this, he was finished. He'd never pick up a gun again.

If he weren't a hypocrite he might even let this go. But he wasn't strong enough to leave it be. He couldn't allow his sister's death to go unavenged. If that meant he was a hypocrite, then that's what it meant. He could live more peacefully with that than he could with the knowledge that his sister's killer still walked the streets.

He'd do this—he'd find justice for his sister—and then he'd walk away from violence forever.

But then he thought about the lives he'd saved, the men still breathing because he'd done what he'd done; the consequences of *their* deaths would have been felt for years as well.

So had he done more good than harm?

He wanted to believe he had, but he didn't know. He *couldn't* know.

He got to his feet and checked the gun. It was drying well, the strips of paper forming a hard shell around his weapon. He flipped it over so the sunlight could dry the other side and then lay down once more. Stared at the ceiling for a while and finally closed his eyes. He tried to think of nothing—tried to calm the TV static in his soul.

But images of Layla kept flashing through his mind, and with them came all of the related emotions, a contradictory tangle of them that nothing could unknot.

◼ Once the weapon had dried as much as it was going to—once the sun had set—James took it from the windowsill and carried it back to his desk. He sat down and looked at both the rubber band and the spring resting on its metal surface. Thought about how to make a firing mechanism from them. For a long time he did nothing but sit there and stare, moving the two pieces—the rubber band and the spring—around in his mind, trying to figure out this puzzle. Finally, he decided he needed another part. A firing pin.

He got to his feet and turned in slow circles, taking in his surroundings, thinking about what he needed to make his weapon fire.

Toilet. Basin. Desk. Chair. Cot.

Toilet. Basin. Desk. Chair. Cot.

Toilet. Basin.

He walked to the basin and looked at the faucet. In the back of it was a narrow threaded pin used to control the drain stopper. He tried to unscrew it as he'd done when repairing faucets at home, but this one was soldered in place, so he jerked it left and right until he heard the crack of the alloy binding break. He pulled the pin from the faucet and walked back to his desk. Sat down. Put the pin on the desk's surface, about a half inch sticking over the edge, and forced it down with his thumb. The metal dug into the pad, the end breaking through the skin, but still he pushed on it, grunting, until it formed a right angle.

With that done, he went about attaching the makeshift firing pin to his gun. He unwound half of the spring and wrapped it around the gun handle, sliding the straight end of the pin into the half that remained intact. Finally, he broke the rubber band and tied it around the cardboard handle of the gun and the pin. He thumbed back the pin—the threading providing just enough traction for his thumb to hold onto it—let it go, and watched as the bent end snapped into the back of his barrel. If he had extra ammunition, he might test the gun to make sure it worked, but it was probably best that he didn't; he doubted the thing would survive more than a single round.

If it survived even that.

24

Gael Morales drove Danielle and Monica back to Rocha's estate, the trunk loaded with clothes both women had purchased. Monica, busy shopping, hadn't even noticed Danielle's absence from the store; they'd have her to corroborate their story—which was that there was no goddamn story, thank you very much.

Still, he was nervous as he drove.

They were acting as though everything was normal—operating under the assumption that Diego hadn't told Rocha what he'd learned—but they wouldn't know until they reached the estate whether they were correct. Gael might be driving them toward death.

He cracked his window, put a cigarette between his lips, and lit it. Took a deep drag. Exhaled a stream of smoke that twisted and curled toward the window before breaking apart on the hot wind.

Twice today he'd had a gun aimed at his head and one of those times he'd come very close to being killed. Despite having been brought up Catholic—maybe *because* he'd been brought up Catholic—he wasn't a religious man. He went to Sarah's Protestant church on holidays, but that was a social decision rather than a spiritual one. He thought God might exist, but had only doubt for heaven and hell. Still, he found it impossible to separate who he was while alive from who he'd be when dead. Which meant that he thought of himself in darkness, *aware* of the darkness, unable to ever see or touch or smell Sarah again.

Today he'd come very close to that reality. Thinking about it made his chest feel tight.

He forced down all the thoughts and feelings currently swirling through his head and heart, pushed them down, locked them away, and pulled the BMW up to the estate's wrought-iron gate. He punched in the key code. The gate swung open slowly and he guided the car up the cobblestone drive, past the fountain, and into the garage, where he brought it to a stop.

He killed the engine and then sat there, staring through the windshield at nothing, hands gripping the steering wheel. He was afraid to get out of the car, afraid to walk into the house. But he had to do it, and when he did, he had to act like everything was normal. So he told himself that everything *was* normal. Gael Castillo Jimenez might have had a gun pressed against his head, might have come within seconds of death, but he was Gael Morales.

He exhaled a heavy sigh.

Pushed open the car door.

◼ Rocha was sitting on one of the couches in the living room, a bikinied girl on either side of him, his feet kicked up on the coffee table. He held a bottle of beer on his lap, loosely gripped in his right hand. When Gael, Danielle, and Monica stepped through the front door and onto the marble-floored foyer—the girls each carrying a large bag of clothes—he turned his head to look at them.

"How'd it go?"

"About as enjoyable as the Bataan Death March."

Rocha laughed. "Well, it's over now."

Gael pulled out his wallet and slid the man's credit card from a leather pocket. It was wrapped in a receipt. He walked both items over to Rocha and held them out to him. "Girls spent about ninety-eight hundred pesos."

Alejandro waved away the proffered card. "Hold onto it. You'll be using it again. But I'll take the receipt."

Gael handed him the paper and slipped the card back into his wallet. "Anything else you need from me today?"

"Nope. But I might need you to drive the girls to the airport the day after tomorrow."

"No problem. Just let me know when."

"I will."

"If there isn't anything else . . ."

"Go to the bar, hit the whorehouse, go home. You're on your time now."

"Thanks."

Gael turned back to the front door and stepped through it. Walked to his Honda, put on his helmet, and kicked the bike to life. Rode through the fading sunlight to his apartment building. Made his way up the steps and keyed open the front door. Shut the front door behind him and locked it.

His face remained expressionless throughout all of this, but as soon as the dead bolt set with a thwack, he put his back against the door, slid down to the floor, and cried. There was no sound, but tears flowed down his cheeks as the pent-up emotions resulting from today's events poured out of him. After less than five minutes, it was over. He pulled up the front of his shirt and wiped at his cheeks. Lit a Camel. Got to his feet.

His face was once more expressionless.

25

George Rankin drove east toward Juarez. Diego Blanco, directly behind him, and Francis Waters, on the passenger side, sat handcuffed in the back of his car. The blur of the desert streaked by in the fading light of the low sun sinking behind them. The gray strip of road ahead cut a curved path through the orange sand like an asphalt river.

"You can't take me across the border," Blanco said. "I'm a Mexican citizen. Unless you have the paperwork in order, this is kidnapping."

"I have no intention of taking you across the border. Not today."

"What do you intend to do then?"

George glanced in his rearview mirror. Blanco looked back at him with bloodshot eyes, his mouth an angrily penned line.

"What I should do," George said, "is put a bullet through your head. That's what you do with a rabid dog, isn't it?"

"I have three daughters waiting for me at home."

"I know you do. I know everything about you. But you tried to murder my friend and partner. The second you did that, you gave up any expectation of sympathy."

"What about my daughters? They've never hurt anybody."

"You should have thought about your daughters before you took up this line of work."

"I did. That's why I'm *in* this line of work. To feed and clothe them."

"I know plumbers who somehow manage to buy groceries."

"The youngest is only seven."

"So what—you want me to let you go?"

"I know that's not going to happen. As you said, I tried to kill your friend and partner."

"Then why are we talking?"

"Because I believe you're a good man doing what he thinks is best. A good man won't leave little girls to fend for themselves. If you aren't arresting me, and I know you aren't, they'll have nobody to help them. Nobody will know what happened to me. I want you to make sure they're okay."

"What about their mother?"

"She can't even take care of herself."

"The wreckage you leave behind isn't my problem."

But listening to Diego talk about his daughters made him think of Meghan, his own daughter. He and Sheryl had been divorced for ten years now, which meant for a decade he'd seen Meghan at most every other weekend. He'd watched her grow up, but not like present fathers do. Her progress toward adulthood wasn't fluid in his mind. He'd missed so much of it. He saw it more like a photo album or a flip book or a badly animated cartoon that seemed to have frames missing. Twenty-six weekends a year at the most—usually closer to fifteen—piecing together an entire existence. In the last ten years, he probably hadn't spent more than 365 days with his daughter: a year in a decade.

Diego wouldn't even have that. The man wasn't being arrested tonight but he'd end up going to prison and it wouldn't be for weeks or months. The man was looking at decades. The youngest of his daughters might be in her late thirties before he stepped on ground outside a prison compound.

George glanced again in the rearview mirror and saw Diego's face contort with sadness. He lowered his head, putting it between his knees, and made short gasping noises. Perhaps he'd been thinking the same thoughts George had. Only his perspective was different. He wasn't looking at the situation from the outside. He was the one who'd pay.

Unfortunately, that meant his daughters would pay as well.

The man shifted in his seat. Something thumped against the floorboard. Something else thumped against the left back door.

George glanced over his shoulder in time to see Diego pulling his feet through the handcuffs so that his arms were in front of him. He sat up. There was no sadness on his face now, only visible violence. His eyes were cruel and determined. He threw his arms over George's head and pulled back, choking him with the chain of the handcuffs.

It dug into his flesh, cutting off his oxygen.

George gasped for breath, let go of the steering wheel, and instinctively pushed back to lessen the pressure on his throat, forcing the gas pedal to the floorboard.

The engine roared and swerved right, into the desert sand, rolling over shrubbery and rocks, bouncing across the unpaved ground, dust flying up into the air around it.

But George paid none of this any mind.

He was trying to force his fingers down between the chain and his neck. But couldn't do it. He tried to suck in air, but his throat felt like a kinked garden hose. His vision was going gray at the periphery, darkness moving toward the center, and he knew when it did, he'd lose consciousness.

He turned his head to bite the hand, hoping pain would startle the man out of the homicide attempt, but couldn't find the right angle.

He reached for his service weapon, fumbling with the snap, and the gun dropped from the shoulder holster. If it hit the floor, he wouldn't be able to reach it, his head was pulled back, so he went for it blindly, felt his hand wrap around the cool metal.

He shifted the pistol to his right hand.

Diego must have seen this because he redoubled his efforts, putting his knee against the back of the seat and yanking with his full weight, grunting as he did.

Except for the sounds of his grunts and the engine's roar and the car's rattle, the inside of the vehicle was silent. George had never before felt so close to death, and if he were able, he might scream. But sound couldn't escape his clamped-shut throat.

The car continued bouncing through the desert, thumping over a sharp boulder, the left front tire exploding with a pop and a brief hiss.

The sound of it flapping, loose against the desert floor.

George aimed the pistol over his left shoulder and fired off three rounds—his ear going temporarily deaf but for a high-pitched whine like tinnitus—but Diego must have been able to shift out of the line of fire: the pressure didn't lessen.

"Die already, motherfucker," Diego said through gritted teeth.

George dropped his arm so he could fire through the seat under his left arm. The torso was a bigger target than the head and he thought he had some chance of hitting it. He pulled the trigger until his clip was empty.

The car smashed into a large boulder and came to a stop. George flew forward, his throat slamming against the chain. The airbag deployed, suddenly in his face, covering him with white powder. Steam rose out from under the hood.

The pressure on his throat ceased, the arms resting lightly on his shoulders.

He dropped the gun, grabbed the arms, and pulled them from around his head. Heard Diego flop back in his seat. He gasped for breath and rubbed at his throat, which was quickly swelling. Looked into the backseat and saw Diego sitting there with slumped shoulders, arms slack, chin resting on chest. His torso had been Swiss-cheesed with bullet holes.

Francis looked from the dead man beside him to George. His shocked face was splattered with blood. His eyes were wide.

"Just sit there," George croaked, his voice barely audible. "Don't speak."

He shoved the transmission into park and tried to start the car. After three attempts, during which the engine only whined, it coughed, backfired, and roared to life. He reversed away from the boulder, pushed open the driver's-side door, and stepped out of the car.

The sun was low in the sky, now sinking below the horizon, but it was still hot out. A brief wind swept up the desert sand and blew it against his face and body. Black dots swam in front of his eyes, like amoeba, and dizziness overwhelmed him. He stepped left, off balance, and almost fell, but managed, with an awkward shuffle, to keep his feet under him. He rested his hands on his bent knees and took several deep, painful breaths, looking down at the desert floor. At a row of ants marching across the sand. Drool hung from his mouth, snapped, and splashed against the ground. It formed a bead there.

Finally he stood up and rubbed his neck. It felt taut with swelling.

He walked to the front of the car to look at the damage.

The fiberglass bumper had splintered and was hanging off the car on the right side. The grille was shattered. The hood had buckled. The front left tire had to be changed.

He stepped around to the front of the car and pulled the bumper away so it wouldn't drag. Tossed it to the side. Pulled away pieces of the grille. With those things done, he walked around to the trunk and removed the small spare tire, a jack, and a tire iron. He loosened the lug nuts, raised the car, switched out the flat for the spare, and lowered the car.

He walked to the back door on the driver's side, pulled it open, looked down at the dead man. Reached in and dragged the body out, letting it drop limp to the desert floor. A cloud of dust kicked up around him. The line of ants began to march over the open palm. Though rigor mortis had yet to set in, nobody looking at the man would think he was anything but dead.

George turned his attention back to the car. The seat was stained with blood and several bullets—both those that had traveled through Diego and those that had missed him—had punched holes into it that looked almost like cigarette burns. George had signed out the vehicle, which meant the DEA knew he had it, and there was no explaining the damage away.

A man had been killed in this car.

He grabbed the ankles and dragged the body to the back of the car. Hefted it and folded it into the trunk, streaking his pants and shirt and forearms with blood. He frisked the body, found the wallet, and slipped it into his pocket. Walked back to the front of the car and picked up the bumper. Threw it into the trunk on top of the body.

Slammed down the trunk lid.

He leaned down, grabbed a fistful of sand, and rubbed it against his arms and hands to clean off the blood. Once that was done, he dusted himself off, got into the driver's seat and pulled the door shut, his clothes damp with sweat, his heart thumping in his chest. He shoved the deployed airbag back into the steering wheel.

Too many things had gone sideways too quickly. The dead man in his trunk had tried to kill him, but he'd done so under circumstances that might get George into trouble. Diego Blanco was a Mexican citizen. George had no right to have him handcuffed in the back of his car. Had he called La Paz police in, he'd be all right. He'd witnessed an attempted homicide and stopped it. But as soon as he cuffed the man and put him into the back of a DEA sedan, things had entered a legal gray area at best. Only he couldn't call La Paz police in, since every detective on the force and several beat cops besides were in the pocket of the Rocha cartel.

Now the man was dead and in the trunk of his car and George had no idea what he was going to do about it.

■ George drove the car through the desert toward the road. His arms felt weak and rubbery. His mind was turning. He glanced in the rearview mirror and looked at Francis Waters. Man hadn't said a word since George shot Blanco; he was probably still trying to think of a way out of this situation. But he wouldn't find one.

There were people in the DEA—in every law-enforcement agency—who thought their fellow agents—or cops—must be protected from the consequences of their illegal activities. They covered up the theft of drugs and money from evidence lockers, turned a blind eye when their coworkers sold shit back onto the streets, lied in reports about how shootings had gone down.

George was not among them.

He believed dirty cops were worse than the criminal class. Criminals were the opposition, simple as that, and you could at least respect them for owning what they were; dirty cops, on the other hand, used their positions in law enforcement to play both sides. They were Judases, and being Judases, should be sentenced twice as severely as citizens.

George reached the road and turned the wheel right, leaving the bumpy unpaved desert for relatively smooth asphalt. He was still thinking about what to do about the body in his trunk when Francis finally spoke:

"We should talk, George."

"I'd prefer a quiet drive." His voice was both thin and gravelly. His throat throbbed where the chain had been pulled against it, as if there was a ghost of the metal still there.

"You've got a dead body in the trunk."

"Which is no concern of yours."

"But it's a concern of yours and I want you to know that I don't have to tell anybody I saw you kill him in cold blood. I can keep it to myself. But if you take me in, I might have to tell them the truth: you unloaded your weapon into Diego Blanco without cause."

George pulled the car to the side of the road and slid the transmission into park. He turned in his seat and looked at Francis.

"If you think you can blackmail your way out of this situation you're fucking delusional. You've been in Rocha's pocket for who knows how long. You've gotten people killed. You put your weapon to the head of another agent. You're not walking away from this, Francis, and you can tell anybody anything you like. Nobody's gonna believe a word of it. So sit there, keep your fucking mouth shut, and take what's coming to you. Be a man for once in your miserable goddamn life, you duplicitous sack of weasel shit."

Francis Waters only stared.

George turned back around, slid the transmission into drive, and started down the street once more.

The engine rattled and whined.

He thought about what Francis had said. He doubted anyone would believe he'd killed Diego without cause. His neck was swollen and bruised. There was evidence to corroborate what had happened. But George didn't want the truth out any more than he wanted Francis's lies out. He probably wouldn't lose his job—though he might face suspension—but what happened to him if the truth came out was the least of his worries. Mostly he was concerned with Rocha's reaction. Gael was still working for him, still trying to build a solid case, and if circumstances surrounding Blanco's death came out, Rocha would know Gael was undercover.

"Maybe I took the wrong tack," Francis said.

"There's no *right* tack, Francis. Just keep your mouth shut."

"I have close to a quarter million dollars. It's under the black rock in the northeast corner of my backyard. Let me out of here and I'll figure out the rest. Tell Horace Ellison I escaped. Tell him whatever you want to tell him. Just let me out of the car."

"You don't want to run, Francis. We've been through this."

"I don't want to go to prison."

"You're going to prison either way—unless Rocha catches up with you before the DEA does. He won't arrest you. He'll put a bullet in your head and bury you where you drop."

"You think he won't be able to get to me if I'm in prison, where I can't even run, where I'm fucking *caged*?"

"I think you're fucked no matter what you do but staying put requires less energy from everybody. Also, I don't want your money. It's dirty. But I do appreciate you telling me where I can find more evidence to back up my case against you."

Francis didn't respond.

George pulled his cell phone from his pocket and made a call.

26

Coop emptied his duffel bag, tossing clothes onto the bed, and with the bag in hand, made his way out of the hotel room. He checked his watch while he walked. Everybody in the group was supposed to meet in front of the Toyota ten minutes from now, so he expected to sit on the sun-warmed hood in the cool night and smoke a cigarette before the others arrived, but when he stepped into the parking lot and glanced left, he saw them all waiting there.

They were nervous with anticipation and unable to think about anything else. Coop could see it on their faces. He thought that each of them had probably resisted the urge to head out for as long as possible but had finally succumbed. Just like he had. They could concentrate on nothing else anyway; might as well wait by the car.

Bogart was smoking a joint and looking toward the moon, a bone scythe in a purple sky. Pilar was standing with her hands in her pockets, thinking whatever she was thinking, her face expressionless but her eyes flickering with worry. Normal was leaning against the car, arms crossed, right foot tapping against the faded asphalt to the rhythm of an inaudible rock song, two hundred and forty beats per minute.

A second duffel bag sat like a loyal dog on the ground beside him.

If he'd done what he was supposed to do, there'd be bolt cutters, a drill gun, screws, a hammer, and an angle bracket hidden within it.

Coop lit a cigarette and walked toward them.

"Did you get everything?"

"Of course," Normal said. "I don't wanna be doing this, but since it's happening, we might as well do it right."

"You didn't forget anything?"

"I said I got it all."

"I'm just asking."

"Already answered."

"All right, man, forget it. You're worked up about the job."

"I'm not worked up about shit. I just don't like to be second-guessed."

Coop pulled the key from his pocket and thumbed the fob. The doors unlocked. He yanked open the driver's-side door and slid in behind the wheel, tossing the empty duffel bag onto the passenger side floorboard. He reached under the dash and popped the trunk.

Looked in his rearview mirror to see Normal raising the lid. Heard the sound of the second duffel thumping heavily against the carpeted floor. The trunk lid slammed shut.

Pilar got into the front passenger seat.

Bogart and Normal slid onto the back bench seat from opposite sides.

Coop took a drag from his cigarette and started the engine. He cracked the window. Slid the transmission into reverse, backed out of his parking spot, and shoved it into drive. Soon they were rolling out of the parking lot and into the street. Headlights splashing angles of light onto the cracked asphalt. Coop's mind was not on what they were about to do but on what they had planned for tomorrow because, if they failed tonight, they would be stopped before they'd even begun.

He was determined to get James out of that jail. His friend couldn't die in there. What happened after they got James out he didn't know, but they could confront that question when the time came.

"What kind of guns did he have?" Normal asked.

"I didn't get a chance to examine them," Bogart said.

"I just don't wanna be doing this for no reason."

"Whatever we find'll be better than nothing."

"If all he's got is shotguns, we're fucked."

"Not if he's also got deer slugs."

"Jesus Christ, you're optimistic. We'll be firing at eight hundred yards or so and deer slugs are good at what, a hundred max? We'll have to lob them like footballs. Aim ten feet above the target and hope it makes it."

"Can't you take a Xanax or something? You've been yapping like a dog since this shit started."

"Oh, fuck off."

Coop drove past the pawnshop, slowing down to look at it. A dilapidated two-story building. Windows dark. Parking lot empty. He turned a corner, reached the back alley, and made another turn onto the dark, narrow strip of asphalt that ran behind the buildings. He brought the car to a stop, turned off the headlights, and killed the engine. Everybody sat motionless in the silent darkness for what felt like several minutes but was, in fact, less than forty-five seconds.

Finally, Coop took one last drag from his cigarette, flicked the butt out the window. It bounced off a graffiti-covered wall to the left and fell to the asphalt. The ember glowed orange in the darkness. Not even the moonlight reached this narrow alley, cut off by the buildings.

Coop reached down and popped the trunk. Looked at Pilar.

"Mind grabbing the duffel bag at your feet?"

Pilar nodded, grabbed the duffel, and handed it to Coop.

"Let's do this." Coop pushed open the driver's side door, and stepped out into the night.

27

George Rankin, trying to keep his face relaxed, pulled up to the border checkpoint and handed the guard his DEA identification card. He tried not to think about the corpse in his trunk or the fact that a flashlight beam aimed into the backseat would reveal blood and bullet holes. The guy looked at his picture, looked at his face— George flashed a false school-photo smile—and handed the card back.

"All right. Go on through."

George took his foot off the brake pedal and cruised forward. The knot in his stomach loosened. His heart rate began to normalize. He'd known that was how things were likely to go down, but nothing was ever promised, so he didn't feel safe until he'd made it through.

He glanced in his rearview mirror. Francis sat silent in the backseat looking out the passenger window at the night. Behind Francis, through the dirty rear window, George saw the guard kiosks retreat, shrinking until they vanished.

He drove through the El Paso night, wondering if he'd done the right thing when he called Horace Ellison, but he supposed he hadn't had much choice. Francis had witnessed what had happened. It was best if events as they actually happened were on record as soon as possible. If they came from Francis, they'd be distorted to incriminate him. Eventually, one way or another, Ellison would hear about what happened. He was the top man in El Paso, which meant he knew everything.

After fifteen minutes on the road he pulled up to an auto mechanic's garage on Doniphan Drive, CHARLIE NELSON'S AUTO PARTS & REPAIR hand-painted in red on the building's blue stucco façade, below which, in smaller writing, were the words FOREIGN & DOMESTIC. The place should have been closed at this hour, but the roll-up door was wide open and the lights were on inside. George could see Horace Ellison standing beneath them, to the right of the oil-change well in the floor, talking to a blond fellow about forty years old with an unshaven face and a waxed mustache, mesh John Deere cap perched on the back of his head like a trucker yarmulke and a blue grease-stained jumpsuit covering his body.

George pulled the sedan into the driveway and brought it to a stop. Looked at Francis in the rearview mirror. Man looked back at him but said nothing. After he'd heard George talking to Ellison on the phone, he'd seemed to resign himself to his fate. There was no talking himself out of the situation now. He couldn't buy his way out with blood money; couldn't blackmail his way out either.

George pushed open the car door and stepped out into the night. Raised his hand at the two men standing just inside the garage door. It was a strange juxtaposition. Horace Ellison in a well-tailored suit, what remained of his hair neatly trimmed, nails manicured; the other man in a grease-stained jumpsuit, hair curling out from under the cap, black crescents under his fingernails. Of any two men standing next to each other, Ellison and the mechanic were among the least likely.

"You look like you've been suicide-noosed," Ellison said when George stepped into the glow of the garage's overhead lights.

"That's about how I feel."

"We're gonna take care of this mess."

"How we gonna do that?"

"It's not complicated."

"Good. Complicated things have too many parts that can break."

"We're in agreement on that. This is my pal Charlie, by the way. I helped him out of some trouble once. He's gonna let us use his garage for a few minutes so we're not out in the open when we take care of our business."

George nodded in Charlie's direction as the man stuck a Marlboro between his lips and set it on fire.

"Good to meet you," Charlie said through a cloud of exhaled smoke.

"Okay," Ellison said, "formalities are out of the way. Pull the car into the garage."

George walked back to the sedan and slid in behind the wheel. He started the engine.

"What did Ellison say?"

"Nothing," George said. "Just to pull the car into the garage."

He shoved the transmission into drive and pulled the car forward. As soon as his rear bumper had crossed the threshold, Charlie began cranking down the roll-up door with the rusting chain that controlled it. After the lip hit concrete, he flipped a hasp over a staple and threaded a padlock through it.

George stepped out of the car again.

"I'm gonna take my leave," Charlie said. "Best if I don't see anything you guys might be up to. I'll be in the office if you need me."

"Thanks again, Charlie," Ellison said.

"Anytime." The mechanic pushed through a blue metal door and disappeared. The door swung shut behind him and latched with a soft click.

Horace walked to the sedan and pulled open the rear passenger door. "You stay right where you are, Waters. The door's open so you can listen, but you aren't part of this conversation. As far as I'm concerned, you're no better than a corner boy selling bindles, and handcuffed in the back of a car's where you belong. You gave up your right to call yourself a part of the DEA the moment you put the barrel of your gun against another agent's head. You understand me?"

"Yes, sir."

Ellison turned to George. "Here's the deal. If the shooting happened in Mexico, we're in a legally complicated mess. Mexican police would have to get involved and word would, inevitably, get to Rocha. You know this and I know this, which is why I had you come across the border. The way I see it, Blanco and Francis were having themselves a secret conversation here in El Paso. Waters, piece of shit that he is, decided to sell out Gael for a couple grand. You knew if it got back to Rocha, Gael would be in serious trouble, so you handcuffed both of them and put them into your car. Blanco managed to tuck his feet through his arms, tried to strangle you while you were driving, and you shot him. All that changes is the why and where. The what, which is the only thing that'll be investigated, stays exactly the same. You with me?"

"That leaves out the fact that Waters had women killed and threatened to murder another DEA agent."

"I know it does, which is why he's gonna go along with our story. He'll be relieved of duty and spend maybe three months in a minimum security prison, an unbelievable deal for a man whose crimes could put him away for life."

George didn't like it. It was exactly the kind of false report he hated. He felt crooked just thinking about it. But it had to be done. To protect Gael.

"Okay," George said.

"Okay," Ellison said. "We have to get some things in order. Pop the trunk."

28

The three men—Bogart, Coop, and Normal—walked to the pawn-shop's back door while Pilar slid into the driver's seat, their designated getaway driver. Coop carried the empty duffel bag. Normal carried the one holding the tools they'd need. When they arrived at the door, Coop noticed a large sign plastered to the left of the door. ADVERTENCIA in white on a red background below which were the words CUIDADO EL PERRO.

"Did you see a dog earlier?" Coop asked Bogart.

"Nope."

"Then let's hope the sign is bullshit."

"Let's," Normal said as he set down the duffel bag and unzipped it.

He pulled out the angle bracket, the drill gun, and a box of wood screws. Sat on his haunches and examined the door frame. But so far as Coop could tell, Normal wasn't seeing what he was looking for. He cursed under his breath, squinting at the inch-wide painted frame. After a brief moment of nothing, he ran his hand down the edge.

"There it is."

"What is it?"

"Just a slight bump. Where the button was installed."

Coop nodded. Normal had earlier told him about the alarm system in his parents' house. Each exterior door had a button installed on the hinge side of the door frame. It was pushed down when a door was shut. Once the alarm was set, the button had to stay down if you didn't want a visit from the police.

Because Normal used to sneak in and out of the house through the back door, he'd found a way to bypass the alarm system. Slide an angle bracket into place over the button and screw it down to keep said button from being released when the door was opened.

Simple, but it worked.

Coop just hoped it worked tonight as well; there was a lot more at stake than being grounded for two weeks because he'd sneaked out to smoke pot and skateboard with friends.

Normal lined the bracket up and tried to push it between the door and the door frame about six inches above the bottom hinge. It was a tight fit, however, and wouldn't slide in on its own, so he pulled the hammer from the duffel bag and began to pound the bracket into place.

By the third hammer strike, Coop could hear growling coming from the other side of the door. By the fifth, deep, angry, ferocious barking—the barking of a very large dog.

"I guess the sign wasn't bullshit."

"We should have brought some meat," Normal said as he finished hammering the bracket into place. Finally he got the elbow flush with the door frame.

"We didn't know there'd be a dog."

"Which is why we shouldn't be doing this. We don't have enough information, man."

"We also don't have time to collect it."

"I think there might be some pork rinds in the passenger door."

"You mind checking, Bogart?"

Bogart nodded and headed toward the car while Normal pulled

several wood screws from a box and picked up the drill gun. He put three screws into his mouth. The fourth he lined up in one of the bracket holes and pressed the drill gun against it.

"Hope I can get through this stucco with wood screws," he said through pinched lips that held the screws in place. "Concrete screws with tighter threading would have worked better."

"You should have bought concrete screws."

"I'd never been here before and I'm not exactly an experienced burglar. Not sure how I was supposed to know what I'd be dealing with."

"Should have prepared for all possibilities."

"Shut the fuck up, Coop."

"Then stop complaining about shit we can't change."

Normal glanced at him angrily but said no more. He pulled the trigger on the drill gun. For a long time, the screw only spun on the surface of the stucco, held in place by Normal's fingers, but finally—Normal thrusting his weight into it—the pressure put a deep enough hole in the stucco that the threads caught, and it twisted into the wall. Once it was in place, Normal looked at the finger and thumb that had been holding the screw. Thread-shaped cuts in the pads oozed blood. He rubbed his fingers together, pulled a screw from his mouth, and repeated the process.

The dog continued to bark furiously on the other side of the door and—based on the sounds—it was lunging as well. Coop could hear thumping and what he thought were either teeth or nails scraping against the door's metal surface.

Bogart returned with a half-eaten bag of jalapeño pork rinds.

Once Normal had finished screwing the bracket into place, he tossed the drill gun into the duffel and came out with bolt cutters. A padlock above the door had been threaded through a staple to hold the hasp in place. He handed the bolt cutters to Coop and wiped the blood from his fingers onto his shorts.

Coop tossed the empty duffel he'd been unconsciously holding, pinched the padlock between the bolt cutters' blades, and pulled the handles together with as much force as he was able. The shackle held for a long time, the blades merely denting the metal. But finally, in one fluid motion, it gave all at once, the handles squeezed together, and the padlock fell to the asphalt with a rattling clack.

Coop threw the bolt cutters down. They landed on top of the tool bag. He tried the door handle but it was, of course, locked. It made sense that they wouldn't catch a fucking break.

The scratching and barking continued.

Coop looked from Bogart to Normal. "Either of you know how to pick a lock?"

Normal said, "I do."

He grabbed the hammer and began pounding at the door handle, banging at it again and again. It bent and then snapped away, the screws pulling out of the metal door, revealing the lock's inner workings. He flipped the hammer, stuck the claw end into the door, and pried out the lock. It clattered to the asphalt in pieces.

"Smooth as warm butter," Normal said. "Now let's get this shit done and get out of here. We've been at it too long already, making way too much fucking noise. Police are probably on their way."

The dog thumped against the door, already on the attack, and Coop had to hold it in place to keep the beast from lunging through and attacking.

"Give me the pork rinds."

Bogart handed him the bag. He sat on his haunches and eased the door back about six inches, keeping his right foot against the outside to hold it in place in case the dog lunged again, and said, "Good doggy—you're such a *good* doggy." He poured the pork rinds through the gap and into the darkness on the other side.

The dog growled, barked two more times, and sniffed at the pork rinds. Finally it began to eat. Coop pulled open the door, slowly and cautiously, but the dog—some sort of boxer mix, its body taut with thick muscles—only glanced at him, growled briefly, and went back to eating the pork rinds.

Normal shoved all the tools into one duffel bag and zipped it up. He strapped it over his shoulder. Coop grabbed the empty bag and pulled open the door.

An explosion from within, like interior thunder, and a flash of light.

"*¡Métetelo por el culo!*"

Coop threw himself back, against the outside wall to the left of the door while Bogart and Normal dove to the ground and crawled to protection.

Another blast.

Coop didn't know what to do now. The pawnshop's owner was inside, armed, and not the least bit bashful about squeezing his trigger. He should have considered that. This was a two-story building, which meant there was probably an apartment on the second floor, and as much noise as they'd been making, of course the proprietor had heard them. They were unarmed and unprepared for battle, but they had to get inside. They had to get to the guns or James was going to die tomorrow. Problem was, he didn't want any of *them* to die tonight.

He was thinking through what their next move should be when the pain came. He looked down at his right shoulder and saw half a dozen spots of blood on his shirt, each of them spreading in the cotton. Shotgun pellets.

"Fuck."

"What is it?" Bogart said.

"I'm shot. Don't think it's bad, though."

"We still doing this?" Normal said.

"We have to," Coop said.

"Then what's the plan?"

Coop looked toward their car, Pilar's face like a moon floating in the darkness behind the glass as she sat watching him. He had to figure something out or he would lose his best friend. Pilar would lose the man she loved.

From inside the pawnshop: "*Revelar hagáis, cabrones. ¡Sus madres son putas!*" The son of a bitch was just waiting for them. He had all the time in the world and a loaded shotgun to back him.

Finally Coop made a decision. He looked to the other side of the door where Bogart and Normal were now standing, their backs against the stucco wall. They were looking at him, waiting. He inhaled, exhaled, and then ran past the door.

Another shotgun blast. The sound of pellets thwacking against the door.

"Here's the deal," Coop whispered once he was standing with the other two men. "I don't think this guy called the cops. If he had, they'd be here already. We were working the door for more than ten minutes. He's only one man. We can take him."

"He's one man but he's got a fucking shotgun," Normal said.

"We take him from two sides. Motherfucker can't aim the barrel in opposite directions at once. I'm going to the front. Gonna break the window—"

"Someone drives by and sees you, we're fucked," Normal said.

"It's our only option—and once I break the glass the alarm's gonna sound anyway. I'll draw him toward the front of the store, you guys come at him from behind."

"I'll come at him from behind," Normal said. "Bogart can go straight for the guns."

"Makes sense," Coop said, handing the empty duffel to Bogart.

"Let's do it, then," Bogart said.

"Okay." Coop ran to the corner of the building and made his way down a narrow walkway between two buildings, stepping over an abandoned bicycle and a stack of bald tires to reach the front. As he walked, he also picked up a large stone. An old Ford Pinto, green-painted but rusting, rolled by on the street, but so far as Coop could tell, the old lady behind the wheel didn't so much as glance in his direction.

He waited for the car to pass, watching its red taillights shrink and then disappear around a corner. Glanced in the other direction and saw only the empty street, not even a single car in sight. This wasn't surprising. None of the businesses on this strip of road were open. A red light hung from a cable stretched across an intersection in the distance.

It turned green, but nobody drove across.

Coop pulled back and threw the rock.

The window shattered, great and small shards of glass falling both to the sidewalk outside the store and on top of the merchandise displayed on the other side.

An alarm siren began to wail.

Coop picked up an electric guitar to use as a weapon and stepped into the darkness.

◼ Normal pulled the hammer from the duffel bag, wiped his sweaty palm against his shorts so his hand wouldn't slip, and gripped the wooden handle tight in his fist. He dropped the tool bag to the asphalt—he could grab it on his way out—stood with his back against the stucco wall, and waited. He closed his eyes, preparing himself mentally for what came next.

"You okay?" Bogart whispered.

"Let's just be ready. You need to go straight for the guns when we get in there. I'll go for the motherfucker shooting at us. Once the alarm sounds, we won't have a lot of—"

Shattering glass from the other side of the building. An alarm wailing.

Normal inhaled, exhaled—waiting for the man to respond to the break-in through the front window—and stepped around the door. Bogart followed.

He glanced inside but it was so dark he could see almost nothing. He put his hand through the door, waved it, and when no one tried to shoot him, stepped into the pawnshop.

He took a second step and a third. He blinked, trying to hasten the adjustment of his eyes to this darkness, and continued forward, carefully rolling his Emericas across the floor, trying to walk in complete silence despite the wailing alarm. Its rhythmic cry would hide some sound, but any noise he made between its pulsing scream would be heard.

At the other end of an aisle of shelves he saw a silhouette. The pawnshop's owner walking away. If the man glanced over his shoulder and saw him, he was dead. Man could simply swing around and blast him. But he hadn't glanced over his shoulder yet. He was making his way toward the front of the store.

Normal couldn't let him reach it. Coop was in the storefront unarmed.

Normal glanced at Bogart and held up a finger. Wait a minute.

Bogart nodded.

Normal increased his pace, still being careful not to make any noise, closing the distance between himself and the pawnshop's owner. He raised the hammer, ready to strike a blow.

The pawnshop's owner reached out and grabbed the doorknob. He pulled open the door, revealing a moonlighted storefront, and he must have caught movement because he raised his shotgun and pulled the trigger.

An empty shell clattered to the floor.

Normal rushed up behind him and swung down with all his force.

The hammer struck the back right side of the man's head and Normal could feel bone resist briefly and then shatter, leaving a hammer-shaped dent in the skull. The man dropped first to his knees and then forward, like a felled tree. He hoped the man wasn't dead, but if he was, it was still better than Coop getting—

A growl, a ferocious bark, and sharp pain stabbing into his calf muscle.

The motherfucking dog.

It had clamped down on his calf muscle with its vise-strong jaw and was whipping its head back and forth, tearing at the muscle.

He let out a scream and turned on the dog, whose jaw was locked on his calf, and swung down the hammer with all his strength, hitting the dog on the left side of its muscle-thick neck, but though it yelped through its clenched teeth, it didn't let go. It only whipped its head back and forth harder, trying to do serious damage, trying to incapacitate him by tearing away the muscle. Even as his leg screamed with pain—even as he swung back the hammer again to strike another blow—he was thinking about where he could strike in order to stop the attack without killing the thing. Its owner had been attacked in his home. The dog was only protecting its territory.

But before he had a chance to swing again he heard the crack of a small-caliber pistol being discharged and a red dot appeared in the dog's head, just below the right eye. The dog yelped once and went limp, its jaw still clamped on Normal's calf.

Normal looked from the dog to Bogart, who stood with a duffel bag strapped over his left shoulder, gun barrels jutting from it, and a .22 in his right hand.

"You didn't have to kill it," Normal said.

"A thank-you would be nice."

"You didn't have to kill it," he said again, but the truth was, shooting it in the head—killing it quickly—was probably more humane than anything he'd have done. He reached down and pried the dog's jaw off his leg. Blood, hot and viscid, poured down his leg and soaked into his sock. He looked up at Bogart. "Thank you."

Coop stepped through the door, saw the man on the floor, and tossed aside an electric guitar he'd been carrying.

The alarm was still screaming but in the space between the wails, Normal thought he could hear police sirens in the distance—but drawing nearer.

"Let's get the fuck out of here," he said, took two steps, and fell to his knees.

■ Coop and Bogart, each with a hand hooked under one of Normal's arms, dragged him out into the alley and toward the car as blood dripped from his leg and spattered to the ground behind them. Once they were outside, it became obvious just how close the police were. Six or seven blocks at the most and approaching at eighty miles per hour.

When they reached the car, Coop pulled open the front passenger door and they shoved Normal toward it. Bogart yanked open the rear passenger door and slid in. Coop followed.

Before he could even reach right and grab the door handle to yank it shut, Pilar had slammed the transmission into gear and gassed the car. They rolled toward the opposite end of the alley in darkness. Coop noticed that Pilar hadn't turned on the headlights.

As they reached the end of the alley and turned right, toward the main road, three La Paz police cruisers flew by from the left, lights flashing and sirens wailing. Pilar waited for them to pass and then turned onto the street, driving away from the pawnshop even as another police car drove by them.

Coop kept expecting one of the cop cars to burn a U-turn and come after them, but none of them did. He looked over his shoulder to the rear window and saw them screeching to a smoking-tire stop in front of the pawnshop.

After about a quarter mile, Pilar flipped on the headlights.

29

George Rankin stood outside his car, which was parked on the shoulder of the road, and emptied a clip toward a chain-linked lot where nothing had been built, angling his gun downward so the bullets would hit the dirt thirty or forty feet away. This was the middle of the city, and while he wanted to make sure the neighbors heard both gunfire and the sound of the crash, he didn't want wild rounds to strike random people or buildings. He reached down and picked up the empty shells, counting them as he did. Walked back to his car, pulling his cell phone from his pocket, and slid in behind the wheel.

He dialed Horace Ellison. "I'm here, shots fired, about to call the local police."

"All right. Our guys will be on the way soon."

George glanced in the rearview mirror. Francis was looking back at him, face spattered with blood. Diego Blanco, being dead, was sitting with slumped shoulders and blank eyes.

George started the engine, slid the car into gear, and drove into a telephone pole at about fifteen miles per hour. He whipped forward but the seat belt locked and held him in place. He pulled the airbag from the steering column so it looked as though it had just deployed. After taking a brief moment to collect himself, readying himself for what came next, he said, "Okay," and made his second call.

"El Paso Police Department. What is your emergency?"

"My name is Special Agent George Rankin. I'm with the DEA, Intelligence Division, and I just shot and killed a suspect in my custody. I spoke with my superior and he instructed me to call the local police. He's also sending men down here to conduct an internal investigation."

◼ The ambulance arrived before the police. It swerved down the street, lights flashing, and came to a stop behind the sedan. Two EMTs stepped from the vehicle and walked toward him. He was leaning against his car, hands in pockets.

"I already told the police, the guy's dead."

One of the EMTs put on latex gloves, pulled open the back door, and checked the pulse. After less than fifteen seconds he said:

"Dead as dead gets."

The first police car arrived five minutes later, pulling to a stop left of the sedan. Two beat cops—one in his thirties with a relaxed demeanor, the other in his early twenties and wound up with tension—stepped from the car. The older cop took the lead, walked over to George, and asked him what happened. George explained the situation and the guy looked into the sedan to confirm there was a dead guy inside. Once it was confirmed, he grabbed the radio from his shoulder, thumbed the button, and spoke into it, saying they had a corpse.

"Detective should be here soon. Mind if I get a statement from your witness?"

"No, go ahead, do your business."

"Thanks," he said. He started walking around the back of the car, paused, and looked over his shoulder at George. "He's not dangerous, is he?"

"He should be fine."

About the time the first responders finished cordoning off the area, the homicide detective, the meat wagon, and the DEA boys, including Horace Ellison, arrived on the scene, pulling their cars to the shoulder of the road.

George was sitting on the back of the ambulance holding an ice pack on his neck while one of the EMTs took his pulse.

The detective, a guy of about fifty in an ill-fitting department-store suit, walked to the sedan, looked inside at Diego, and then wandered over to George.

"What the hell happened?"

"My agent placated an angry suspect is what happened." Horace Ellison walked over, introduced himself to the detective, whose name was Winton Smith, and said he was going to listen in if the man didn't mind.

"No problem."

George gave his statement.

"Can I see your neck?"

George removed the ice pack.

"Jesus, that guy did a number on you."

"I'm just glad I walked away."

"Looks to me like a justified shooting. Don't see no need to get up your ass about it after the night you've had. I might have you come down to the station tomorrow to help me dot the tangos and cross the Indias, but that'll be about it, yeah?" He looked to Horace Ellison. "You're not gonna give this guy a hard time about saving his own life, are you?"

"Probably give him a medal, shooting a motherfucker like that."

The detective laughed. "Mind if I get a statement from the witness?"

"No, go ahead, but then I gotta get him into an interrogation room. We need to find out how much more he's revealed to the cartel, make sure our man is safe."

"I understand."

"Also, please make sure nobody leaks any information to the

media. If this guy's identity is revealed, it'll put a good man in serious danger."

"I'll seal lips with a needle and thread if I have to."

■ A news van and a tow truck arrived one after the other as Diego Blanco's body was being pulled from the sedan and placed on a gurney.

Detective Winton Smith shouted, "Cover that corpse. News crew can't get a shot of the face," even as a cameraman was stepping from the van. Smith walked over and met both the cameraman and the reporter, a blond woman in a low-cut blouse, and said, "We have no comment. Do *not* talk to my officers."

■ Horace drove George home. They sat silently in the car for the first half of the journey, George looking out the passenger window into the dark night, at the shadow-covered buildings streaking by. He was tired.

Finally, Ellison spoke: "Don't think that could have gone much better."

"I hate to let Waters off the hook for what he did."

"He's not off the hook for anything, George."

"He won't be charged. He can't be."

"There's other ways to make a man pay for his crimes. We know what he is."

Ellison pulled the car into George's driveway.

"Put some more ice on that neck and get some sleep. I think you should see a doctor tomorrow. Don't be a tough guy. Your neck looks like a boa constrictor that swallowed a goat."

"Okay."

George pushed open the passenger door and stepped outside. He waved at Ellison as the man backed his car out of the driveway, then stood and watched as the taillights receded. Finally he walked to his front door, unlocked it, and stepped inside.

30

Pilar woke to the sound of her wailing alarm clock, opened her eyes, and stared at the dark ceiling. For a moment, she only lay there, unmoving. Finally she reached over and slapped it silent. She sat up, knuckled her eyes, and picked at the rheum in the corners. It was four o'clock in the morning—she'd gotten three hours' sleep—and the window was still dark. A pain behind her left eye throbbed. Today was the day they got James out. Or failed to get James out. She turned, put her feet over the edge of the bed, and stepped onto the carpet.

She padded to the bathroom and washed her face.

When that was done, she got dressed, putting on 501s, a tank top from Express that said MAS AMOR POR FAVOR, and red Vans Gumsole sneakers. She gazed at herself in the mirror. She looked tired, with bags under her eyes, but she supposed that was to be expected under the circumstances. No need to bother with makeup. The day's activities didn't require it.

She pushed out into the hallway and took the three steps left to Normal's room. She tapped her knuckles on the wood.

Normal pulled open the door from the other side.

He was already dressed and ready to go, wearing cutoff shorts and a T-shirt that said I LIKE TO PARTY AND BY PARTY I MEAN TAKE NAPS. The front of the shirt was dotted with small holes. He used his shirts to twist open bottles of beer and the bottle caps inevitably damaged the cotton. Almost all of his shirts—all the ones Pilar had seen—looked moth-eaten.

His left calf was gauzed and taped, the gauze dotted with a dozen dots of burgundy where blood had seeped through. Pilar had treated the wound last night, after stopping at a drugstore and picking up supplies. She'd poured Listerine over the bite, used Super Glue to seal the deepest, longest rips in the flesh—the dog had really gone at him—and wrapped it. He'd taken ibuprofen, a shot of NyQuil, and gone to bed. She'd been worried the NyQuil would keep him asleep even after his alarm sounded, but he'd obviously been up for a while. She'd seen him just out of bed, and sleep still clung to him for half an hour afterward as he wandered around bleary-eyed and incoherent.

Normal was a self-contradictory person, which was one of the things she liked about him. He'd pick his nose, wipe boogers on his shorts, laugh at idiotic jokes, and burp in nice restaurants. But when he had to take things seriously, he did, and he often displayed a competency that was surprising when juxtaposed with his day-to-day personality.

"How you feeling, Pilar?"

"Nervous."

Normal nodded. "Me too."

She looked at his blue eyes to see if he was teasing her, but saw only tension flittering behind them.

He leaned forward, hugged her, and said, "It'll be okay. I know I've been the squeaky wheel on this shopping cart, but that doesn't mean I don't care about you and James. I consider you both friends. I love you guys. We're gonna get him out today."

For a moment Pilar only stood stiff, but this was the first time since James was arrested that somebody'd acknowledged what she must be going through, and the emotions she'd kept locked away rushed out of her. She wrapped her arms around him and cried into his shoulder.

"Do you think we will?"

"I do. Now let's get out of here."

Pilar pulled away, wiped at her eyes, and said, "Thank you."

"You're the first woman who ever thanked me for making her cry."

◼ Pilar drove them through the dark morning, the eastern horizon ahead of them fading to purple, the sun not yet visible but bleaching the black night with its illumination. Normal had put *Swordfishtrombones* into the CD player, and "16 Shells from a Thirty-Ought-Six" was thumping through the speakers. Normal cracked his window, sipped the paper cup of coffee he'd gotten from the machine in Hotel Amigo's lobby before they left, and though he grimaced at the taste, took a second sip.

It was a forty-minute drive, but neither of them spoke.

◼ Pilar parked the car in front of a brick building in Juarez, the sign above the door only three letters long, A.T.C., a chain-linked lot next to the building holding about twenty armored trucks. She killed the engine and turned the knob to shut off the headlights. She pushed open the driver's-side door and stepped out into the cool morning.

Though the sun had now breached the horizon, the streetlamps still glowed, halos of light hanging around them.

She walked around the car as Normal pushed out the front passenger door. They met on the sidewalk and together made their way up the concrete path to the front of the building. There were lights on inside, but no one visible at the front desk. Pilar knocked on the glass door.

The inside remained still and empty.

She knocked again and her uncle Arturo pushed out of a room that opened onto the hallway behind the lobby—probably a bathroom—and looked toward the front door. He saw her through the glass, smiled, and raised his hand in greeting before waddling over. When he reached the front door, he unlocked it and pushed it open. He held out his arms and said in Spanish, "Maria, you look beautiful. How long has it been?"

"Almost nine years."

"Nine years!"

He wrapped her in a tight hug, held her there a long moment, and then pushed her away again, holding her shoulders in his thick-fingered hands. He looked her up and down. "You're a woman now, aren't you? My God."

"How was your flight from Mexico City?"

"I don't know. I had three cocktails before takeoff and slept through it."

"This is my friend, Normal," Pilar said, waving her arm toward him.

Uncle Arturo stuck out his hand and said in English, "Any friend of Maria's is a friend of Arturo's. It is good to meet you, Normal."

Normal shook his hand and said, "Good to meet you too, sir."

"Sir! No, please—Arturo."

After a few more minutes of conversation, Arturo walked them out to the lot where the trucks were parked. They were much more intimidating close up than they were from the street. Hulking beasts. He showed them the vehicle he'd arranged for them to use, a large black-and-white BATT-XL with A.T.C. on each side door above an image of the company's security-badge logo.

"Let me show you everything." He swung open the rear doors.

The inside was lined with two bench seats, between which two safes and a hydraulic lift—a sniper step—sat bolted to the floor. Above the seats, in each wall, were three small windows. Below each window was a hatch through which one could stick the barrel of a rifle. In the center of the roof was another hatch. A man—or woman—could stand on the sniper step, open the hatch, and shoot with a 360-degree view. At the front of the truck were two bucket seats that faced the double-paned windshield.

"This beast," Uncle Arturo said, "offers fifty-caliber protection, an armored firewall at the front end, a rear deployment bumper, front and rear door lockout ability, flip-out running boards, gun ports, a blast mitigating floor to protect against ricochets, four-by-four capabilities, a sniper step and roof hatch, and a three hundred and sixty-two horsepower engine that takes regular unleaded fuel. You could drive this son of a bitch into hell and beat the devil."

"Yeah—but what's the gas mileage?" Normal said.

Uncle Arturo laughed. "Eight miles per gallon, give or take."

"Can't have everything, I guess."

"I will ask that you cover anything that can identify the vehicle and remove the license plate before you do what you need to do."

Pilar, who'd been very nervous about what they were going to attempt today, felt much better than she had before seeing the truck. They might still fail—failure was always a possibility—but if the breakout *could* be done, this armored truck would do it.

She hugged her uncle tightly in her arms and said, "Thank you so much. You don't know what this means to me."

"We're family, Maria."

■ Pilar drove the Toyota while Normal followed her in the armored truck. It was five thirty when they left Juarez and ten minutes past six when they reached La Paz. If Coop's information from yesterday was correct, they had almost five hours to wait until James was in the yard, in a place they could get to him.

She hoped he wasn't killed before then.

31

George Rankin parked his car in front of the house and killed the engine. He looked through the passenger window. It was a two-story white stucco place in the generic suburb style of the mid-1990s with a river-stone front yard and a shrub garden in front of the porch.

He pushed out the driver's-side door and made his way up the driveway to the side of the house, stepping over a coiled hose to get to the cedar gate. He unlatched the gate and stepped into the back-yard, which was sheeted with brownish grass.

He walked to the northeast corner, where a young ironwood had recently been planted. The dirt around it was covered in mulch and the mulch framed in by a circle of stones. One of those stones, un-like the others, was polished obsidian. He sat on his haunches, picked up the obsidian, and set it to the side. Beneath it lay a small square of plywood, which he also lifted and set aside. Under the plywood was a hole, one foot square, maybe two and a half feet deep, and lined with sheet metal to keep it from falling in on itself.

Inside the hole, shoved in sideways, were two cash boxes.

George reached inside and pulled them out. Set them down side by side on the grass. Flipped them open.

The one on the left was packed with banded stacks of hundred-dollar bills. The one on the right had enough space for maybe two more stacks before it too, was full. Each stack held ten thousand dollars.

George dumped the cash boxes into the grass, and after counting them, put the stacks of money back inside. There were twenty-two of them, which translated to two hundred and twenty thousand dollars. For a moment—for no more than ten seconds—George thought about keeping the money. He was a good person and this was dirty money, but dirty money spent just as well as clean money, and sometimes it was much easier to come by.

But in the end he knew he couldn't keep it.

He closed the cash boxes, latched them, and with one in each hand, got to his feet and walked back to his car.

■ He arrived in La Paz about ten minutes to seven, still thinking he had enough time to get to work if he made this quick. He parked his car on the street, and with one banded bundle of cash tucked into the inside pocket of his suit coat, strode toward the apartment building Rocha's employees lived in.

He walked to apartment 223, knocked on the door, and stood there waiting. He was about to knock a second time when he heard the dead bolt retract. The door swung open, revealing Diego Blanco's oldest daughter.

The girl was sixteen years old and very pretty. She had short black hair and wore a pair of black tights, a red skirt he'd be upset to see Meghan wearing, and a black T-shirt.

"My dad isn't here," she said in Spanish.

"I'm not looking for your dad," he said in very poor Spanish. "Do you speak English?"

"Yeah—who are looking for?"

"Are you Sophia?"

The girl took a step back. "Who are you?"

"That's not important."

"What do you want?"

"I want to talk to you, but before I can, I need to know you can keep a secret."

"If you're some kind of pervert, I swear to God—"

"I'm not. I have a daughter not much younger than you. This isn't about anything like that. Can you keep a secret? I'm serious."

The girl nodded.

"Your dad got himself into a little trouble. He doesn't want anyone to know about it, especially Rocha, but he wants to make sure you and your sisters are okay. He asked me to bring you some money." George reached into his pocket and pulled out the stack. "He said this should be more than enough for you and your sisters to take care of yourselves while he's away. It's ten thousand American dollars. But if he has to stay away longer than expected, he'll get you more. You have to be the grown-up right now. Can you do that?"

The girl nodded.

"Good." George held the money out and she took it. "Your dad is counting on you."

"Okay."

"Okay." George turned around and walked back to his car.

He wasn't sure how he felt about lying to the girl, and he wasn't sure how he felt about putting so much responsibility on her shoulders—she was only a child and now expected to take care of other children—but he didn't see an alternative.

He unlocked his car, got in, and started the engine.

32

Gael Morales stepped out of his apartment in time to see an ingot silver Ford Taurus pulling away from the curb, and while he knew George Rankin had one in the same color, he couldn't see who might be behind the wheel. He looked right and saw Sophia, Diego's oldest daughter, standing in her front door, looking out at the street.

She glanced toward him and raised a hand. He nodded. She stepped back into the apartment and swung the door closed. It latched with a click.

Gael walked down the concrete steps and out to the street where his Honda was parked. He put on his helmet and kicked the motorcycle to life. Toed it into first, throttled out into the street, and made his way east, toward Rocha's estate.

The sun was floating over the horizon, a bright hole-punch in the sky, and he had to squint to see as he rode toward it. When he reached the estate, he parked his bike, walked up to the front door, past two armed guards, and made his way inside. His stomach was a knot.

Rocha didn't know what he was, not yet, but the man wasn't stupid, and things had already started to go bad. Gael wasn't certain—he didn't know what Rocha knew—but he might have enough pieces that, if he decided to put them together, he'd be able to figure out Gael Morales wasn't who he said he was.

Which meant every day was dangerous.

Rocha was sitting on the couch in a pair of boxer briefs and a terry cloth bathrobe, his feet kicked up on the coffee table, holding a mug of coffee in his hand and watching the morning news. He glanced toward Gael as he took a sip.

"Have you seen Diego?"

"Today?"

"Of course today."

"No."

"He's supposed to be here."

"I haven't seen him."

"So you said. Did he talk to you about the pickup?"

Gael shook his head.

"Motherfucker. He was supposed to talk to you about a job."

"What kind of job?"

"If he doesn't show up in the next fifteen minutes, I'll talk to you about it. You'll have to do it alone. In the meantime go to the kitchen and have a cup of coffee. I need to be left alone."

Gael nodded and walked to the kitchen. He poured himself a cup of coffee and stood by the counter sipping it, waiting for Diego to arrive while knowing Diego wouldn't arrive.

The coffee was good.

■ An hour later, Gael was pulling Rocha's BMW into an alleyway behind a warehouse in Juarez, a Remington 1911 sitting on the passenger seat beside him. He was here to pick up heroin, heroin put into condoms that Danielle and Monica would swallow. Danielle would then fly to Los Angeles and Monica to Chicago. What made this dangerous was the Juarez cartel. If they knew about this shipment—and it had passed through enough hands that someone might have talked—they might take this opportunity to steal it. It'd happened before. Wait until the heroin is out of the warehouse and make your move. Shoot everyone you see, get the junk, and get the fuck out. Here's a little taste of death, teach you to operate in our city.

No suspicious cars on the street, no one who might be checking out the place standing around suspiciously, but still: he was wary and his stomach was in a knot. He parked the car, grabbed the 1911, and pushed open the driver's-side door.

As soon as he stepped into the morning sun, he tucked the Remington into his 527s and looked toward the warehouse.

It was a concrete structure with three loading docks in back, a rubber bumper bolted to the concrete in front of each, so that when trailers were backed up to them, no damage would be done either to the trailer or the concrete. The roll-up doors were all closed.

Rocha didn't like drugs in cars with his name on the title—he tried to keep all illegal substances away from anything that could be connected to him as a person—but nobody seemed to know what had happened to either Diego Blanco or his truck.

Gael knew, of course, but he wasn't talking.

He was, however, thinking. The truck was parked in the department store lot. It was surrounded by other vehicles, which meant it might not be discovered for a while, but it *would* be discovered. The question was what would happen next. Gael didn't know the answer to that question, but he disliked at least one of the possibilities. If not all of them.

He had to get rid of it. Tonight, after dark, he had to go to the department store, get into the truck, and drive it somewhere it wouldn't be discovered. If it was found in town, Rocha would know something had happened to Diego. He'd know it was a possibility, at the very least, and that was troublesome enough. Rocha would start asking questions and some of the answers could get Gael killed.

Could get Gael Castillo Jimenez killed. But he wasn't Gael Castillo Jimenez today. He was Gael Morales, and he had a heroin shipment to pick up.

He walked to the warehouse, up three concrete steps, and knocked on a brown-painted metal door just to the right of the loading docks. The dead bolt retracted. The door swung open. Standing on the other side was a Mexican man of about forty-five years old, a few inches shorter than Gael, Glasgow smile etched up both cheeks.

"I'm here for the shipment," Gael said in Spanish.

The man nodded him into the warehouse, closed and locked the door behind him, and started walking away.

Gael followed.

◼ Next time Gael got in behind the wheel, he had a cardboard box on the passenger floorboard with fifty condoms in it, twenty-five for each of the women traveling tomorrow. Each condom held twenty-five grams of heroin at a wholesale value of a hundred and twenty dollars per gram, meaning each woman would be traveling with about seventy-five thousand dollars' worth of junk in her stomach. If even one of those twenty-five condoms broke, someone was dead. On the other hand, Gael now had inside information—absolute proof—of Rocha's international drug running. This was only a small part of his operation, but even this was enough to put him away for a very long time. Every day Gael might be in more danger, but every day he also got more evidence against Rocha. Soon it would be time to wrap up this case.

He started the car, shoved it into gear, and pulled out of the alleyway, making a left onto the sun-faded street.

◼ The powder-blue Ford pickup was parked on the cobblestone driveway in front of the house. Gael saw it as he drove up toward the pissing fountain: a dinosaur of a vehicle, dented, battered, rust eating away at the front-left quarter panel. His heart pounded in his chest, and despite the BMW's air conditioner blasting against him, sweated beaded on his forehead. His first thought, stupid though it might be, was that Diego had come back. His second thought, equally as panic-inducing but much more likely, was that Rocha had found the truck and knew that something had happened to Diego.

He could have done something about it last night. He'd had both the time and the opportunity to get rid of the truck, but he hadn't thought to do it. It was an idiotic oversight, but also one that any-body could've made. He was juggling a dozen balls. That he'd dropped one was unsurprising. But that didn't mean he'd forgive himself for it. He'd fucked up big and his fuck-up had the potential to have serious consequences.

The BMW came to a stop in the shade of the garage, and after shoving the transmission into park, killing the engine, and picking up the box of heroin, Gael stepped out of the vehicle.

He told himself the consequences wouldn't be for him. They'd be for Gael Castillo Jimenez. He'd heard of the guy, of course, but his name was Gael Morales. Maybe distantly related to that other fellow, but so fucking what? They lived separate lives. Let Castillo Jimenez deal with the consequences of his own actions.

He inhaled, exhaled, and made his way into the house. Walked to the kitchen and set down the box. Turned around—and there was Alejandro Rocha, standing in the doorway.

"Diego finally showed up then. Where'd he say he was?"

"Diego's not here."

"Saw his truck out front."

"The *truck* is here. Diego's not."

"I don't understand."

"When's the last time you saw Diego, Gael?"

He tried to read Rocha's expression but found he couldn't. The face was expressionless, the eyes dull as unpolished stones. He might have been thinking anything.

"Yesterday—not long before I took the girls out, I guess."

"You sure?" The tone suggesting that Rocha knew otherwise.

"Yeah, why?"

"Do you know where his truck was?"

"How would I know that?"

"Now isn't the time to be a smart-ass. Do you know where his truck was?"

"No."

"I'm surprised you didn't see it yesterday."

"Where was it?"

"Care to take a wild guess?"

Gael shook his head. "No point in it. I got no idea."

"Why do I feel like you're being less than honest with me?"

"I don't know. I've got no reason to lie to you."

"I'm not quite convinced that's true. Do you know how long Diego's worked for me?"

"No."

"Twelve years. Do you know how long you've worked for me?"

"Six months."

"That's right. Six months. You don't really know a person after six months, do you?"

"I guess it depends on the person and how much time you spend together."

"No, it doesn't. You *can't* really know a person after six months. Most people present a simplified, shallow version of themselves, a version that's easy to understand. It's how we function in society. But everybody knows that a man's public image—how he projects himself—is at best only a small part of him, the part that others might accept in a civil society. Leave out the instinctive racism. Leave out the rape fantasies. Leave out the violent urges and the complex feelings you have about yourself. People amongst other people are playing a role. If they're honest people the role they're playing is a part of who they are. If they're dishonest, the character they present is an outright lie. Which is why people wait years to get married. People hide themselves, Gael. Some people hide themselves so well even *they* don't know who they really are, but I don't think you're one of those. You strike me as being too self-aware for such obliviousness. But that doesn't mean you haven't hidden yourself from me. It doesn't mean you didn't hide yourself from Diego. Who are you?"

"Mr. Rocha, I swear to God, I have no idea what's going on here. I don't know what you're talking about. But there's been some kind of misunderstanding."

"What's going on here is we're having a conversation. Is Diego still alive?"

"I don't know. I don't know where he is, I don't know where you found his truck, I don't know a fucking thing, so how could I know whether he's alive or not?"

"His truck was in the department store parking lot."

"Okay."

"People say it'd been there since yesterday—and you were there yesterday."

"But I had no idea it was there."

"Danielle Preston told me a different story."

"Danielle Preston's a lying bitch."

"Maybe," Rocha said. "But I'm not convinced." He reached forward, pulled the Remington from Gael's belt, and pointed it at his face. "So convince me."

33

Coop drove the armored truck while Pilar sat in the passenger seat beside him and Bogart, in back, looked through weapons and ammunition to see what they had available, duffel bag unzipped at his feet, the engine rumbling deep as they rolled along cracked asphalt. Coop looked in his side-view mirror to the rented Toyota, Normal at the wheel. The breakout had been Coop's idea, and he still thought it was their only option—they couldn't let James die—but a large part of him couldn't quite believe they were doing this. A large part of him still hadn't processed what went down last night at the pawnshop, and now they were rolling toward something even more dangerous—much more dangerous—facing not one man, but at least four armed guards in towers and another half dozen in the yard.

The street ahead bent right. Coop turned the wheel and felt a throb of pain in his right pectoral muscle and shoulder as shotgun-damaged muscles worked. Pilar had pulled the pellets out last night with a tweezer—what pellets weren't too deep to get to—and he'd cleaned and dressed the wounds. Didn't think he'd have to be treated by a doctor—hoped not, as doctors were required to notify authorities of gunshot wounds—but for now it was uncomfortable.

They continued another five miles before Coop swerved off the asphalt and rolled through desert toward a large rock formation in the distance that jutted from the flat earth like some ancient culture's church.

Normal followed in the Toyota, staying back a good distance to keep the thick cloud of dust kicked up by the armored truck off his windshield, weaving left and right around rocks and shrubs. The windshield wipers swept back and forth across the glass.

When they reached the rock formation, both vehicles came to a stop. They were about a half mile off the road.

Coop cracked his window and lit a cigarette. He glanced toward the side-view mirror. Normal stepped out of the Toyota, locked it, and shoved the key into his pocket. He limped toward the back of the armored truck, and then disappeared behind it. Bogart opened the back for him and he climbed inside.

Coop looked over his shoulder as Bogart swung the door shut. He exhaled through his nostrils, smoke swirling around his head.

"How you guys doing?"

Normal shrugged.

"Good, man," Bogart said.

Coop had seen Normal like this several times before. It was how he got before an assignment. He switched off emotionally, like a house at night, one light after another going out, one room after another going dark. He functioned, but he wasn't really there. It meant he was ready to do what he had to do to get the job done.

Coop looked at his Timex. It was ten o'clock, still an hour until inmates hit the yard. They'd stay here for the time being, hidden from view, and prepare.

Normal sat on the bench seat in back and picked up an M1903 Springfield, an old weapon but a reliable one.

"We got thirty-aught-six rounds?" Normal asked.

Bogart held up a box.

"We got a scope that'll fit this bitch?"

"We got a Buehler I think'll work."

"Lemme see it."

While Normal worked on getting the Springfield ready, Bogart picked up an already scoped Remington 700 with a twenty-six-inch barrel.

Normal looked toward Coop, face still expressionless, as it would remain until this was finished. "Think anybody'll hear gunfire if we calibrate out here?"

Coop shrugged. "Doesn't matter if they do. It's gotta be done."

So Bogart and Normal loaded their weapons and stepped out of the back of the truck.

■ Using binoculars and a laser pointer—they didn't have a bore sighter available—they removed the bolts from their weapons and bore sighted them against a boulder with a dark spot near its center about twenty-five yards away, lining up their sights' crosshairs with the red dot of the laser pointer, which was barely visible in the bright light, even at such a short distance. Once this was finished, they went about narrowing their rifles' accuracy, working from one hundred yards to five hundred, to a thousand. It was a tedious process, each of them firing five rounds per test, but if they didn't do it they wouldn't hit a barn at distance.

With their rifles ready, they got back into the truck.

It was ten forty-five.

34

When George Rankin reached his cubicle, cup of coffee in hand, he found a sheet of paper laying across his computer's keyboard, information on the social security number Mulligan Shoibli had used to open his bank account and get a Visa card. The number was originally assigned to a man named Marcus Shawn. Born in 1962. Died, at the age of forty-five, in 2007. Both transitions—into life and out of it—had occurred in Chicago, Illinois.

George fell into his desk chair, set the paper from the SSA to the left, set his coffee to the right after taking a sip, and turned on his iMac. He ran a records search for Marcus Shawn and found a string of arrests, from assault to car theft to drug possession to possession with intent to sell: guy was a regular Renaissance man of petty crime.

In October 2006 the DEA began to investigate both Marcus Shawn and his older brother, Leonard, a pharmacist in Northbrook, under suspicion they were selling prescription narcotics on the streets of Chicago.

In 2007, on March 8, the Drug Enforcement Agency got themselves a no-knock warrant. They executed the warrant at two thirty in the morning on March 9, and after a DEA agent was hit in the back of the head with a Louisville Slugger while attempting to climb through a window, Marcus Shawn was shot twenty-eight times. He was declared dead on arrival at Loyola University Hospital at five minutes past three. DEA agents found Adderall, Ambien, and Oxy-Contin in his home, with a combined street value of less than five hundred dollars.

The lead agent on the case was Horace Ellison.

Chicago had been nagging at George Rankin since he heard the place was connected to Shoibli. Now he knew why—or thought he did.

He hadn't immediately connected it to the chief of intelligence—despite the fact that he knew Ellison had transferred from there—because one tended to think men wearing the same color jersey as you were on your team. But it was naïve to make such assumptions and he should have known better, especially with so much money involved.

It made sense that Mulligan Shoibli would be DEA, especially if Shoibli was the real power behind the Rocha cartel, and a man in Horace Ellison's position would have access to all sorts of information that could keep the cartel running for years. It was no wonder that the Rocha cartel had operated so quietly for so long. No wonder Rocha had been able to slip through the cracks for years while simultaneously trafficking millions of dollars in cocaine and heroin and marijuana a month.

Even if he had to behave as though his organization was under investigation—George had brought this case to Ellison, and it'd been strong enough even at the beginning that rejecting it out of hand would have been suspicious—he could work to undermine said investigation at every step while staying hidden in shadows.

He could feed Rocha just enough information to trip up the investigation at every step. No wonder George and Gael had been working at an indictment unsuccessfully for years. No wonder incriminating evidence had slipped through their fingers again and again.

Ellison might not have been willing to tell Rocha who the undercover agent in his midst was—Rocha was likely to kill him and a dead (or missing) DEA agent would only draw more attention to La Paz—but the man had known there was one, and he'd known what the limits of his activities might be. Known what the DEA could and couldn't get him for.

But there were still questions.

Like whether Francis Waters had been working for Horace Ellison or Alejandro Rocha.

Like why Horace Ellison had allowed this information from the SSA to reach George's desk in the first place. Maybe he thought George wouldn't put the pieces together, but that was a risky assumption, and didn't make sense if Ellison had been so careful about remaining undetected to this point. Maybe . . .

George got to his feet, walked to the elevator, and pushed the call button. He waited for about thirty seconds before the doors opened, and once they had, stepped into the elevator car and pushed the button for the lower level.

He stepped out of the elevator, walked to the desk at the front of the holding-cell corridor, and picked up a pen to sign in, but before he did this, he examined the sheet. Only four people had signed in to visit arrestees so far today, and none of them was Horace Ellison. None of them either, had come down to visit Francis Waters.

George scrawled his name, the name of the man he was here to visit, and the current time in the form's three columns. He looked at the whiteboard chart on the wall, written in green dry erase marker, telling him which cell Francis Waters was in. He made his way down the corridor, pulling his key ring from his pocket as he walked.

He reached the door, keyed the lock, and pulled open the door.

Francis Waters was hanging by his neck. He had, based on the evidence at hand, stood on his cot, knocked the drop-ceiling tiles aside, knotted one end of his necktie around a steel beam running the length of the crawlway above, and the other end around his throat, after which he'd stepped off the cot and hanged until he was dead.

Urine had pooled on the vinyl floor under his feet.

George stood in the doorway unmoving for too long but a finger twitch in Francis Waters's right hand yanked him from his paralysis. The man wasn't dead. George ran to where Francis hung and grabbed the legs. He lifted his weight off the necktie noose and yelled out:

"I need some fucking help in here! I need some *help!*"

35

Gael Morales stared down the barrel of the gun to the darkness that would greet him if Rocha squeezed the trigger. He'd had guns pointed at his head all too frequently these last couple days. But he thought this entire situation was coming to a head. He thought it would be finished soon. All he had to do was get to the end alive.

"Listen to me," Gael said.

"I'm all ears, Gael, if that's your real name."

"I never saw the truck. I drove to the department store and parked. Danielle and Monica went inside. I sat in the car smoking and listening to the radio for two hours. They came out and we drove back here. That's it. If Danielle is telling you a different story, she's lying. For all I know, she's the reason Diego's missing. Whatever the fuck she's selling you, it's all packaging. The box is empty. You know me, Alejandro. I've been working for you every day for six months and never once have I done anything to make you suspicious of me. I'm a man making a living by doing his job—that's all I am—and I think we can both agree that I do my job well. I'm on time, I do what I'm told, and I do it well and without complaint. You shouldn't be pointing that gun at me. If anything, you should be pointing it at Danielle—because she's the bitch who's lying to you."

◼ Alejandro thought about Gael's words. He wanted to believe them—partly because he liked the guy and partly because they made sense. Francis Waters was supposed to have approached Danielle Preston yesterday. If he had, and if she'd agreed to talk, Diego would have gone for her. It was possible that she'd somehow managed to get the upper hand. Even good men sometimes made stupid mistakes, and in this line of work, a stupid mistake could cost you your life. But if she'd gotten the upper hand, what had become of Diego?

"Don't fucking move," he said, pulling his cell phone from his pocket. He dialed Francis and put the phone to his ear. It rang five times before going to voice mail. He ended the call and replaced the phone. He didn't know what to do. So, for almost a full minute, he simply stood there aiming his gun at Gael Morales.

Finally he said, "I want you to kill her."

"What?"

"Danielle Preston. If she's lying to me—if you're not DEA—I want you to prove it to me. Put a bullet in her head. That's not a problem, is it? If she's willing to lie, willing to tell me lies that'll get you killed, you should *want* her dead."

◼ Gael looked past the gun to Rocha's face. He swallowed and heard a dry click in his throat.

"What about the trip she's supposed to make tomorrow?"

"If she can't be trusted, she's not going. I'll send someone else."

"Fine," Gael said. "I've got no feelings for the bitch."

What he said wasn't a lie. Gael Castillo Jimenez might like Danielle Preston. Gael Castillo Jimenez *did* like her. But Gael Morales had no feelings about her one way or the other.

Alejandro Rocha looked him in the eyes, examined his face, and after what felt like a long time, decided he was telling the truth.

"Good," he said.

36

Normal sat in the back of the armored truck, staring blankly at the wall opposite, thinking nothing as Coop parked near the base of hills that surrounded the jail. As soon as the truck came to a stop, he got to his feet while still holding the Springfield, opened the back, and jumped out to the desert floor, the sun overhead shining down on him hot and bright. His left calf muscle throbbed with pain, and though he was aware of it on some level, it barely registered consciously.

He began his trek up the hill toward his shooting position, Emericas sliding through the sand, hearing but barely registering Bogart walking behind him. When they reached the large boulders near the crest of the hill, they got into place behind them, setting up their rifles, positioning their bodies for comfort.

Normal looked through his scope to the guard towers. It was five minutes to eleven and the guards were now in place, rifles in hand, though none of the prisoners were in the yard yet. He watched the guards standing there, moving his scope from one to the other, lining up their heads in his crosshairs, his index finger resting on his rifle's trigger guard. In the Marines, he wasn't a shooter but a spotter, but he had no doubt he'd be able to take them out—one, two, three, four—in only a few seconds. However, he didn't want to take anyone out. He would if he had to, but these were not his enemies, and would only become his enemies when they threatened his friends.

Unfortunately, that would happen soon enough.

■ James walked with the other prisoners from his cell block, all of them in a single-file line, one guard leading the way and one guard behind. His makeshift pistol was tucked into his sock, and he felt it must be very conspicuous, felt the way the leg of his jumpsuit moved against it must be unnatural, but there'd been no other place to hide it. Anyway, nobody had said anything, which meant nobody had seen anything. If they did, he was fucked. But if he didn't do this, he also was fucked, so it wasn't really much of a risk.

The guards led them through the corridors, the only sounds the rhythmic thump of footsteps. It reminded James of marching with his company in boot camp, reminded him of drill instructors chanting cadence:

> *Left, left, left—right.*
> *If I die in a combat zone, box me up and ship me home.*
> *Issue my rifle to another Marine; it served me well and I know it's clean.*
> *Put me into my Dress Blues, comb my hair and shine my shoes.*
> *Pin my medals upon my chest and tell my momma I done my best.*
> *When I get to heaven, St. Pete will say, "How'd you earn your living, how'd you earn your pay?"*
> *I'll reply as I take my knife, "Get outta my way 'fore I take your life."*
> *He'll open the gate and let me pass, and if God don't like it I'll whoop His ass.*
> *Left, left, left—right.*

The lead guard pushed through the door that led onto the yard. The inmates filtered out and headed to the free weights, the basketball court, and the naked ground where they played soccer. James himself walked to the back fence, kicking through the desert sand, wondering if he'd have an opportunity to make his move. Or if he'd have to *create* an opportunity.

He knew that doing what he intended to do would probably end in his death, but possibly dead was better than definitely dead, and if he didn't get out of here, he was certain he'd be killed sooner or later. He stood with his back against the fence for a few minutes, watching the other inmates. He scanned the yard, looking at the guards who lined its perimeter. He watched as the inmates from one of the other cell blocks filtered out onto the yard. He reached down and scratched his ankle, palming his makeshift pistol, keeping it hidden as he stood up again.

His heart thudded in his chest. His mouth was dry. It was hard to swallow.

He looked toward the guard in the far left corner. That was the man he needed to get to. If he could put his pistol into the guard's back and make him understand both that it was real and that he was willing to shoot it, he might lead James into the nearest building, and just on the other side of it was the employee parking lot. He'd get the man's car keys and drive away. He'd have to crash straight through the gates to get off the compound, and as soon as he did, there'd be people after him, maybe people shooting, but that was something he could deal with when it happened. *If* it happened. The chances of getting even that far were minimal at best.

He was about to make his move—about to begin strolling over casually—when Pedro, the man who'd lost his daughter, leaned against the fence beside him.

"They're coming for you. I heard talk earlier."

"Who's coming?"

Pedro nodded toward the basketball court. James looked and saw a group of five men walking toward him, their pace deliberate.

Fulanito—the man with no name—was at the center of the group, clearly leading the others.

It looked like James might not have the opportunity to even attempt his breakout. He might have to use his single bullet on the leader of this group. In fact, he was almost certain of it. His grip on the makeshift pistol in his hand tightened. His heart rate increased, thudded against the wall of his chest. He could feel the pressure of his throbbing veins in his forehead.

"You should walk away, Pedro."

"I'm not going to do that."

"You don't even know me."

"I'm not leaving you here to get murdered. I'm not a coward." Pedro shook his right arm and when James glanced over, he saw a sharpened toothbrush slide into the man's waiting palm. He gripped it not like someone would hold a knife, but as one might hold an ice pick, blade jutting from the pinky-side of his grip.

Fulanito and the others continued toward them, spreading out as they did, so that neither he nor Pedro could easily walk away, so that they couldn't walk away at all without a confrontation. Fulanito smiled as he approached, his Ping-Pong ball eyes alight with dark humor.

"I told you I'd make certain that I was the one to kill you."

"You did—and you were wrong." James raised the makeshift pistol and aimed it at the nameless motherfucker's face. He thumbed back his firing pin.

Fulanito actually laughed. "What do you think you're going to accomplish with—"

James released the firing pin. It snapped forward.

The gun exploded, pieces of the barrel and shreds of paper suddenly falling around them like confetti. The shell shot out the back of the pistol and thwacked against James's neck, burning it. But a hole appeared in Fulanito's left cheek, and blood began to ooze from the hole. The smile was gone. The eyes were dazed.

"What—" The word left Fulanito's mouth plaintively. He

dropped to his knees. He collapsed forward. A cloud of dust exploded around him.

■ Coop shoved the transmission into gear, released the clutch, and footed the gas. He ground the gears as he shoved his way through them quickly, trying to gain speed. He honked his horn so the people standing in front of the fence would get out of the way. He aimed the truck at a gap between two of the vehicles parked in front of the fence, knowing he would hit them both but hoping they wouldn't slow him down.

■ Bogart watched through his scope as one of the towered guards aimed his rifle at James, who had just—somehow—shot a man in the head with a toy gun that looked like it was made out of paper. He didn't want to kill anybody today—he only wanted to make sure none of his friends died—so he lined the guard's right hand up in his crosshairs even as the guard moved his finger from the trigger guard to the trigger.

Bogart fired off a round. For a full second—for what felt like a full second—nothing happened. Finally, the bullet finished its long journey. The hand exploded, a mist of blood hanging in the air. The guard dropped his rifle.

■ James looked at the four men coming at both him and Pedro, the four men left alive. Each of them held a shiv, and each of them was ready, body tense with muscle.

James threw down the remains of his gun, waited for someone to make a move. His back was against the fence—he had nowhere to go—which meant he'd have to fight. But that was fine because a large part of him *wanted* to fight. He had as much violence in him as any man, more than most, and the only thing that kept it from erupting was the thin membrane of conscience that held it in place, the thin membrane between urge and action, and that membrane had torn open.

"Let's go, you fucks," James said.

One of the four men, bald motherfucker with a face like a bull-dog, lunged at James with his weapon.

James jumped aside, grabbed the wrist, and twisted it even as he punched the guy in the nose—one, two, three times—with quick but powerful jabs, the cartilage bending and snapping with the final blow. A sheet of blood poured down his face.

The man yanked his arm away and swung again.

James knocked the blow aside with the swipe of an arm and brought his foot up between the legs, lifting the motherfucker off the ground.

When the guy came back down, his knees buckled. He dropped to the ground, clenching at his groin, forgetting the weapon he'd left lying in the dust.

James stepped forward and swung down his fist as hard as he could, punching the temple and knocking the motherfucker out.

But in doing so, he felt a knuckle in his middle finger break.

He didn't care. He leaned down to pick up the shiv.

Another of the men came at him, his mouth either grinning or grimacing, it was impossible to tell which. Missing teeth made him look like a building with broken windows. But Pedro brought down his fist like a sledgehammer, burying the sharpened toothbrush in the man's throat, and blood gushed out around it to the rhythm of his heartbeat, a carotid geyser, and the man grabbed at his neck as he fell to the ground.

He'd be dead in a second. Good.

James swung back around to face the last two men who would kill him.

They stepped forward, weapons gripped in their fists.

◼ Normal aimed his Springfield at the yard, panning the area. Guards were running toward James from all directions. He squeezed his trigger, leading one of the guard's by a good distance, and al-most a second later his round struck a foot. The guard he'd shot collapsed and his momentum flung him forward into the dirt. He rolled through a cloud of dust, silently screaming.

Normal yanked back the bolt. An empty shell arced through the air. He chambered a new round. He panned the yard, found a second guard, squeezed his trigger a second time.

He couldn't let them reach James. If they managed to grab him, it would make getting him out close to impossible. If they managed to grab him, there'd be a tangle of movement, and it would be impossible to get shots off without the risk of killing James.

If they managed to grab him, it was over.

Normal panned across the yard, found a third guard. Guy was yanking a sap from his belt as he ran toward James.

Normal squeezed his trigger.

◼ Coop cringed as the armored truck barreled toward the fences, aimed at the four-foot space between a Ford Pinto station wagon and a small Dodge truck. It slammed into both vehicles simultaneously, the sound like thunder. The armored truck pushed both aside, rolling over the front edge of the Ford and flipping the Dodge onto its side. It tore through the fences like tracing paper. He spun the wheel left and slammed his foot on the brake pedal. A large plume of dust drifted around them.

Guards aimed their weapons from their tower perches and fired, dotting the windshield glass with their bullets.

◼ Bogart lined one of the guards up in his crosshairs, exhaled steadily, and in the space between breaths, the space between heartbeats, he squeezed his trigger. The rifle pulsed against the crook of his shoulder. Through his sight he saw a mist of blood hanging in the air. The guard fell to his knees, dropping his rifle to the ground below.

Bogart panned to another tower, to another guard.

◼ Pilar ran to the back of the armored truck with a pistol in hand and swung open the doors. She looked out onto the yard and saw

James and three Mexican men staring at her. For a moment, for what felt like a long moment, nobody moved. They only stared.

Finally Pilar shouted, "Come *on*, James! Let's go! This isn't a fucking picnic!"

■ James looked from Pilar to the yard surrounding him, taking everything in. Guards were shooting and being shot. Prisoners were screaming and rioting. One ran to the foot of a guard tower and picked up a dropped rifle and began shooting at the guards on the ground. One in the back. One in the face. He shot another prisoner in the abdomen. He fired into the air. He was screaming while he shot off rounds. Other prisoners tackled yet another guard and held him down while he was pummeled. James took this all in in less than a second, and then grabbed Pedro by the arm and said, "Let's get the fuck out of here."

He ran toward the armored truck, pulling Pedro with him.

They reached the truck and climbed into the back.

But one of the men who'd attacked him, one of the last two standing, grabbed him by the ankle and began pulling him back out.

Pilar shot him in the face.

James scrambled back into the truck.

Pilar slammed shut the doors.

Coop looked over his shoulder and shouted: "We good?"

"Go!" Pilar shouted back.

The transmission was slammed into gear. The engine roared as the truck barreled forward, turning in a half circle.

■ Coop glanced in his side-view mirror and saw several guards in bulletproof vests rushing from one of the buildings. They had rifles in their hands. They stuck them into the crooks of their shoulders and began firing at the truck. The bullets thwacked against its armored exterior. Prisoners began rushing them and they shot the prisoners.

Coop slammed the truck through the fences.

More prisoners began to run through the hole and out into the desert.

■ Normal got to his feet as the armored truck rolled toward him, a cloud of dust kicked up in its wake and drifting on the hot summer breeze. It was followed by running prisoners, looking over their shoulders, shouting.

"Let's go," Normal said.

He and Bogart began to make their way down the hill, feet sliding through the sand.

Guards down in the yard—wearing bulletproof vests, bearing rifles—shot at the truck and at the prisoners escaping on foot.

Chaos in the yard.

The armored truck came to a rumbling stop near the base of the hill, sliding sidewise in the sand. The doors swung open.

As Normal and Bogart ran toward it, guards began to shoot at them, their bullets kicking up chunks of earth at their feet.

Pilar, James, and some Mexican guy with James shot through the portholes in the side of the truck. Guards took rounds to their vests, were kicked off their feet.

Normal's left calf was now screaming with pain.

He and Bogart jumped into the back of the truck. Bullets thwacked against it even as Pilar pulled shut the door and it roared away from the jail.

37

George Rankin sat down in his desk chair and looked at his blank computer monitor. He thought about what Francis Waters had said to him before he'd died on the floor in his cell while waiting for medics to arrive—either one or two words, George wasn't sure he'd heard correctly. It might have been *Ellison*. But it could also have been *Edison* or *a lesson*. It could have been none of those words, the sound leaving Waters's mouth, as it had, with a gurgle of frothy blood that then rolled from the corners of his mouth and dripped to the vinyl floor. If it was *Ellison*, it might have been an accusation—*Ellison is behind all of this*—but it didn't have to be. There were any number of things that might have followed or preceded the word. The man had been near death, his brain oxygen-starved, he might have been talking about nothing at all.

But George decided he had to check the camera recordings to see if someone had visited the holding cells without first signing in. If Francis knew something, Ellison—or whoever was behind this, but it almost had to be Ellison—would want him dead. He'd want whatever secret Francis knew to die with him.

It was possible, of course, that Francis had simply ended his life because of the situation he was in. As a disgraced DEA agent, he'd lose not only his career but his entire life as he knew it. Even if he survived jail, which was questionable, he'd come out with nothing and no way of getting anything back. His trial and inevitable conviction would be news. His friends from the DEA would be his friends no more. Because he'd earned money selling information to a drug cartel, his finances and home would be seized. He might find a job, but it wouldn't be in law enforcement. It probably wouldn't be any kind of skilled position. Nobody would trust him.

The man had certainly had time to think about all of this overnight, while he lay on the cot in his holding cell, which meant he'd also had plenty of reasons to kill himself.

But George wasn't about to take the situation at face value. There was at least one person out there who might have a reason for wanting Francis dead, and George was pretty sure he knew who that person was.

38

James was sitting in the backseat of the Toyota, squeezed in between Normal and Bogart, when Coop pulled into Hotel Amigo's
parking lot. Pilar was in the front passenger seat. Nobody said anything as Coop brought the car to a stop and killed the engine.

After they'd roared away from the jail, Coop had driven down the
street at high speeds before he jerked the car right, pulling off the
road and heading through the desert. He'd parked the armored truck
behind a large rock formation standing alone in the sand like the
last structure on earth—all that remained of some ancient civilization.

He killed the engine and gave James a set of civilian clothes, a
pair of cutoff sweatpants and a Captain America T-shirt, and James
quickly stripped out of his prison jumpsuit, shedding himself of it,
feeling like a different person once he was no longer dressed like a
prisoner, and changed into the clothes Coop had given him.

Coop and Bogart wiped down the truck of fingerprints and everybody got out, stepping into the bright daylight. Normal put the
weapons into the Toyota's trunk.

James and Pedro stood under the hot sun for a moment, looking at each other, neither knowing what to say. Pedro had saved his life, helped to save his life, but James sensed that now that he was out of jail, he intended to part company with them.

"You can come with us," James said. "We'll squeeze you into the car."

"No," Pedro said. "You have your thing to do. I think I should handle mine."

"Where are you gonna go?"

"I'm going to find the men who killed my daughter."

"Let us drive you into town."

Pedro shook his head. "I think I'd rather be alone."

"We're in the middle of nowhere. You have no food or water."

Pedro turned his hands so his palms were facing up—it looked as though he were waiting for something to be placed in them—and stared down at his bandaged wrists. His eyes were sad.

"Everything that could be done to me *has* been done to me. I've lost everything already. There are no worse fates. Good luck, James."

He turned and walked away, walked south, deeper into the desert. James watched him for a moment, but knew there was no time. They had to get out of here and in a hurry. The farther they got from the jail, the safer he was. The safer they all were.

He and the others got into the Toyota. Coop drove out to the street. But when he glanced right, he saw a line of police cars rushing at him from La Paz, so rather than heading toward town right away, he drove across the street and parked on the north shoulder, car facing west, facing the jail. He put on the emergency flashers and they waited.

Several police cars flew by with their sirens wailing and lights flashing.

The last two in the line pulled off the road only ten yards in front of the Toyota, dust swirling around them. A cop stepped out of each vehicle. James's heart thudded in his chest as he watched them through the dirty windshield. One of the cops popped his trunk and removed a spike strip. He and the second cop spread it across the street.

Once they were done with this, they both glanced toward the Toyota, and spoke to one another. They walked to the car. James hadn't been out of jail fifteen minutes and he was about to go back. Unless they incapacitated the cops. The easiest way to do that was to kill them, but James wanted no part in murdering men who were only doing their job. He'd rather go back to jail. One of the cops knocked on the driver's-side window.

Coop looked over his shoulder, said, "Be cool," and rolled down the window "What's going on?" he said to the cops. "We were on our way to visit a friend."

"There has been a breakout. You need to turn around and head back to the city."

"A breakout? What happened?"

"Turn your car around, sir, and head back to La Paz."

Coop nodded. "Okay."

He turned the car around in the dirt. James looked south to the desert, but Pedro was already gone. Vanished from the horizon.

Nobody talked.

James couldn't be certain but he'd be willing to bet that none of them had anticipated the chaos the breakout had resulted in. They'd been thinking only about getting him out of jail before he was murdered. They'd failed to consider how other prisoners in the yard might respond. But this sort of operation was unpredictable. The Marines in the car had known that, even if Pilar didn't—or hadn't. They'd taken villages in Afghanistan in order to capture al-Qaeda members and it was never pretty. But maybe the fact that they weren't in Afghanistan made them forget what this sort of operation looked like in the real world. It always seemed so neat on paper—get in, do your thing, get out—but plans and reality never aligned.

Reality was always much uglier, and it was always much messier.

The only good thing about the chaos was that authorities wouldn't be looking only for James. At least half the prisoners in the yard had escaped through the fence, which meant La Paz police force would be spread thin. Even though most of them were on foot—some had probably stolen cars from employees or visitors—many would reach La Paz. There'd be break-ins, clothes missing from lines as escapees tried to get out of their jumpsuits, and random assaults. There'd be robberies, and as night fell, burglaries. None of this was good for the people of La Paz, but it was—in a way—good for James.

It was good for everybody in the car.

Even after the others pushed their way out of the Toyota, stepping onto the Hotel Amigo parking lot, James sat in the empty car and stared straight ahead through the dirty windshield and thought about what had happened. Very recently he'd been in jail, sure he was going to die. But now he was both alive and free.

He pushed out into the sunlight.

Coop said, "You okay?"

James nodded and they made their way into the hotel.

■ James and Pilar lay on the bed in her room. They were on their sides, facing one another. James was looking into her eyes, stroking her arm, thinking about the fact that when he woke up this morning, he was pretty sure he'd never see her again. He leaned forward and kissed her mouth. Ran his fingers through her hair.

"I missed you."

"I missed you too," Pilar said. But then she pulled away, rolled onto her back, and looked up at the ceiling. She exhaled a heavy sigh.

"What's wrong?"

For a long moment, she only stared at nothing, her mind seeming far away, but finally said, "I have to tell you something."

"What is it?" His head was suddenly spinning with possibilities. She had to tell him something, but she also didn't *want* to tell him. It made his stomach feel tight.

She glanced toward him, but quickly broke eye contact.

"You can just tell me."

"I—I almost had sex with someone else."

"You what?"

"You'd broken up with me. I was angry and hurt and I—"

"Pilar."

She turned to look at him. Tears stood out in her eyes. He didn't think the emotion she was feeling had as much to do with her admission—or the guilt she felt about it—as it had to do with what they'd just gone through. She wasn't a soldier or a Marine, she was a civilian, and only an hour ago she'd helped to break him out of jail, and shot someone in the process.

"What?" she said.

"Whatever you did or didn't do isn't important. I don't wanna hear about it. I don't want details. It makes me sick to my stomach to think about you with another man. But whatever happened is as much my fault as yours. I broke up with you and left for Mexico. You didn't know where I was or what I was doing. I'm sorry for the way I reacted to my sister's death. I'm sorry for the way I made you feel. *You* have nothing to be sorry for." He stopped talking a moment, swallowed. "Now let's never mention it again."

"Okay," she said. She rolled back toward him. She leaned in and kissed his mouth. "I love you, James Murphy."

"I love *you*, Pilar."

■ Later, as they lay in bed with their fingers interlaced between them, James stared at the ceiling and thought about his sister. He was out of jail now—he was free—but the charges against him still stood, and now he'd broken out of jail, which would only add time to his eventual sentence. When he was done with Rocha, he had to make a decision. Either he'd flee to a country that didn't have an extradition treaty with Mexico or turn himself in. With Rocha dead, he wouldn't be in danger of being murdered in prison, he wouldn't be in more danger than everybody else, but first he had to take care of business. It was why he'd come to Mexico in the first place, and he was a man who finished what he started. Rocha needed to pay for what he'd done to Layla, needed to be prevented from doing the same to anyone else.

"What are you thinking?" Pilar said.

"What time is it?"

Pilar looked at the clock on her nightstand. "Two thirty."

James sat up and ran his fingers through his hair. His body felt bruised and tired from his fight in the yard and he was tempted to fall asleep beside Pilar—a large part of him wanted to do just that: fall asleep beside the woman he loved and forget about everything else—but now that he was out of jail, there was something in him that demanded action.

"What are you doing?"

James got to his feet, picked up his clothes, and began slipping back into them. "I'm gonna borrow Coop's car and drive to Rocha's estate."

"And do what?"

"Nothing. Not tonight."

"Then what's the point?"

"I don't know," James said. "It's just something I need to do."

"You shouldn't be out in public. If the police see you—"

"The police will be occupied with escaped prisoners who are actually committing crimes. I'm just gonna drive by the estate."

"I just got you back, James," Pilar said. "I don't want you to go out that door. I—I don't want you to go after Rocha."

James sat on the bed, leaned over, and kissed her. Stroked her neck. He said, "I have to."

"You could get yourself killed."

"I can't walk away when I know the man responsible for Layla's death is breathing the same air as me."

"It was an overdose."

"I don't believe that. I've had time to think about it and I don't believe that anymore."

"Maybe you don't believe it because you need to justify what you plan to do."

"I don't need justification."

"Why would he kill her?"

"I don't know, but I do know that four days before she turned up dead in El Paso, she was here in La Paz and she didn't sound like she had any intention of leaving. I talked to her on the phone, Pilar, and I knew her better than anybody else in the world. Something happened after we last talked, and maybe I don't know what, but I do know that Rocha is responsible. He killed my sister, he stole her life, and I'm gonna take his as payment."

"I can't talk you out of this, can I?"

"No."

"I'll never forgive you if you get yourself killed."

"I won't."

He walked to the door and stepped through it.

39

Gael Morales and Danielle Preston stepped out through the front door, Alejandro Rocha walking behind them with a gun in his hand. Gael hadn't said a word to Danielle, nor she to him, since this had begun, but they'd shared a few knowing looks, and that was enough to tell Gael that she'd said what she had to save her own ass, just like he'd done. They were in a bad situation, two people who should be working together forced by circumstance to bury the other. But because the situation was what it was, Gael was determined to bury her. He wasn't going to die today.

They walked down the steps and across the cobblestone drive-way to the garage.

"You're driving, Gael," Rocha said, throwing him the key to the BMW. "Danielle, you get into the front passenger seat."

They all got into the car, Rocha slipping into the back, keeping his gun at the ready. Gael started the engine, slid the transmission into reverse, and backed out of the garage. He shoved it into drive and they began to roll toward the estate's wrought-iron gate.

Rocha hadn't explained what he was going to do but Gael didn't need an explanation. He knew what came next. He knew what the two possibilities were, anyway. Rocha would have him drive out to the desert and he would either have Gael kill Danielle in order to prove he wasn't a DEA agent or he would simply put a bullet in both their heads and be done with it.

If Gael were in Rocha's position, he thought he'd do the latter. It made sense. Kill both potential sources of trouble and wash your hands of the entire situation. When things got complicated, it was almost always best to simplify them in the most efficient way possible. It was how one survived. The more parts a machine had, the greater the chances it would break down at some point. If you could cut out parts and ensure it still worked, you should.

They reached the gate and it squeaked open. Gael stopped the car at the end of the driveway and said, "What do you want me to do?"

"Turn left."

Gael pulled the car out into the street.

■ James was driving the Toyota while Coop sat in the passenger seat, smoking a cigarette, looking out the window. James glanced at him, but the man said nothing, only sat there and thought his thoughts.

"I should thank you," James said. "I'd probably be dead if it wasn't for you."

"You'd have done the same for me."

James had asked if he could borrow the Toyota, but Coop insisted on coming along. He'd also insisted that they both be armed, so they each had a pistol tucked into the front of their pants, James a Ruger LCP 380 and Coop a Kahr CW9. He didn't expect that either of them would use their weapons, but considering their situation, he supposed it was best to be prepared.

He was driving east on Calle Herboso, about to roll through a green light at El Dorado, when a man in a gray jumpsuit ran in front of the car. James slammed on the brakes, screeching to a stop. The man ran up to the driver's-side door, yanked it open with his left hand while he held a knife gripped in his right, and told him to get the fuck out of the car.

James aimed his pistol at the man's face and said, "You're trying to jack the wrong vehicle, pal."

Guy looked from his face to the pistol in his hand, turned, and ran.

James pulled shut the car door and continued on.

Five minutes and three turns of the steering wheel later, James made a left onto Avenida la Armonia, the street on which Rocha lived, his estate about half a mile up on the right.

"What's your plan exactly?" Coop said.

"No plan. I just wanna see it."

Coop nodded.

James looked back to the street ahead. A white BMW pulled out of the wrought-iron gate that blocked the entrance to Rocha's estate. It made a left out of the driveway and rolled toward them. James slowed down and squinted through the glass, trying to see the faces of the people in the approaching car. They were too far, so he braked completely, not giving a shit that he was in the middle of the street, blocking the lane, and picked up the binoculars from the center console. He put them to his eyes, adjusted the focus, and looked. A man and a woman he didn't recognize in the front seats, but sitting in the backseat, holding a gun, was someone he did recognize. Rocha was in that car.

"Motherfucker."

"What is it?"

James glanced at him. "Buckle up."

"What are you gonna do?"

James moved his foot from the brake pedal to the gas, forcing it to the floorboard. "Buckle the fuck up, Coop."

Coop strapped the belt over his shoulder, clipped it.

James felt his stomach knot with anticipation. All he felt now was the determination to get to this man right now. He didn't think of consequences. He didn't think of anything that might come after this moment. He had laid eyes on the man who had killed his sister, and for the first time, he was in a position to do something about it.

The car screamed down the faded asphalt, the distance between the two vehicles cut in half—and then cut in half again.

Once the cars were close enough that a collision would be unavoidable, James yanked the car left, screeching into the oncoming lane, and pulled his hands from the wheel so his arms wouldn't be broken.

Less than a second later came the crash. It thundered through the vehicle. The airbags deployed. Glass shattered. James was flung forward, slammed against his seat belt, and then jerked back into his seat. Smoke rose from the hood.

He looked right and saw Coop sitting there dazed. "You all right?"

Coop nodded.

"Then let's go." He pushed open the driver's-side door and shoved out of the car. He walked around to the back of the BMW, pulled open the door, and yanked Rocha from the car, throwing him to the street before the man had even recovered from the shock of the accident.

Rocha, sitting on the street, looked up at him. Blood dripped from his nose, covered the lower half of his face. James aimed the gun. Rocha's eyes were bright with fear.

"You killed my sister. Now you're gonna pay for it."

"Diego Blanco killed your sister."

These words made James hesitate—not because he questioned what he intended to do but because they were a confirmation that Layla had been murdered—and for a moment, he stood there and absorbed what they meant.

"Why?"

"She was gonna talk to the DEA."

"You fucking coward," James said. He put the barrel of the gun against Rocha's forehead. "I don't care who did the job, it was done because *you* ordered it. Diego Blanco was just your weapon of choice."

"I didn't order it. Mulligan Shoibli ordered it."

"Fucking liar," James said.

"I swear to God."

"James." At the sound of Coop's voice, James glanced over his shoulder. "What do you want me to do?"

"Get the driver out of the car."

"And the woman?"

"Leave her."

Coop nodded, pulled his pistol from his belt, and walked to the BMW.

James turned his attention back to Rocha. "Who the fuck is Mulligan Shoibli?"

"I don't know—I don't know his real name—but he ordered her killed. I know you think I am, but I'm not in charge of this organization."

"I don't believe you."

"I can prove it."

"Get to proving it then. You've got thirty seconds so you better talk fast."

"I can do it here, but I can also get you to him."

James considered this. He knew there was a chance—maybe a good chance—Rocha was saying whatever he could to save his own ass. But even the possibility that he might kill the wrong man bothered him. It wasn't that Rocha didn't deserve to die—even if he was telling the truth, he did—it was that James wanted the man at the top to pay for what had been done to his sister. Everybody else down the line was a tool, but the man who ordered her dead was the reason it had happened. His *decision* made it happen, which meant he was responsible for everything that followed.

But, be that as it may, this couldn't be handled in the street. The risks were too great.

James took a step but kept his pistol aimed. "Stand up."

Rocha got to his feet.

■ Gael sat behind the wheel of the BMW, dazed, and watched as a tall man with a pistol walked to the side of the car, yanked open the door, and pulled Rocha out into the street. He watched as a black man got out of the passenger side of the car that had run into the BMW. Watched as that man pulled a pistol from his belt and walked toward him. The man pulled open the driver's-side door of the BMW and looked down at him. "Let's go."

"You don't understand what—" Gael began.

"Explain it to me later. Let's go."

Gael stepped out of the vehicle. He looked at the man currently aiming a pistol at his face. This guy wasn't part of a rival cartel. He wasn't a career criminal at all. Gael had encountered enough of them that he knew when he was dealing with one.

"Turn around."

Gael did as he was told and the guy frisked him.

"Okay, go stand with your buddy."

"He's not my buddy."

"Go stand with your fucking pal then. I don't give a shit what you call him."

"You don't understand," he said again.

"I don't *need* to understand," the guy said. "I need you to fucking *listen*."

"Okay."

■ James watched the driver walk over and stand next to Rocha. Watched Rocha give the man an untrusting look. "Did you have anything to do with this?"

"I don't even know what this is," the driver said.

"Shut the fuck up, both of you," James said. "Coop, can you open the trunk of our car? Transfer the guns to the backseat."

"Got it," Coop said.

James heard his footsteps fading, heard the sound of the trunk unlatching. The hinges creaking as it swung open. The duffel of rifles and pistols being pulled from the trunk and being tossed into the backseat. To Rocha and the other man he said, "I think you both see where this is going. Let's get this done."

Both men started walking toward the Toyota, and while they did,

James kept his gun trained, ready to squeeze the trigger if necessary. He followed the men to the back of the Toyota and the open trunk.

Rocha looked from the trunk to James and James motioned with his pistol that Rocha should climb in. After a moment's hesitation, he did.

"You too," James said to the driver.

"Can you listen to me for a second?"

"I'll listen to you for ten."

"I know it looks like I work for Rocha," he said, "but my name is Gael Castillo Jimenez and I'm an undercover DEA agent. Or I *was* an undercover DEA agent. Rocha found out today and he was making me drive to the desert so he could kill me—kill me and the woman in the car, who'd agreed to talk to me. If you put me in that trunk with him, one of us is gonna be dead when we get wherever we're going. I understand if you don't believe me. I understand if you don't trust me. Keep the gun on me if you want, but let me ride in front—or make me drive. I won't try anything."

James thought about this for a moment—thought about the look Rocha had given the man—and decided, if not to actually trust the guy, then to operate as though he did for the time being.

"Fine," he said. "Close the trunk."

Gael slammed the trunk lid down on Rocha.

"Coop, give him the key."

Coop tossed the Toyota's key to Gael.

"My friend and I are gonna ride in back. You'll drive."

"That's fine."

■ Gael slid in behind the wheel of the Toyota Corolla while the two men who'd abducted Rocha got into the backseat. He was in almost exactly the same situation he'd been in ten minutes ago, except these people didn't want him dead. He might have been able to manipulate the situation with Rocha, he thought he would have been able to, but this eliminated that need.

"Start the car."

Gael tore away the airbag, tossing it to the passenger floorboard, and stuck the key into the ignition, turning the key. The engine whined, turned over slowly, but for what felt like a long time refused to spark. Finally, all at once, it did. Gael had been pumping the gas, so once it started, it roared.

"Do you know how to get to Hotel Amigo?"

"I do."

"Then get us there."

"No," Coop said. "Too many people. There's an empty building on the west side of Hidalgo, just north of El Tule."

"The old church," Gael said.

"Okay," James said. "We'll go there."

Gael put the car into gear and backed it away from the accident. Something at the front of the car dragged against the road, but he wasn't worried about it. He wasn't worried about anything.

He finally knew how to bring this case to an end.

He shoved the transmission into drive, and rolled around the wreckage. Something under the hood thumped, and smoke rose from the grille, but he thought the car would make it. When he reached Calle de Oro, he made a left. The old church was only three miles away.

40

James kept the pistol aimed at Gael as the man pulled the Toyota to a stop behind the old church, a wood-sided building covered in graffiti, its windows boarded up with plywood, its asphalt shingle roof collapsing inward.

James glanced at Coop. "How'd you know this place was here?"

"Saw it when I drove into town."

James nodded, and said, "Keep an eye on this guy."

Coop raised his weapon and trained it on the man behind the wheel. As soon as he did, James pushed out of the car. The lot on which the church sat was littered with trash—rusting Coke cans, convenience store cups, a few mismatched hubcaps, several dirty diapers. A few desert shrubs erupted from cracks in the earth.

James walked to the church and paced its perimeter. The windows and both doors, front and back, had been boarded up at one point, but someone had already ripped the plywood off the back entrance. James stepped inside.

It was dark and smelled of wood rot. Sunlight slanted in through the collapsing roof, dust motes drifting through an array of beams.

Several of the pews had been knocked over. Bibles and hymnals lay open on the floor like dead birds with their wings spread. A breeze blew in through the open back door and pages flapped. The sound of their ruffling vibrated through the air. Several used condoms littered the floor like popped balloons after the party was finished. Graffiti had been spray painted across the walls.

Two doors interrupted the otherwise solid back wall. James walked to the one nearest and pushed it open to find an office with a desk, a chair, and a shelf of books, a lamp on the desk with a rotting paper shade, and an overhead fan with sagging fiberboard blades.

He walked to the next door and pushed that one open to find what looked like the room for Sunday school. A low table and small plastic chairs filled the center of the room. There were children's books stacked on a shelf in the back of the room. Games littered the floor.

A few bats clung to the ceiling.

The place was perfect.

■ Coop was sitting in the back of the car, thinking about what was happening here, when he decided he needed to call the others. They needed to get down here, find perches from which they could shoot, and be ready in case everything went sideways, as he had a feeling everything would. He had a bad feeling about this. It knotted his stomach and made his muscles tense.

"Give me the car key," he said to the man behind the wheel— Gael Castillo Jimenez—while keeping his pistol trained on him. Ignoring the thumping from the trunk, the calls for release. The man behind the wheel pulled the key from the ignition and handed it back to him.

"Now just sit here."

Coop pushed out of the car and into the hot day, sweat immediately beading on his face and body. He kept the pistol aimed at Gael while, with his other hand, he pulled his cell phone from his pocket. He thumbed through his contacts, dialed Normal. The phone rang four full times, and he started to think Normal wouldn't pick up, when the fifth ring was cut off.

"Coop."

"Normal, I need you and Bogart to get down here."

"Where's here?"

"The old church on Hidalgo and El Tule."

"What about Pilar?"

"Don't tell her anything. Just get down here."

"What's going on? I thought you guys were going for a drive."

"Things change. I'll explain when you get here."

"Okay, we're on our way."

The line went dead. Coop put the phone back into his pocket.

He glanced from the car and the man inside it to the church and saw James walking back toward him, his shirt damp with sweat.

"Who were you just talking to?"

"Normal."

"What's up?"

"I told him to come down here—he and Bogart might be useful."

"What are you thinking?"

"I'm thinking this is a tense situation and we don't know what's gonna happen. I want them perched on buildings with a view of the church in case anything goes bad. Better to have them here and ready, even if we don't end up needing them, than to find ourselves in trouble with no way out. We've got the guns in the car."

James nodded. "Okay. Let's get these fuckers into the church."

■ James and Coop led Rocha and Gael into the church at gunpoint. In the main room, he told Coop to keep Gael there while he interrogated Rocha. He then led Rocha into the back office and tied him to the desk chair using the electrical cords from the lamps.

"Tell me about Mulligan Shoibli."

Rocha looked up at him from the chair, his wrists bound to its arms, his legs pulled back under the chair and tied to its hydraulic center post. His hair hung down in his face, damp and sweaty. He looked pathetic and James almost allowed himself to feel sorry for the motherfucker. But he pushed that feeling aside. This man was either responsible for ordering Layla's death or was part of the chain of command that had gotten her killed. Either way, Layla was dead in part or fully because of the man's actions. So fuck him straight to hell.

"You're supposed to be dead," Rocha said.

"I told you I wasn't going to die today."

"The day isn't over."

"Tell me about Mulligan Shoibli."

"I don't know much about him. He works for the DEA. It's how I've been able to stay in business. He keeps up to date on what's going on with the investigation and he tells me what I need to do. I stay visible as the front of the operation in order to keep him in shadows. Because I do this, because I take all the risks, I get forty percent of the take, which is more than enough to keep me in the lifestyle I want."

"How do you contact him?"

"He contacts me."

"How?"

"He calls me. Every week we get new cell phones in order to talk to one another. Prepaid burners. Either Diego Blanco or Gael Morales—Gael Castillo Jimenez, the motherfucker—pick up a new phone from a locker at a bus station in Juarez every week and bring it to me. Only Mulligan Shoibli has the number. If it rings, it's him. Different number every time."

"Have you ever met in person?"

"No."

"Why did he want Layla dead?"

"I already told you, she was gonna talk to the DEA."

"You said he *works* for the DEA."

"He does—which is how he's been able to kill witnesses before they can testify. You have to understand, he can get information, he can manipulate information, but he also has to maintain his anonymity. He can't do anything overtly suspicious."

"Why are you telling me all this?"

"I'm a pragmatic man, Mr. Murphy. I have no loyalty to Mulligan Shoibli. The simple truth is that I'd rather you kill him than me. I'm more than willing to help make that happen, provided I can walk away from this."

"Do you have the cell phone on you now?"

"In my coat pocket."

James reached into the pocket and removed the prepaid cell phone. He slipped it into the pocket of his cutoff sweatpants.

■ James opened the office door and looked out at the main room. Coop and Gael were sitting on opposite ends of the same pew, Coop with his pistol trained on the son of a bitch. James called to him. Coop got to his feet and walked over.

"What's up?"

"Watch Rocha while I talk to Jimenez."

Coop nodded and stepped past him, heading into the office where Rocha was tied to the chair. James pulled the door shut and made his way to the pew on which Gael was sitting. James settled in at the opposite end. He kept his pistol in hand, resting it casually on his thigh, but he made certain it was aimed at the man to whom he was speaking. Gael Castillo Jimenez might well be DEA—it seemed likely he was—but James was in a situation where he could trust nobody but his closest friends.

"Let's talk."

"Okay," Gael said.

"You tell me you're DEA."

"I am. I've been undercover with the Rocha cartel for six months."

"Can you prove it?"

Gael was silent for a long moment as he thought over the situation. His eyes looked troubled. Finally he said, "Fuck it—yeah. Let me call my stateside man in El Paso and he can confirm it."

"You have your phone?"

"In my pocket."

"Go ahead and grab it—but no sudden moves."

Gael reached into his Levi's and pulled out a cell phone. He slid his thumb across its smooth surface, hit the phone button, hit the keypad button, and dialed a number from memory.

He put the phone to his ear.

"No," James said. "Put it on speaker."

Gael nodded, hit the speaker button.

They waited while it rang.

◾ George Rankin was at his desk watching footage from the security camera downstairs when he felt the phone in his pocket vibrate. He'd been sitting there staring at the screen as almost nothing happened for more than three hours, so he was glad for the interruption. The man at the desk in front of the holding cells wasn't a DEA agent but a civilian guard. His job mostly involved reading comic books. For hours George had watched as he flipped through a *Watchmen* omnibus, and then half of the first volume of Art Spiegelman's *Maus* (the only comic George had read since he was a teenager), only looking up when a DEA agent emerged from the elevator, signed in, and headed back. He reached into his pocket, pulled out his phone, and saw a number he didn't recognize.

"Hello?"

"George. You're on speaker phone."

He recognized the voice but knew better than to identify him by name when he didn't know the circumstances under which he was calling. "Where are you?"

"I'm in La Paz."

"What's going on?"

"I'm with somebody. I need you to tell him my name."

George's heart was suddenly pounding in his chest. His mouth dry, tongue like a cactus paddle. He had no idea what was going on, but whatever it was, it couldn't be good.

"Gael Morales," George said.

"No—I want you to tell him my real name. Tell him who I am. It's fine."

George didn't know what to do. He couldn't imagine a scenario in which Gael would need George to corroborate his actual identity while working undercover. But he had to trust that the man knew what he was doing. Gael would have been able to avoid this call if he'd felt he needed to, which meant, whatever the situation was, it was one Gael had under control.

"George?"

"Your name is Gael Castillo Jimenez. You're an undercover special agent for the Drug Enforcement Administration, Intelligence Division. You've been investigating the Rocha cartel for the last six months. My name is George Rankin, I'm currently sitting in my office in the DEA building on Fort Bliss, in El Paso, Texas, and I'm your stateside contact on this case. If necessary, I can call from my office phone so the DEA caller identification comes up on your cell phone screen. Is that all the information you need conveyed?"

George glanced toward his computer screen and saw Lou Billingham, the deputy chief of intelligence, walk by the desk without signing in, watched him disappear into the corridor. He paused the video. He asked himself if Lou Billingham might be behind all this. It was possible. The man had access to same information George himself did. He could have intentionally used a social security number and other information that would circumstantially implicate Horace Ellison. On the other hand, Ellison could have let all of this information reach George so that—

A new voice, the mouth closer to the speaker: "George Rankin, my name is James Murphy. We're talking privately now, and I have to tell you, I think we've got ourselves a helluva situation."

"You're in jail."

"You've heard of me then."

"I have—and you're in jail."

"I *was* in jail."

George didn't say anything for a moment.

"George?"

"What's the situation, Mr. Murphy?"

"The situation is this. I have Alejandro Rocha tied to a chair in an old church in La Paz. I'd planned on killing him, but if I had, we wouldn't be talking now. The reason I didn't is because he mentioned a man named Mulligan Shoibli. Is that someone you've heard of?"

"I'm coming down there, don't do anything stupid."

George hung up his cell phone, got to his feet, and slipped it into his pocket.

◼ James handed Gael his cell phone. He looked at the man sitting across from him. He was a DEA agent like he'd said—or else he'd planned ahead for a scenario like this. If it was the latter, the man he'd spoken to might be on his way down here to rescue Rocha or . . .

Or any number of things. He didn't know what.

But he did know this: he was glad Bogart and Normal were on their way too.

"Is it all right if I step out and grab a cigarette?" Gael asked.

"No," James said. "Wait until my friends get here so they can keep an eye on you, then I don't care."

Gael nodded.

James had Rocha tied to a chair. He was holding a probable DEA agent at gunpoint. A second DEA agent was on his way down here. Part of him wanted to walk back to the office, put the barrel of his gun against Rocha's forehead, pull the trigger, and be done with it. He'd broken out of jail. He was wanted for crimes that would get him locked away for thirty years—his life was ruined. Killing the son of a bitch wouldn't do much to make it worse, even with a DEA agent as a witness.

But there was that niggling fear that Rocha was telling the truth about Mulligan Shoibli. If James walked to the back office and put a bullet in Rocha's head, he might be killing the only man who could get him to the person who'd ordered Layla's death.

Bogart and Normal pushed through the back door.

"What the fuck is going on now?" Normal said.

41

George decided he needed to have Horace Ellison and Lou Bill-ingham come down to La Paz with him. One of them was Mulligan Shoibli, and since James Murphy had Alejandro Rocha tied to a chair, tied to a chair and talking, he thought they might be able to figure out which one of them it was. The other could offer support if things got ugly—*when* things got ugly.

He walked to Horace Ellison's office first, and knocked on the door.

"What is it?"

◼ They were in the parking lot when Lou Billingham said, "I'll catch up with you guys in a minute. I need to call my wife, let her know I'll be late."

"Make it quick," Ellison said.

"I will."

George and Ellison continued to the car, George getting in behind the wheel and Ellison slipping into the shotgun seat.

* * *

◘ James was sitting alone in the main room of the church. Normal and Bogart had found perches from which to shoot. Bogart on the roof of the primary school just across Durango. Normal on the roof of El Niño's Pizza just across Hidalgo. Both of them had a good view of the church's back door. Gael was standing outside smoking a cigarette. Coop was in the office keeping an eye on Rocha.

James didn't like the situation he was in at all.

Based on George Rankin's reaction when he mentioned Shoibli, the man had heard of him, and he might be able to help figure out just who the son of a bitch was, but if he did, he'd also arrest the fucker, which would put him out of James's reach. He didn't want the son of a bitch in prison. He wanted him dead.

One of the cell phones in James's pocket began to ring. He pulled it out. It was Rocha's burner, which meant it was Mulligan Shoibli calling.

James's heart thudded in his chest. The phone in his hand was ringing, and if Rocha had been telling the truth, the man responsible for Layla's death was on the other end of the line. James exhaled a long, trembling sigh, and then thumbed the green button.

He put the phone to his ear and said, "Hello?"

But the person on the other end of the line didn't say anything.

"Answer me, motherfucker."

The call ended.

James pulled the phone away from his ear. He stared at it for a long moment and thought about returning the call, but he knew Mulligan Shoibli wouldn't pick up, so he slipped the phone back into his pocket. He'd wait until George Rankin got here. It was the only thing *to* do. He only hoped that, if they figured this thing out, he had the chance to kill the motherfucker before he was put back into prison himself—or had to run to avoid prison.

◘ George sat behind the wheel and watched as, across the parking lot, Lou Billingham slid his cell phone back into his pocket and made his way to the car. He slipped into the backseat, apologized, and fasted his seat belt.

George started the car and backed out of the parking spot.

While he drove toward La Paz, he thought more about the evidence he had. It was clear to him that Mulligan Shoibli was in this car, but he still didn't know for sure whether Billingham or Ellison was the man behind all of this.

The evidence against Ellison was circumstantial. The social security number Shoibli had used belonged to a man Ellison had spent months investigating. The address Shoibli had used was a bar in Chicago only a quarter mile from the DEA offices out of which Ellison had worked for five years before being transferred to El Paso.

But though these facts might seem to implicate Ellison, they almost did the opposite in George's mind. A man running a drug cartel from the shadows would be careful to ensure there was no paper trial connecting him to his false identity, and even if he'd created that identity thinking no one would seriously investigate it, once Ellison knew it was being investigated, he could have worked to keep this information out of George's hands.

Of course, there was also the question of arrogance. A man who'd been getting away with what Shoibli had been getting away with for years might start to believe he was smarter than everybody else, and a man who thought he was smarter than everybody else often made stupid mistakes, sure that nobody would see through his cleverness.

On the other hand, Lou Billingham had visited the holding cells without signing in at the front desk. The time stamp on the footage indicated that he'd made this visit only half an hour before Francis Waters hanged himself. The question was what Lou Billingham had said to the man during their conversation.

It was entirely possible that, knowing it might eventually come out that a DEA man was behind this cartel, Billingham had created Mulligan Shoibli in order to point at Ellison. The evidence was entirely circumstantial, but a grand jury might also find it compelling.

It made sense in a way. Not only would Ellison take the fall for another man's crimes, but Billingham would then move up to become chief of intelligence, putting him in an even better position to control things in Mexico.

They reached the border about a half hour before sunset, but George had a feeling the day was only getting started.

42

James heard a car rumble to a stop outside. He drew his pistol and aimed it at the back door. Three men in suits stepped in with their hands raised. One of them, the youngest of the three, stepped forward.

"James Murphy," he said.

"George Rankin—who are the two men with you?"

Gael, who'd been sitting on the pew across from James, got to his feet and said, "Horace Ellison, chief of intelligence, and Lou Billingham, deputy chief of intelligence." He walked over to the men. James let him. He shook hands with George and patted him on the shoulder. "It's good to see you. We've got a fucking mess on our hands."

"I think that's a bit of an understatement."

Gael shook hands with Horace Ellison and Lou Billingham, patting both of them on the shoulder as well. He said, "The man with the gun is James Murphy. Rocha killed his sister. He's not gonna do anything stupid. He's just a man grieving a loss. We can clear up the situation with him. He treated me well, despite the stressful circumstances, so I don't want anything to go bad with him. Rocha's in an office in back. One of Mr. Murphy's friends is keeping an eye on him. Two more of Mr. Murphy's friends are watching the church from nearby. They're armed. My goal, plain and simple, is to get everybody out of here alive, and I think we can do it."

"I think the situation is more complicated than you know," George said. "Have you heard of a man called Mulligan Shoibli?"

Gael shook his head. "No."

"I think we need to bring Rocha out here."

James said, "That's a good idea."

He walked to the back office and knocked on the door. Coop opened it, looked out into the room and said, "Who the fuck are these people?"

"DEA."

"Jesus."

"Can you bring Rocha out here?"

Coop nodded, walked to the chair Rocha was sitting in, and rolled it out into the church's main room. Rocha sat in the chair, saying nothing, looking from one face to another. Finally he smiled at James and said, "I guess you're not gonna be able to kill me now, no matter what else happens. Let me state too, that I'm willing to cooperate with law enforcement in any way as long as you keep me alive. If James Murphy kills me, you'll never get to Mulligan Shoibli."

"Shut the fuck up, Rocha," George said, his voice angry, and because of those words James decided he liked the guy.

"What the hell are we doing here?" Ellison said.

"We're going to clear up this situation," George said. "Somebody in this room is Mulligan Shoibli, I'm sure of it, and I'm gonna find out who."

"What do you mean someone in this room?" Ellison said. "You're treating me like a fucking suspect, Rankin? After what I did to get you out of that mess with Diego Blanco?"

"What mess with Diego Blanco?" Rocha said.

"Shut the fuck up," George said to Rocha. To Horace Ellison he said, "You *are* a suspect, sir. You and Billingham both. Somebody at the El Paso office is Mulligan Shoibli and I have evidence that implicates both of you."

"I've spent my whole career fighting scumbags like this guy," Ellison said, nodding at Rocha, "and you're gonna bring me down here and accuse me of—"

"I'm not accusing anybody of anything, sir," George said. "I'm just following the evidence and it pointed at—"

James said, "How do you spell Shoibli?"

George told him and said, "Why does that matter?"

James swung his pistol around and aimed it at Lou Billingham. He thumbed off the safety. As he did this, Horace and George both instinctively drew their own weapons and aimed them at James. Coop, seeing this, drew his and aimed it at Horace.

Nobody moved.

"Put down your weapon, Mr. Murphy," Horace Ellison said.

"Keep your hands out of your pockets," James said to Billingham, ignoring Horace's words. He then reached into his own pocket.

"Keep your hand where I can see it," George said.

"What am I gonna do, George, pull another gun?"

Coop said, "Let's all just lower our weapons and talk this through. Nothing has to get violent here."

James pulled Rocha's burner from his pocket.

"What are you doing, Mr. Murphy?" George said.

"Mulligan Shoibli is an anagram for Lou Billingham." He held up the cell phone. "This is Rocha's. The only person who might call it is Mulligan Shoibli. It rang about an hour ago and I picked up, but nobody spoke. I'm gonna return the call now."

"You can't honestly think—" Lou Billingham began.

"Shut up," James said. He pushed the button.

Seconds passed.

Guns remained raised. The room was silent but tense.

Then—after what felt like an eternity—something in Lou Billingham's pocket began to ring.

"You motherfucker," James said, stepping toward him, ready to

273

fire a round into his forehead, consequences be damned. But George stepped in front of him, stepped in front of the barrel, aiming his own weapon.

"Don't do this, Mr. Murphy," George said. "I know you want revenge. I know you want the man who killed your sister to pay for what he did, but it can't happen like this. We'll arrest him. He'll be tried. He'll spend the rest of his life in prison, and I can almost guarantee you this, it won't be a very long life."

While George was standing between James and his target, Lou Billingham ran out the back door.

43

James, ignoring the gun in Rankin's hands, shoved him aside and sprinted out the door after Billingham. The man ran to a black sedan and was pulling open the driver's-side door when James heard a gunshot from either Bogart or Normal. The door handle exploded and Billingham yanked his hand back. James dove, tackled him, and sitting on his chest, put the barrel of his pistol into the man's mouth.

"You motherfucker," James said, "you're gonna pay for—"

But Rankin tackled him, knocking him off Billingham, and held his wrists to the ground. "Don't do it, James—not here and not like this."

"Get the fuck off of me, motherfucker."

But Rankin leaned in close and said, "You kill him here, you're going to prison. I know the charges against you in La Paz are bogus—the drug charges anyway—and the DEA knows that La Paz cops are dirty. We can get the charges dropped by threatening a conspiracy indictment against them—every one of them by name. An entire Mexican police force charged with conspiracy in an international drug trafficking case—the federal government will lean on them hard to leave you alone. But if you kill Billingham, your life is over. He's a cop. I don't care how sympathetic your reasons are for doing what you want to do, killing a cop—even a dirty motherfucker like Billingham—will get you locked away for the rest of your life. He's gonna pay, I promise you that. But don't throw *your* fucking life away."

James exhaled a long sigh.

He said, "I'm okay. Get off me."

"You sure?"

"Get the fuck off me."

Rankin got to his feet and held out a hand. James grabbed it and allowed the man to pull him up.

While all this was going on, Horace and Gael handcuffed Billingham and put him into the back of the black sedan. James looked at him through the glass and felt nothing.

He glanced toward Rankin. "What now?"

"We have Alejandro Rocha in our custody. He's a pragmatic man. He'll testify to get a reduced sentence. We have Gael's testimony, and information he's given us about how the organization is run. We'll be able to put a case together—a good case. You need to go home and live your life. I'll make sure the man who killed your sister pays. It won't be with a bullet to the head. It'll be through the court system. But you remember, your sister's body was found in El Paso, and Texas still has the death penalty."

44

The charges against James in Mexico were dropped just like George Rankin had said they'd be. He and the others headed back to El Paso. Headed back to Fort Bliss. James had been on leave because of his sister's funeral—and even if he hadn't been, his false arrest meant he had a legitimate reason for being absent—but the others were expecting to be court-martialed. Instead, they were reprimanded strongly and told they'd been irresponsible and if they missed a single shift from now until their discharge, they *would* be court-martialed—and they'd also get a foot right up the ass.

Though his absence wasn't at issue, James was still in serious trouble, and faced court-martial for stealing a weapon from base. His trial lasted three hours and he was sentenced to a month in the brig. It would have been six months, but people were sympathetic to his reasons for doing what he did. He served his time patiently.

Once out of the brig and back at work on Fort Bliss, awaiting his next deployment, James kept up with the news coming out of La Paz, and with Pilar sitting beside him on their couch, learned about Rocha giving up people in Chicago, El Paso, Los Angeles, and New

York. The DEA seized his bank accounts, recovering two million dollars, and during a search of his home, also found four million dollars in cash and his well-kept records—five years of careful book-keeping.

His records indicated that over nine million dollars had been provided to Mulligan Shoibli, either in the form of wire transfers or cash drops, but the only account with any money in it was the one they'd already had record of, and it only held half a million dollars. The other accounts, they discovered, had already been emptied.

James waited for news about Lou Billingham to surface, but it never did. The DEA was apparently keeping that aspect of the case under wraps for as long as they could.

He wasn't all that surprised.

■ Two weeks after his son was born, Gael Castillo Jimenez knocked on Horace Ellison's office door. He sat down in an uncomfortable chair and looked across the desk's tidy surface to the man on the other side. Ellison looked back with blank eyes, waiting.

The silence stretched for fifteen seconds. "Are we having a staring contest or did you come in here to talk to me about something?"

Gael exhaled a sigh. He said, "I can't do it anymore. I have to quit."

Ellison nodded. "I've been waiting for this. You have a family now. You have a son. You look at him and you think about your wife raising him alone because you've been killed on the job. It makes your chest feel tight. It makes your stomach ache. I've seen it happen to other men and was waiting for it to happen to you."

"I'll get my cases in order and I'll be available to whoever takes them over. I just can't do it anymore."

"Fine. Pain in my ass, but like I said, I've been waiting for this."

"Okay." Gael got to his feet and started for the door.

"What are you gonna do?"

"Excuse me?"

"For work—what's next for you?"

"I don't know. Sarah's gonna go back to work in three weeks. Thought I might be a stay-at-home dad for a while and figure it out."

"Good luck."

"Thank you, sir."

■ Four months later, James took a taxi to El Paso International Airport. He arrived at 10:30 for an 11:33 flight to Atlanta, where he had a connection. He didn't check any luggage. His carry-on bag held almost everything he'd need. He also carried with him a guitar in a hard case he'd bought at a pawnshop for fifty dollars. There was one item he couldn't take with him, but he'd mailed it to his destination hotel four days earlier, and when he arrived, the three separate packages should be waiting at the front desk for him. All he'd have to do then was assemble the pieces.

He sat at his gate and waited. He tried to read but found he couldn't concentrate. He waited until almost everyone else had boarded the plane, picked up his duffel bag and guitar, and walked to the counter. He handed his ticket over. The woman he handed it to scanned it and handed it back. She smiled and said, "Have a nice flight."

"I'm sure I will," he said.

He boarded the plane, one of the flight attendants taking his guitar and storing it for him, found his seat, stowed his luggage, and sat down.

45

James Murphy landed in Grand Cayman and took a taxi to a Comfort Suites hotel about a block away from a beach with water bluer than the sky. He'd never been to George Town before, never been to the Cayman Islands at all—he'd only traveled internationally while in the employ of the Marine Corps and they weren't exactly famous for sending folks to beautiful destinations—but he liked it immediately. He looked at the sea between the buildings as they drove. He almost wished he could spend more time here. But he had to be back on base by Monday, and anyway, when you visited a place with the sole purpose of killing a man, it was best not to linger once the job was done.

When the taxi arrived at the hotel, he paid the driver, and stepped out into the eighty-degree weather. The driver popped the trunk and pulled out his duffel bag and his guitar. James took them and walked into the lobby, made his way to the counter, and told the woman he had a reservation.

"Name?"

"James Murphy."

He checked in and the woman told him they'd received three packages for him earlier that day. He took the boxes and—overloaded with stuff—made his way to his first-floor hotel room. He set the boxes, his duffel bag, and the guitar on the bed and walked back to the door. He attached the chain lock.

Once the three boxes were open, he went about reassembling the rifle he'd broken down and shipped to himself. The Cayman Islands had very strict gun laws, and if he was caught with this rifle, he'd be facing a minimum of ten years in prison. But his chances of being caught now were minimal. His worry had been the mail—and the rifle had made it through.

He opened his guitar case. Inside the case was a cheap acoustic-electric guitar. Before leaving for the airport, he'd drilled holes into one of the pickups and slid bullets down into it, one under each string. He'd run it through the X-ray belt at the airport without incident, though a TSA agent had made him throw out his double-edged safety blades, so he wouldn't be shaving while in George Town. His stomach had been in a knot until he cleared security.

But once he did, it loosened up.

Now he was here. He knew which hotel his target was staying at, and he'd be watching for the next twenty-four hours. Or less if he got the chance to kill the motherfucker before his time ran out, and he hoped like hell he did.

He slid the six bullets from the guitar and pulled the guitar from its case. He loaded the rifle and shoved it into the case, stuffing pillows around it so the rifle wouldn't rattle. He closed and latched the case, grabbed it by the handle, and stepped out of his room.

He walked out to the street and thought about everything that happened at the old church in Mexico. He thought about the fact that when Gael Castillo Jimenez had shaken hands with Lou Billingham, he'd had the opportunity to slip Mulligan Shoibli's cell phone into his pocket. He thought about Alejandro Rocha telling him that Gael had been going to Juarez to pick up the burners. He thought about the fact that as an undercover DEA agent, he had more access to both worlds than anybody else. He thought about his months of watching the man since then—almost certain Gael Castillo Jimenez was Mulligan Shoibli but needing more proof before he could allow himself to squeeze his trigger.

Now—six months after everything that happened in Mexico— the man was in George Town, Grand Cayman, and James was certain he was here to clean up his financial affairs. His wife Sarah might believe they'd brought their four-month-old son here for a brief getaway, but James knew more of the story than she did.

It was unfortunate that in getting justice for Layla, James would be creating a widow and a fatherless child, but that was death for you, the effects always rippling outward from the point of impact, sometimes for years and sometimes for decades.

Gael had brought this on himself—and he'd brought it on his family.

James walked six blocks, crossed the street, and made his way into a resort hotel across from the one in which the man he wished to kill was staying.

He took the elevator to the top floor.

■ George Rankin had been waiting months for Gael to fuck up and finally he had. In a way it broke his heart. Gael was his friend— Gael *had* been his friend—and he'd wanted to be wrong about his suspicions. But he hadn't been wrong. Gael had visited six banks in the last three days. He'd walk in with an empty duffel bag in hand and come out with a full one. He'd walk into the next with his full duffel bag and come out empty-handed. George figured he'd emptied his bank accounts some time ago, put the money into safe deposit boxes, and waited. He'd been patient for a man living on his wife's earnings as a hair stylist. Nine million dollars he didn't touch for six months. George was impressed in a way.

But then he went and touched it.

George knew it would happen as soon as Gael booked his ticket to Grand Cayman. Here was a small island with a population of forty thousand, but somehow it managed to support six hundred banks, one bank for every sixty-six inhabitants. There was a reason forty thousand offshore companies were registered in the Cayman Islands.

Gael was currently out on the beach with his family. Two agents—dressed in shorts and flip-flops—were watching him.

George himself was sitting in a van with four more agents, ready to move the moment they could be sure of taking Gael in without injury to his wife or son—or to any innocent bystanders. The time would come soon. He was sure of it.

■ Gael sat on a towel on the beach and watched Sarah play with Grayson, their beautiful baby boy. He could hardly believe he had a son. He could hardly believe he'd gotten away with what he'd gotten away with. It'd been a little rocky at times. He'd come close to getting himself killed. But in the end, it had paid off. Paid off big.

When you were undercover, you learned to be the person you were pretending to be, which meant internally you were two people at once.

For years, he'd been both Gael Castillo Jimenez and Mulligan Shoibli. He'd built a drug empire while simultaneously fighting drug traffickers. It had been a good arrangement. On the one hand, he was making the world less violent by taking down the worst of the cartels, or trying to, and on the other hand, he was clearing a path for his own organization. Even he wasn't certain what his true motives had been at first. He'd told himself that drugs were impossible to stop, told himself that if he didn't fill the hole left in the drug trade by his arrests, that someone much worse would fill it. He might as well make a little money. But he wasn't sure. The different parts of himself didn't communicate much with one another.

For a long time, things had run smoothly. He'd operated under the radar, using what he knew about the DEA to keep himself and the organization invisible.

Eventually, however, George Rankin took an interest in the Rocha cartel.

He knew that meant the days of the organization were numbered—and he knew too, that it would eventually come out that someone at the DEA was the real power behind it. Fortunately, he'd prepared for that eventuality. He'd created evidence—circumstantial though it was—that could be pointed at either Horace Ellison or Lou Billingham, depending on the circumstances under which it was discovered, and trusted that when the time came, he'd be able to frame one of them. He'd gotten himself assigned to the case and gone undercover, becoming three people rather than two, and he'd manipulated circumstances and evidence as well as he could. He knew Rocha had to go down, and knowing this, he knew too that it meant Rocha could never find out who he was. The man was a pragmatist, with no moral center, and he'd do whatever he had to in order to survive. Which meant Gael had been at constant risk of death.

He knew too that he had to provide evidence that would take Rocha down—but that would take him down in an acceptable manner. The DEA was already aware of him, already working to nail him, so Gael's job was to make sure he didn't get nailed down too.

He watched Sarah and Grayson splashing in the water and he smiled.

He wondered, not for the first time, what Sarah would think if she found out what he was really capable of, what she would do if she found out who he really was.

But there was no place in his mind for such thoughts.

He was Gael Castillo Jimenez. He was a husband and a father.

Mulligan Shoibli was some other person, someone from his past.

He glanced left and saw a man in pink swim trunks and flip-flops watching him. The man wore Ray-Bans, so Gael couldn't see his eyes, but he seemed to be watching him. He touched his right ear and moved his mouth as if speaking—but there was no one around to listen.

For a moment, he thought nothing about it. A strange man was standing on the beach, touching his ear, and talking to himself.

But two seconds later, he understood.

He hadn't gotten away with anything. Not yet.

He turned away from the agent and looked back toward Sarah

and Grayson playing in the water. He smiled at them and waved with his right hand while with his left he reached into his beach bag. It held towels and sunblock and powdered formula in a plastic container and a few bottles, a small jug of water and swimming diapers. It also held a .25 caliber pistol, which was hidden within a cut-out section of a James Patterson novel. He'd bought it illegally because he knew he'd be transporting great sums of money and wanted protection, and since then, had been carrying it with him. He'd spent years with a gun on his person and felt naked without one anymore. He'd thought it pointless to carry the weapon here—it was just something he did because it made him feel better—but now he was glad he had it.

He glanced right, casually, to see if he was being watched by anyone else. There was another man about forty yards away, and though he didn't do anything as obvious as touch his ear while looking at him, Gael knew a DEA agent when he saw one—now that he was looking for one. He slipped the novel out of his beach bag, opened it, pretending to read, and slid the .25 into his pocket. He pretended to read for five minutes, smoking a cigarette while he did so, watching the agents from the corners of his eyes. He slipped into the Original Penguin polo shirt that had been resting on the towel beside him. He got to his feet and waved at Sarah.

He walked down to the water and when he got to Sarah he said, "I'm a little tired from all this sun. I think I'm gonna go in and take a nap."

"Grayson and I are gonna stay out a little while longer. He just loves this water."

"Okay."

Gael looked down at his son. His son giggled at him and slapped his tiny palm against the water's surface.

"I'll see you in a little bit, Gray," Gael said. He leaned down and kissed his son's forehead. He kissed Sarah's mouth. "All right. Have fun, kids."

"You okay, Gael?"

"Yeah, why?"

"I dunno, you seem a little . . . off."

"Just the sun, I guess."

"Okay. Go take that nap."

"I will."

He took a drag from his cigarette, turned around, and headed back toward the hotel. He flicked the cigarette away and slipped his hand into his pocket. He wasn't sure what he was going to do, but he knew this: he'd never see his wife or son again. If he got away, he'd have to disappear. If he didn't, he'd be in prison for the rest of his life.

He didn't like it, but he'd already come to accept it.

What he hadn't accepted was that he was going to be taken down. The DEA was going to make its move soon, he knew that much, but he still had hope. He still believed he had a chance.

A white van parked on the street about half a block south of the hotel.

He saw it and stopped.

If he went to the hotel, they'd rush out of the van and arrest him.

He couldn't let that happen.

They were watching him. They were waiting for their moment. Well—he'd choose their moment for them. He'd make it happen so that he could control the circumstances. He glanced over his shoulder toward the beach. Sarah and Grayson playing in the water. About ten yards from them, a Jet Ski was parked on the sand. He could ride it out into the water, circle the island. He could get to his bank, collect money and identification from a safe deposit box, and disappear. Really, it was his only option. That or allow himself to be taken down, which he wasn't about to do.

The agents on the beach weren't armed. They were there only to watch him, which meant he could use one of them as a shield— better than using a civilian.

Well—fuck it. Let's do this.

He pulled the .25, aimed at the van, and shot out the right rear tire. The gun emitted only a small pop, like a firecracker, and then the tire was flat.

Gael turned and ran.

He glanced over his shoulder and saw DEA agents rushing out of the van's back door. Five of them, including George Rankin, and he had five rounds left in his weapon. He could make this work. He ran toward the agent nearest the Jet Ski. Sarah was standing in the water, holding Grayson in her arms, watching him. But he pushed her out of his mind.

The agent looked up at him, positioned himself to tackle Gael, but even as Gael ran, he aimed at the guy's leg and pulled his trigger.

A mist of blood hung in the air.

People all around turned their heads to look.

The agent started to drop to his knees, but before he could, Gael wrapped his free arm around the man's neck, and holding the agent against his chest, spun around to see where George and the others were.

About thirty yards behind them. Wearing suits and ties on the beach.

Gael put his pistol against his hostage's temple.

Now he had four bullets in his gun and five armed agents coming after him.

George Rankin walked toward him. "It's over, Gael."

"It's not over until I say it's over, George."

"There's no way out of this."

"Stop walking toward me," Gael said, even as he backed toward the Jet Ski.

George took another step.

Gael aimed at one of the agents standing behind George, all of them now with their weapons drawn, and fired off a round.

Hit the motherfucker in the stomach. He grunted and bent over at the waist but didn't fall. Did not even drop his weapon.

"I said to stop walking toward me."

"Okay, okay," George said. "Don't shoot anyone else."

"All you guys need to drop your fucking guns."

"If you don't come in today, we'll get you six months from now."

"I'll take those six months, George. Throw your fucking weapon into the water—all of you, throw your fucking weapons into the water or I'll shoot someone else, and this time I'll aim between the eyes."

"Okay, Gael," George said. "Okay."

George threw his pistol into the water.

Three of the other agents followed his lead. The fourth had finally dropped to his knees, and was watching blood bloom on his shirt, still holding his gun in hand.

"Somebody throw his piece into the water."

One of the other agents threw it.

Gael, who'd continued to back away, was now beside the Jet Ski. People all over the beach were standing and watching. He glanced toward Sarah. Grayson was crying in her arms while she looked at him with sad eyes. But he was surprised to see there was no confusion on her face. He'd tried to hide what he was from her, but he saw now that she'd known. At least on some level she had. He turned away from her, unable to bear the sadness in her eyes.

"I'm going to have to shoot you guys now."

"Gael, you don't need to shoot anybody. We're unarmed. We did what you asked."

"Right now you are. I'm sorry, George, but I need to get off this island."

Police sirens wailed in the distance. The local police on their way.

Gael aimed his pistol at one of the agents. He squeezed his trigger. The bullet hit the agent in the throat.

◼ James had been watching the hotel, but movement on the beach drew his attention. He panned his rifle toward it. He saw Gael run toward the water. He saw him shoot a man in swim trunks. He saw him grab the man by the throat and use him as a shield while five DEA men—all of them in suits—ran after him.

James estimated that they were fifteen hundred yards away—two hundred yards short of a mile. He'd made such shots on the range, but never in the real world. He'd never been expected to. But he'd have to do it now.

Gael shot one of the DEA agents in the stomach.

James adjusted his sight.

The DEA agents threw their guns into the water.

James licked his finger and held it up into the air, trying to judge the wind. At this distance, it would be enough to make him miss.

Gael shot one of the agents in the throat.

James lined him up in his crosshairs, then shifted slightly up and to the right to account for distance and wind.

Gael aimed at another agent.

James exhaled, and just as the last of the breath was leaving his lungs, he squeezed the trigger.

Nothing happened for a moment, then Gael's head kicked back, a mist of blood hung in the air, and he dropped to the beach.

Water ran up over his body and then retreated again.

James shoved his rifle into the guitar case, clipped it shut, and walked away.

EPILOGUE

Later that night, James disassembled his rifle, shoved the parts into the guitar case, and walked down to the water. He set the guitar case on the sand, opened it, and went about throwing the pieces into the ocean. When it was finished, he stood on the beach and looked out at the black water. For six months, he'd wanted nothing so much as he'd wanted the man who killed his sister to die. Now he had died, and James didn't know what to feel. The anger, the need for vengeance, was gone, but it had been replaced by nothing. He only felt hollow and didn't know what he was supposed to fill that emptiness with.

He closed his eyes, and projected on the wall of his skull, saw Pilar smiling at him, her brown eyes full of love.

He opened his eyes and looked out at the black water a moment longer. Turned around and headed back to the hotel, leaving the guitar case where it lay.

■ The next day, with a duffel bag hanging off his shoulder, he boarded a flight that would take him back to Atlanta, where he'd catch a second flight, that one taking him to El Paso. To Pilar.

He walked down the aisle to his seat. When he reached his row, he looked down.

George Rankin looked up at him from the window seat. His face was haggard, tired, but there was a slight smile touching his lips all the same.

"James Murphy."

"Special Agent George Rankin. Quite a coincidence."

"Not a coincidence at all. I figured only you would've made that shot so I checked passenger lists."

James stowed his duffel bag and sat down.

"What shot are you talking about?"

"So it's like that, is it?"

"Like what? I'm honestly confused by this conversation."

"Okay," George said. "Forget it."

"How are your agents?"

George smiled. "Looks like everybody's gonna live. They're staying here to recover."

"There are worse places to get well."

"I'd say."

Fifteen minutes later, their plane took to the sky. When the flight attendant arrived with the drink cart, George Rankin bought James a scotch.

■ James stepped out of the terminal and saw Pilar waiting for him by a taxicab. She smiled and opened her arms. He hugged her. He inhaled the scent of her neck, the scent of her perfume. Petite Cherie. Every time he smelled it, he thought of her. He kissed her neck.

He thought of Layla. He thought of the man who'd killed her. Some lives were stolen and when a life was stolen, you made the person who stole it pay, and the cost of a life was another life. That's what he'd believed. He wasn't sure he believed it anymore. That hollow feeling inside made him question the rightness of that belief.

But what was done was done. It was time to move forward. It was time to fill his life with something else. He'd lived with violence for years; it was time to live a different kind of life.

A better kind of life.

"Let's go home," he said.